USA TODAY Bestselling Author

Dale Mayer

HEROES FOR HIRE

CARSON'S CHOICE: HEROES FOR HIRE, BOOK 27
Dale Mayer
Valley Publishing Ltd.

Copyright © 2022

ISBN-13: 978-1-773365-63-3
Print Edition

Books in This Series:

About This Book

Carson is pleasantly surprised by the job Levi assigns him, until Carson hears all the details. An elderly friend of Ice's believes someone is out to kill her. But she has no proof, no suspects, no motives. The police think she's imagining things and won't look into the case any further. However, after meeting this lady … and her granddaughter, Carson has his own suspicions.

Eva doesn't want Carson in the house. She doesn't want anyone in the house, if she were honest. As an artist, she loves her space, her freedom, and especially her privacy. This man is a distraction and soon could become so much more—her muse. And that is dangerous on various levels.

But, if his presence saves her grandmother, then Eva will do anything to keep her safe even put up with the man that makes her feel things she had never expected.

Prologue

ONCE AGAIN IN the massive dining room at their compound, Levi looked over at Tomas and Amber, sitting close together at the huge dining room table. "Ah, the magic strikes again?"

"Maybe," Tomas said, with a nod. "Although I didn't know anything about your matchmaking plans, so a little more warning would have been nice."

"Nope," Ice stated, as she joined them, walking from the big kitchen area. "It happens with or without warning. You just can't escape it." She looked over at Carson and grinned. "You are next."

"Like hell," he replied. "I just started working for you guys. I'm not next at all."

"Yep, you are," Levi confirmed. "It always happens, so you might as well just accept it now."

"I haven't met anybody," Carson noted, shaking his head. "So it's hardly an issue at the moment."

"Well, you're likely to, on this next job," Ice added seriously.

He looked at her and smiled. "Oh, boy, what have you got planned for me?"

"Only the best for an old friend," she teased, smiling back at him.

He groaned. "That could mean anything, though."

"True," she said, with a bright smile. "We've got an interesting case."

He shook his head. "I'm not convinced. Sounds more like a job you're just trying to give me to get me out of your hair."

"If that were the case," she said, "I would just put you to work out on the back forty. But, in this case, we have an old friend of mine. She's local, so she's in town here, but she thinks somebody is trying to kill her."

He stared at her. "Do we do that kind of job?"

"Not often, but, like I said, we're doing it as a favor for a friend. She's eighty-two."

He winced. "And?"

"I think she could be right."

He stared at her in shock and asked, "What about the police?"

"She already talked to them. She has no proof, no motive, no nothing. There are no suspects and nothing for them to go on. I've been talking to the police myself," she admitted. "They don't know how they can help because they don't have anything to go on with any of this. They can drive by her place every once in a while, but that's it."

"So, I'll provide security to an eighty-two-year-old woman, who thinks somebody is trying to kill her?" he asked in horror.

"And her granddaughter."

He narrowed his gaze at Ice. "What granddaughter?"

"Her name is Eva, and she's an art student."

"*Great*," he replied. "That'll get her a job and a steady income—not."

She laughed. "Oh, I wouldn't say anything about that until you see her art," Ice said, with a bright smile. "But the bottom line is that they need somebody there to see if anything's going on or not."

"Somebody who's not connected. A fresh pair of eyes, I presume?" Carson asked.

Ice nodded. "Exactly. So I said I'd send you in for a week, but, beyond that, I can't do much more."

"Even at that," he noted, "that's generous of you."

"Like I said, she's a friend. And her influence helps us quite a bit too," she added. "I help my friends whenever I can."

"Good enough," Carson said. "How hard can it be?"

"I wouldn't say that because it could be serious. She has a lot of money, and I don't know if that has anything to do with the threats or not. I haven't delved into her financials or anything else because she is such a good friend," she explained, with a wry smile. "If you find anything or see anything that's suspicious or if you think something's going on that needs further investigation, you let me know, and I'll be on it in a heartbeat," she stated.

"And when am I going?" he asked.

"Now," she said, looking at her watch. "By the time you get there and get settled in, you should be just in time."

"For what?"

At that, Levi started to laugh. "I noticed Ice left this part to the last." He looked at his wife affectionately, as she grinned.

"For the haunting," she added.

"*Haunting*?" Carson asked.

"Yeah," she stated, staring at him intently. "Apparently things go bump in the night. So I want you to find out what it is, who is behind it, and whether any of those bumps are intended to kill her."

"If she's that old, anything like that could cause a heart attack," he noted cautiously.

She nodded. "And that's for you to figure out. Oh, and, by the way, say hi to Eva for me."

Chapter 1

C ARSON DUGGAN DROVE up the long driveway through a big steel gate and on to the other side, feeling the might and the grandeur of the beautiful estate, although he didn't see much in high-tech security at the entrance. And, if any were hidden along this driveway, how was somebody getting in and trying to kill the grandmother?

The case felt odd. A favor for a friend, yet someone eighty-two years old, possibly nervous and imagining things.

So was this for real, or was it more a case of paranoia? Could she just be making it up? For what though? Attention? It wouldn't be the first time he had dealt with someone who had a mental disorder, and was likely not the last. Whatever it may be, he didn't want to mention this mental health topic.

Not considering the relationship this old friend had with Ice.

Carson didn't want to say anything before he had the lay of the land. According to Ice and Levi, this grandmother was in full command of her faculties and very sharp mentally. Yet, Carson was told, this had been going on for quite a while.

Apparently the police had investigated and found no evidence. While they wanted to help her, the lack of evidence was concerning.

As Carson drove up to the huge mansion, he was awed by the might and beauty of the place. Admiring the stately architecture, he pulled closer to the huge garage, out of the main accessway. He'd seen a lot of pretty impressive houses in his day, but this one was different.

It would have been an incredible house in its day, but now it had more of a faded-glory look to it, likely the home this woman had lived in for most of her life. Some people had these enduring lifestyles that Carson knew little of, personally. He had always moved from place to place, with plenty of ups and downs that he had shared with his family.

This was someone else's life, and enduring stability was here, with an ageless quality to it. It was also stupendously gorgeous. As he stood in the driveway, he admired the place, looking around at the entire front of it, which had a massive entranceway. A series of long windows were on the left and on the right, before disappearing around to another wall which then jutted yet again.

It looked like the house was developed with a step design. The segmental layout gave it a different look, and, as he studied it closely, he noticed that all but one of the windows appeared to be closed.

He hoped some kind of security was on each one of them. He had already spotted cameras up in the corners near the main entrance. With that logged in his brain, he walked up and pushed the doorbell. It opened soon afterward, a striking young woman staring at him suspiciously.

He realized that she may have seen him pull up and may have also watched him standing here, staring at the house. He gave her a gentle smile. "Hi, I'm Carson. Levi sent me."

She continued to frown at him. "I really think this is a fool's errand," she stated crossly.

"You must be Eva. So, you don't think that your grandmother is in any kind of danger?"

She hesitated, then shrugged. "I don't know about that," she murmured, "but the police don't seem to think so."

"Or could it be that you just don't want anybody up in your space?" Seeing the guilty look crossing her features, he nodded. "Listen. I get that nobody wants their life probed in such a manner, but there is also a cost for feigning ignorance."

She flushed. "I'm not pretending, nor am I ignorant." She shot him a flat look. "But I sure as hell hope this is nowhere near as severe as Grandma seems to make it out to be."

"Do you think she's making it up?" he asked curiously, finding himself more and more curious about Eva.

Eva seemed to think about it, then shook her head. "No, I guess not. It's not really her style."

"In that case," he added, "maybe we should let her be the judge of whether this is a fool's errand or not."

Her gaze searched him; then she gave a clipped nod and stepped back slightly. "I don't mean to make it sound like I don't believe her," she explained. "She's a very special person, and I've never had any reason to doubt her before."

"So, why do you doubt her now?"

She shrugged. "Because I also believe in the police, and they seem to think that nothing's wrong."

"And, in that case, I should put things to rest this week."

"Be my guest," she conceded, with a loud sigh. "After all, you'll be living in our space."

Such an obvious note of disapproval filled her tone that he couldn't help but grin at her. "I'll try to stay out of your personal space," he stated.

She rolled her eyes at that. "Yeah, well, you must do better than this, but that's not likely to happen."

"Why is that?" he asked.

"Because what you're trying to do is impossible," she said. "No matter how much I don't like it, staying out of my personal space isn't very likely to happen, even if you try."

He withheld his comment, as he stepped inside, then turned to look around. "How many visitors do you get?"

"Not very many. Mostly just deliveries," she murmured.

"So just the two of you live here alone?"

She nodded, then shrugged. "Except for our housekeeper, who has been here since forever."

"What does *since forever* mean?" he asked.

"Twenty-plus years, I think," she murmured.

He noted that because it was rare for anybody employed that long to turn on their employer, unless some changes had been stirred up recently. In which case, somebody could be afraid of those new changes. People were always afraid to face up to change. "And who is the housekeeper?"

"Flora," she replied immediately.

At that mention, an aged woman bustled forward and gave him a bright, affable smile. "I heard my name." She looked Carson up and down, and then gave Eva a frown.

Eva rolled her eyes at that. "Okay. I know I promised I wouldn't open the door, but he didn't look suspicious."

"You know full well that you're not supposed to," Flora reprimanded her.

"But I'm expecting a parcel," Eva added, with a sigh, looking uncomfortable. She turned toward Carson. "So pardon me for being excited. Of course that's the only thing that lets my guard down."

"So, you aren't supposed to open the door? Is that correct?"

"Yes, and don't you dare make any more rules for me."
Eva glared at him. "They are hard enough to follow as it is."

"Apparently somebody tried already, and it didn't
work," he noted mildly, "so I'm not sure anything I say will
make a difference."

She stared at him in surprise.

"I'll let it go, for now."

"Good," she snapped. "Then maybe we will get along
better than I thought." And, with that, she stepped to the
door, looked outside once more, and groaned. "Where the
hell is it?" She nearly bounced up and down with impa-
tience.

"Is there no tracking on whatever you're waiting for?" he
asked.

"Yes, there is, and it was supposed to be delivered this
morning. So far it's not here."

"Well, maybe give them a chance," Flora suggested, with
a cheerful smile. She motioned to Carson. "Come in. Come
in now, so I can close the door. You don't need to stand here
in the entranceway," she added. "You are expected, and Aida
is waiting for you."

He followed her a little farther into the hallway, where
he put down his bag. "I'll collect this later, if you don't
mind."

"Of course." Flora nodded, then looked at the bag. "It
will be safe there. Chances are, I won't lift it anyway."

He smiled at her. "No reason why you should either."

She shrugged. "In my day I would have, ... but I'm
afraid those days are long gone."

"And again, not an issue," he stated. "I can pull my own
weight, while I'm here."

"But there's not a whole lot you'll need to do," Flora shared. "I handle the cooking, cleaning, and laundry, although, I must admit, we do have cleaners who come in to help once a week. That makes my job a whole lot easier."

Considering the size of the house, he could understand that. "It is a large place and way too much for one person."

"When I was young," Flora added, "I could do most of it on my own, but the years do tend to catch up to us."

He didn't say anything but figured the woman in front of him had to be close to sixty, if not a few years older than that. He followed her into another room, what he thought would have been called the drawing room in the good old days. As he stepped inside, he noted an older woman, sitting at a big office desk.

He smiled at her and stated in a calm and amiable voice, "Carson Duggan, ma'am, reporting for duty." She looked up and flashed him a smile that made him aware of an elegant passage of time. She clearly would have been a catch in her day, an absolute knockout.

She motioned him in. "Come in. Come in." Then she turned to Flora. "Maybe some coffee, please?" Flora immediately nodded her head and disappeared.

Aida looked him over, once the housekeeper was gone. "I presume you drink coffee."

"Coffee is fine," he agreed. "I think everybody does, don't they?"

"No." She shook her head. "And I'm always quite suspicious of people who don't."

He burst out laughing. "Not a problem with me. Coffee is a mainstay in my world."

Aida continued to study him thoroughly, her eyes taking on a sharp gleam.

Had she been forty years younger, he would have considered her motives, but instead she seemed to almost assess his capabilities based on his physical appearance and demeanor. "I can assure you that I am perfectly capable of doing the job, if that's what you're wondering," he stated gently.

She beamed at him. "Good. I have yet to see you in action, but I must admit. You don't look much ... like a security guard."

"I'm not," he confirmed. "However, you matter a lot to Levi and Ice, so they've sent me to give you a hand."

A charming dimple appeared. "Indeed. Ice is such a sweetheart, and, if I still had it in me, I'd give her a run for her money over Levi."

Carson burst out laughing. "And I suspect she'd run you right out of town," he teased, with a big grin.

The dimple appeared again, and this time she laughed herself. "Isn't that the truth? Still, it's nice to know that they are around, looking after me as best they can. And I do understand that they can't do it for very long. I mean, a huge cost is involved in keeping you here."

"It's not so much that, but what if I can't solve it within this week? They'll be more than a little disappointed in me," he noted, trying to engage in small talk. In the back of his mind, he knew that honesty would matter the most. "They want to ensure we get to the bottom of whatever is going on here quickly, so we can get it resolved."

"And I would love that more than anything," she agreed, now looking angry. "I'm not sure what's going on myself, but it's getting worse—the noises here and the sense of someone following me when I'm out and about."

Just then Flora arrived, pushing a tea cart, laden with a

big pot of coffee and cups. Something was very old-worldly about the way she poured the two cups, handed one to him and then placed one on Aida's desk. He realized he had moved into a completely different world from the one that he knew.

Seeing the house from the outside was one thing; seeing it and being with them on the inside was a completely different thing. Yet now? He felt almost an eerie feeling to it.

As soon as Flora left, Aida turned and looked at him expectantly.

He nodded, then pulled out his notepad and began. "I have the file from Ice and Levi. I've also read the police file and the threatening email and the letter you shared with them, plus saw the photos of the dead birds found on your doorstep. And, while that is good to a certain point, I do need to hear, from your perspective, just what you think is going on here."

"I think somebody is trying to kill me," she stated immediately.

"How so?"

She stopped, considered him, and asked, "I presume we're talking motive?"

"Yes. What motive would someone have for killing you?"

"I'm not sure," she admitted. "I have made a few enemies over the years. I didn't think I had any who were intent on revenge or whatever until recently, but, then again, no one was trying to kill me before."

"Okay, that's a good place to start. How have you made enemies?"

"It's my work. I have a charity that I run," she murmured, "and a lot of money passes through my hands."

"Money is always a great motivator, for good and for evil."

She nodded. "The thing is, I don't have any particular suspicions of who it could be," she added. "I handed over the files of anybody we've had complaints from to the police and to Levi and Ice."

"Good. I know that both the cops and Ice are working on that angle, running background checks on everything they can get their hands on. But, so far, nothing major has been found, so we've nobody to go after at this point. That is a problem, and it's always distressing because we need a clear-cut idea of who's doing this, if possible."

"Wouldn't that be nice," she agreed bitterly, with more strength than he expected. "So, that's your job now, young man." She picked up her coffee cup. "Next question."

"Here we go then. Who is set to gain from your death?" he asked bluntly. "Have you made any recent changes to your will?"

Her eyes widened. "You are a sharp nut." She nodded. "I like that."

Slowly he let out a breath, trying not to let her see that he was happy that at least he'd made the right call. "I tend to be clear and direct," he told her calmly. "No point in doing this if we'll only have half the information."

"No, you're quite right there," she agreed. "You should know that I have made recent changes to my will. Basically the bulk of my estate goes to my granddaughter."

"Are there other family members or friends who would not like that dispensation?"

"Not any close relations. My only son was killed in a car accident quite a few years ago," she murmured, "and my granddaughter has been living with me ever since."

"And when you say *quite a few years*, are we saying your granddaughter has been here since she was a child?"

"Since she was a teenager, I guess," she replied, thinking hard. "Well, maybe when she was about ten or eleven, I think, when she started living with me."

"So, your son died, Eva's father, but what about her mother? Your daughter-in-law?"

"She was in a coma for a very long time. And, yes, I did pay all the medical bills associated with her care."

His eyebrows shot up. "Any particular reason for that?"

"Because she was my daughter-in-law," she stated equally bluntly. "I had the funds, and my son was a fool who didn't have enough medical insurance. The costs of keeping her alive all those years ... were pretty expensive," she admitted. "She passed away a few years ago."

"Was there any animosity from her—or Eva's other grandparents—that you still looked after your granddaughter for all these years?"

"Eva's maternal grandparents died long ago. So, if my daughter-in-law didn't like the arrangements I had made, she never said anything to me," she murmured. "But, of course, how do you ever really know what's in the back of somebody's mind?"

He had to admit that she had a point there. "Okay, and who else gets part of your estate at your passing?"

She looked at him and shrugged. "Obviously Flora, who was just here, is getting something. I mean, she's been in service with me for a very long time."

"And is it enough for her to retire on?"

She looked at him and then slowly nodded. "I guess, if she's frugal with it."

"Is that so?"

"No, I might need to change that," she stated, looking thoughtful.

"Change what?"

"Well, you're right. I don't know if it is enough for her to retire on, and she needs to retire in peace. She's done nothing but look after me for the last two decades—and has been taking care of my granddaughter since she came here. It would only make sense that she probably doesn't have a whole lot of other money."

"She might, or she might not," he noted. "That's not necessarily your responsibility."

"No, it's not, but you make a good point. That is something I probably should spend a bit of time considering in a little more detail. I would want her to live the time she had left, without scrimping."

"And certainly now would be a better time to do it, if you seriously think that somebody is out there, trying to kill you."

She stared at him directly, as she pulled down her reading glasses from atop her head, the chain dangling around her neck. "Young man, let's get this straight. Neither of us would have gotten so far down this pathway if I didn't firmly believe that someone was intent on killing me."

"Good. I needed to hear you say that."

She regarded him for another long moment, then nodded. "So that question won't ever arise again, will it?"

He shook his head. "As long as you are objective, it won't. No reason we should go there, but I can't promise you will always like what I have to say."

"We should be good there as well."

And Carson realized then that, of all the things he'd said so far, she did believe that. "Your granddaughter doesn't

15

seem to think she is in any particular danger."

"She's young." Aida gave an airy wave of her hand. "She also spends most of her time caught up in her art."

"I understand that she's a student."

"Not for long," she added. "She's just completed her degree. Not that she ever needed a degree, and I did find it odd that she went ahead and got one."

"Maybe it wasn't so much to have a degree as much as to be on a path with some structure and to learn what she could out there in the world."

"I don't know, but you may be right," she admitted. "Regardless, my granddaughter is very talented."

He reserved judgment on that. In his lifetime, he'd certainly heard more than a few people raving with unapologetic bias about their talented someone, only to reveal ordinary results.

She looked at him, first with a laugh, then a smile. "You'll see," she stated serenely.

He nodded. "I suspect I will. What about any of her boyfriends?"

Aida rolled her eyes. "I have them thoroughly vetted by Levi. Even with that precaution, I find I can't tolerate any of them. Luckily Eva is too devoted to her art to give them much time, so they don't last long. Thankfully. However, I do believe Eva needs a social life outside of watching me work and Flora manage the household. So, in that vein, college was good for her."

"Other than Flora, who else do you have in your bequests who I need to know about?"

"Just the charities. I run one huge nonprofit that involves many charities within its umbrella."

"And, out of your estate, what percentage do the charities get?"

She stopped, thought about it, and shrugged. "Less than half."

"Are there any particular charities that you think would potentially disapprove of that dispersion of your estate?"

"They should be glad they're getting anything at all," she snapped, looking at him over her glasses again.

"True, but that doesn't mean someone doesn't think they should have a bigger piece of the pie," he argued, "particularly if there are those you're personally involved with and who have no one else set to look after them, once you are gone."

She thought about it, shrugged, and noted, "That might be something else I should look at as well, but I'm only really concerned about my granddaughter at the moment."

"You don't have any suspicion that she is the target here, or one of them, do you?" he asked.

She nodded. "I do."

"I presume you have a reason for that." He spoke cautiously, wondering why Aida would jump to someone trying to kill her granddaughter now.

"She's my only living relative," she said simply. "And I know that, when she's off in her art, she can …" Aida stopped, hesitating, then continued. "She can lose track of time." Worry now etched her features. "Eva can get very wrapped up in what she's doing—to the point that she'll often forget to eat, forget to do anything really." Aida raised both hands. "I am very much a business-oriented person, and my granddaughter is … I don't want to say the opposite of me, but, in that particular sense, she is definitely different from me."

"Isn't it nice that there's room in the world for both?" he

mentioned smoothly.

She looked at him and then started to laugh. "Very nicely stated." She chuckled. "I didn't realize diplomacy was an art of yours as well."

"I don't think Levi and Ice would ever consider that to be true." He grinned. "Yet I can manage sometimes."

She smiled, obviously enjoying their conversation. "Well, maybe I'm just being an overly protective mother hen when it comes to Eva. However, she must not be harmed in all this mess targeting me."

Carson easily understood that perspective and nodded.

"We'll show you to your room for now. I presume being on the first floor is the best option for you. Plus, you have access to the entire estate and whatever you need. However, please be aware that my granddaughter's studio is out of bounds."

"That's not a problem," he replied, "as long as I've still got access, when I need it."

She stopped, frowned. "That could be a problem."

"No point in having me here if I can't access each and every inch of this place. I must check it all as I search for potential problems. If I can't enter ..." He stopped, only to continue after a moment. "If I need to see some room in this residence, I must have the freedom to do so."

"I understand that, but she wants her privacy, and she wants nobody in her space," Aida stated.

"I'm all for giving her that," he noted, "and I have no intention of barging in on her, but I can't have any doors off-limits. I can inspect her area while she is there, if that is the only way I am allowed to." He needed to make Aida acknowledge the importance of this, and he would not give an inch. The conversation continued for a while but had diverted to the main charity she ran.

A few minutes into the conversation, Eva walked in, noticed the coffee, and smiled. "I do love that there's always coffee," she stated warmly, as she stepped over, kissed her grandmother on the cheek, and then poured herself a cup.

"As if you need anything else to stimulate you," her grandmother murmured, with an eye roll.

"Hey, it's not my fault I'm a bit on edge over my first show," she admitted. "You know that's big for me."

"It is big," Aida murmured.

At that, Carson turned and addressed Eva. "What's big?" Eva frowned, and he shook his head. "No, no secrets," he declared. "I don't know if this part of your life affects your grandmother—and neither will you—until we sort it out."

Eva glared at him, and Aida chipped in a bit sharply, her facial expression soft, but her voice took on an almost pestering tone. "Come along, Eva. Be nice."

Eva groaned. "I still don't like the idea of having anybody in the house." She looked back at him and glared, but Carson just smiled.

"I am fully vetted," he shared. "I guess I can understand you not wanting strangers living here, even temporarily, but, if not me, you might want to consider having somebody else or even the police."

She shook her head immediately. "I'm just not comfortable having strangers around."

"Understood," he murmured, "and I'll stay out of your way as much as possible, but that won't be an option all the time."

She snorted at that. "Just having you around will make life difficult."

"I'll try not to disrupt your work as much as I can."

At that, she stopped and stared. "You better not disrupt my work at all."

He was somehow amused by her antics, tried not to laugh out loud, and didn't say anything more, just sipping his coffee as he looked from one woman to the other.

Aida smiled at her granddaughter and asked, "So, did your delivery arrive?"

"No," she replied crossly. "I just phoned the courier company, and apparently they wrote down part of the address wrong."

"Oh dear," the older lady murmured. "Isn't that frustrating?"

"It's a contract for my first showing." She looked over at Carson. "Since it really doesn't apply to you, no need to worry."

He stared at her, his gaze flattened, dark, and then he gave a quick nod. "Right. I may well not need to see the details of the show, depending on when and where it's happening and who might be attending."

She stared at him in shock. "That has nothing to do with this. I don't have anything to do with my grandmother's world at all."

"Except that part about you being her only living relative and that you are a major part of her life and that you have lived in the same home with her for sixteen years or so," he argued smoothly, "*and* are the major benefactor in her will."

"That's a low blow." She glared at him.

SOMETHING WAS INTENSELY disturbing about having this man around. Eva didn't want anyone here, but this one was too large, too dominant, too … just too much male.

She had tried hard to talk her grandmother out of having anybody here, but, when it came to her grandmother's security, Eva didn't want to buck the system too much because what if she were wrong?

She sighed, then looked over at her grandmother. "I hope you know what you're doing."

"Not at all," Aida admitted, "which is why we have help."

Eva nodded at that. "I understand that. It's just very distressing to think that anybody could ever want to hurt you."

"And you're living in denial," her grandmother teased. "And I understand that too. I really do. It's much easier to live in denial, but, when something goes wrong, the shock can be really devastating. Followed by the guilt."

At that, Eva winced. "You mean too much to me to have anything like that happen." She walked over and gave her grandmother a gentle hug. "You know how that would completely devastate me, right?"

"I know that, child," she said, patting her awkwardly. "And that's why Carson is here."

Eva nodded, looking at him. "I sure hope you are good at your job."

"I am," he stated smugly, studying her. "Yet I'll also need your cooperation."

"Of course you will," she said. "However, I've already given the police my cooperation. So I'm sure that anything you need from me, you can get from their files."

"I already have that," he noted, "but some information is lacking."

"Like what?" she asked, not liking his tone.

"Your personal life."

"And what's that got to do with anything?" she asked.

21

"If somebody removes your grandmother, there's just you left to inherit," he explained. "And money is a very powerful motivator."

She stared at him, nonplussed. "And what? You actually think somebody would kill my grandmother so that I could inherit more?"

"I don't know if you would inherit *more*," he replied immediately, "but you would inherit whatever you're set to inherit. Would you not?"

"I don't know if I would or not," she stated crossly. "I really don't like discussing anything like that."

"And like your grandmother just noted, denial won't work in this instance."

Eva placed down her coffee cup and faced him. "I'm out of here." She gave him an awkward wave. "You do your investigation, but you better stay away from me."

Carson couldn't contain his laughter. "I'll be up to check out your studio in a little bit."

Chapter 2

E VA STOPPED, THEN spun around to look at him. "What?"

"I need to be familiar with all corners of this property," he explained. "There are no locked doors while I'm here, and I need to know the nooks and crannies, the panic rooms or secret places that others would be most likely to hide in."

Her jaw dropped, and she turned and stared at her grandmother. Aida, however, dropped her gaze to the desk. "Seriously, Grandma?"

Her grandmother looked up and nodded. "Yes. Seriously. If this is what we must do for one week to ensure our safety, then so be it."

Eva stared, shaking her head. "That doesn't put me in a very good spot, does it?" She turned and looked at him. "*Nobody* goes in my studio."

"I will be going in your studio," he declared, with no easing of his inflection. "No way to do my job properly otherwise. I must map out all rooms in this place. I don't know where the threats are coming from, but, in my experience, most come from within," he explained quietly. "I have no interest in your art and certainly not in your life—except to the extent that it becomes part of my investigation. It's not my intent to interfere, yet your life holds the key to solving this as much as Aida's life. So I need to determine the origin of the threats. And, while we're at it, as I mentioned before, I also need to know everything about your personal life."

She shook her head. "Oh my God!" With a horrified expression, she turned and walked out to stand in the hallway. Behind her, she heard him say, "That went well."

Her grandmother burst out laughing. "No, it didn't. And I do understand both sides of it," she murmured, "but I don't really want to leave this world just yet. I think Eva could use me a little bit longer."

"And I presume that's the only reason she hasn't had a full-blown hissy fit."

Eva turned back to see her grandmother give him a quirk of a smile. "Yes, exactly that."

"I'm really not trying to make her life a mess. I'm just trying to protect yours."

"And again that's why she will cooperate in the end, though she won't like it."

With a nod, he stood and stepped out into the hallway and caught sight of Eva.

She took slow deep breaths, trying to control her temper, then moved on him. At the same time, Flora barreled toward Eva, a package in her hand. Eva halted.

"Is this it?" Flora asked, holding out the delivery with both hands.

"Looks like it," Eva said, with a bright smile. She checked the sender's name on it and nodded. "This is it, which almost makes *him* sufferable." She darted a glance at Carson.

"Well, as long as you remember why he's here," Flora reminded her in a commiserating voice.

"Oh, yeah, I get that part, but he's demanding access to

my studio," she complained, looking at Flora with an expression of horror.

"I don't think that he really cares about what you're doing in there," Flora suggested, trying to console Eva. "He just needs to know how this place works. It is a very large property, and you know yourself there's an awful lot to learn about it."

"I still don't understand why he has to have access to my studio," she argued, then she shook her head. "No, of course I do, and that's for Grandma, so fine, whatever. ... I just don't like it."

"And we understand," Flora replied, with a bright smile, "but we also don't want anything to happen to Aida."

"No. God no," Eva murmured, and then, with a shudder, she announced, "I'll be up in my rooms for the rest of the day."

"As long as you come down for dinner," Flora added. "I can't imagine Mr. Carson will take kindly to tracking you down."

Eva glared at Flora. "I know what you're saying, but I won't be on somebody's time frame."

"And I wouldn't want you to be," Flora tried again.

To Eva, it felt like being kicked to the curb. The worst thing in her world was to have anybody disrupt her work and her freedom; yet, at the same time, she also knew that some of this must happen. If she wasn't up against a deadline and struggling to get her last piece done, she wouldn't be so snappy. But she was ...

"Fine. Text me when dinnertime is closer." She turned on her heel and walked away to her studio. "What has happened to my life?" she asked no one in particular.

There weren't any answers here, not easy ones anyway.

Somebody was after her grandmother—or at least her grandmother believed that was so. Surely dead birds were found on doorsteps all around, right? And the email? Well, other than being in her grandma's in-box, it was fairly generic as threats went. Still, Eva wouldn't bet her grandmother's life on these events, no matter how removed any danger felt.

Thus, for the time being, they would all just deal with it—and Carson. Eva hated it and almost felt like life was tinkering with her.

She didn't disbelieve her grandmother, and, if anything was going on, she didn't want to make the wrong call here. Only her grandmother was in Eva's world, and she absolutely adored her. Eva was also a little bit of a control freak with her artwork and so very opposite to everything about Grandma.

Clutching the package tightly to her chest, Eva bolted as fast as she could up to her suite. There, she locked the door, and, as soon as she heard the lock *snap*, she grinned. Carson hadn't arrived yet. Her space was her own, at least in her mind.

She would still do what she needed to do. Whether he liked it or not.

And, with that, she opened the package and reviewed the contract. This was her first-ever showing. She'd held off doing anything until she had stockpiled a decent collection, and then she'd immediately convinced herself that nothing was good enough. She needed to keep working until she got better.

As she saw the progression of her own talent, it was really hard to do anything with her older stuff. But, in this case, she would incorporate old with new, presenting a series of her paintings from beginning to end, her entire show called *Progression*. She loved the fact that they would honor the work she did now, as well as the work she used to do. The whole thing was a huge milestone in so many ways.

Yet also terrifying. She wasn't a child anymore, yet she felt like a child at times, particularly whenever she considered any chance of her grandmother passing on.

Groaning, Eva sat here, staring off into space, wondering if something really was going on to threaten her grandma. And who could it be?

That thought brought Carson's questions about Eva's personal life to the surface. The fact that she had broken off a major relationship would make his eyebrows go up as well. She didn't want to discuss it and almost wished that her grandmother would deal with it, but was that fair?

No. It wasn't fair in any way. Especially not when her grandmother had so many other things to focus on. And Eva didn't want her grandma to worry that one of the biggest problems of her life could be due to Eva.

Her grandmother was a very special person, and just the thought of losing her was already making Eva choke up. She had lost her parents, now this? She grabbed a tissue and held it firmly against her eyes, feeling the fear and grief, knowing that she already had a good chance of losing Aida soon, simply because of her age.

She wanted her grandmother to live for another decade plus, but Eva also knew that the likelihood of that wasn't necessarily great. Her grandmother was aging before her eyes, and this additional mess would just make it that much harder on her. Fear and worry was not good for her. Or Eva.

Sighing, Eva focused on her easel, holding the last piece she must finish for her show—if she could just clear her mind. She and Grandma both had enough on their plates at the moment. And, because of that, Eva would do everything possible to make this investigation work, just for her grandmother's sake.

Including tolerating Carson's presence.

CARSON HAD THE blueprints of the house laid out on the formal dining table, page after page after page.

The place was huge.

The blueprints had been all rolled up and tied with an old silk ribbon, which said much about the age of the drawings as well. But the building itself was fascinating. He tapped several of the layouts, wondering just what it was that he was looking at, when Flora happened to come by. "Do you know what this room here is?" he asked, pointing to the blueprints.

She looked at it and frowned. "I think that's where the second-floor laundry room is now," she murmured. "Some adaptations were done over the years."

"Of course there were." He ran his fingers through his hair. "And how many entrances and exits are there to the house?"

She looked at the blueprints and frowned. "I find these really hard to read."

"Forget the blueprints. Just walk through it in your own mind. You know this place as well as anyone."

"There's one in the kitchen. One through the main hallway to the back of the house to enter the garden. There are the big French doors on either side, plus the front door, and then, around by the pool," she noted, "are those big ten-foot-tall doors."

He stared at her. "Okay, so I haven't seen the pool area yet."

"I can show you now if you want," she offered, then looked at her watch and frowned. "Or you can go look yourself."

"Running out of time?"

"I must get dinner on," she apologized.

"That's fine. I'll wander on my own, as long as I won't spook anybody. Is anybody else staying in the house right now, besides the four of us?"

She shook her head. "No. It is not the cleaners' day today, so you're good to go." She waited for his nod, then left.

Carson slowly walked through the main floor, checking that everything was as he had seen it on the blueprints. There were a few updates, like in the pantry. It looked like there used to be a buttery here too, and then it had been changed into a butler's kitchen, which made sense.

As he wandered from there, he checked out all the outer doors and the locks on the windows just on this first floor. He knew that a bare-bones security system had been installed years ago, and, while it desperately needed an update, so far, everything checked out just as it should. He also didn't see any place for anyone to gain access, unless they had keys. Writing a note about that, he continued to map out the main floor.

When he came around to the stairs, he frowned. "There aren't any stairs at the front entrance," he mumbled to himself, finding that very odd.

Instead, a double circular staircase came all the way up on either side. By the time he made his way up this left-hand staircase, he realized it provided access to servants' quarters but only on part of the second floor. There was another section to this second floor, yet the two parts didn't seem to be connected.

He hadn't seen that on the blueprints either. He frowned, wondering when this update had happened. As he roamed up here, Flora walked out of a room.

She looked at him, then smiled. "I see you found the servants' staircase," she noted cheerfully.

"I wasn't expecting a split staircase."

"Yeah, this house has a lot of secrets." She laughed. "My rooms are here. It's a little confusing at first, but very quickly it starts to make sense."

He nodded. "Is anybody else living up here, besides you?"

"No. Three bedrooms are here. This one's mine."

"May I?"

"Yes, of course. You may walk in and take a look to satisfy yourself that I'm not hiding anything, and then the other two are empty," she stated. "Guest rooms are over on the other side of the house, on the second floor."

"Got it," he said, and, with that, Flora quickly dashed down the stairs. He was amazed at the size of the place—more than ten thousand square feet per the blueprints—and all of it for Aida and Eva.

He wondered about that, but, if they were happy here, who was he to say anything? He did check the other rooms here, and they were empty. When he walked through Flora's room, he found no outside access and no false walls. It all looked seemingly innocent and unassuming. Which, of course, made him suspicious as hell.

There was only the one way up, so taking those stairs back down, he spied a door on one of the landings, built into the paneling. The job was so well done that most people wouldn't know it was even here. He popped it open and stepped through, realizing that he'd come out on a landing that connected both staircases.

Now he made his way upstairs to the other section of the second floor, over the main part of the house. As he went down the hallway, he found yet another hidden door as well. Behind it were stairs going up to the third floor.

Shaking his head, he quickly went through the main portion of the second floor, finding guest bedrooms and what appeared to be Aida's master bedroom.

He did a quick search, checking the windows and the doors and the overall security, then making sure that the room measurements actually lined up with the original blueprints in a way that made sense.

By the time he made his way to the third floor, he'd entered a completely different space—open and airy—and he knew that on this floor would be Eva's studio. As he stepped forward, a door opened, and there she was, glaring at him.

He smiled gently and reminded her, "I'm only here to help."

Her shoulders sagged, and she nodded. "Then you might as well come in, but, after you've seen it, I don't want you back in here ever again."

"If I don't have to, I won't," he replied. As he stepped inside, his gaze was immediately drawn to several easels, but they were all covered up.

He nodded to himself, thinking about how private she must want to keep everything. Whether that was because of the show or because of a lack of confidence, he didn't know. He quickly wandered through, inspecting all the windows, checking the locks and latches, and looking down from here. This floor was at least thirty or forty feet off the ground. He saw no ivy, no latticework. Basically no way to get up quietly. It would take a very large ladder to scale this height. Or a helicopter, which he dismissed due to the noise it would make.

As he worked his way through this suite, he checked out a bathroom and then found a connecting door, which must lead to her bedroom on the other side. "Do you use this entire top floor?"

She nodded, grudgingly. "A lounge is on the other side."

"Your bedroom, correct?" She nodded. "I don't have to check it right now. It can be put off to later. Is anybody else up here ever?"

"No, this is my home."

He stopped, looked at her, and added, "I know you don't want to answer this, but I need to know. Have you ever had a boyfriend or fiancé or anybody who's been up here?"

"I do—or did, I should say. So of course he's been here," she snapped.

"Did he stay the night?"

"No, I respect my grandmother too much for that."

He nodded. "But he did have access."

"Well, yes, in the sense that I was here and that he would come up sometimes to see me."

He nodded. "And does he have a key to the house?"

"No, he does not." She stared at him.

And again he just nodded.

"Do most people hand out access to their homes?" she asked, puzzled.

"Mostly, no," he replied, "but, in some cases—like for a fiancé—then sure. Some people also do it for convenience, so, if they're away, and the plumber needs access, a family member or neighbor could let him in. You know? That sort of thing."

She chewed on her bottom lip and shook her head. "I've never given anyone a key. To me, although it's my home, it is still my grandmother's house, so I would never take such a liberty."

"Good for now. The fewer keys we must track down, the better."

"Good luck with that." Her gaze narrowed. "I know some keys went missing a while back."

"What's a while back? Like how long ago? Do you have any idea where they went?"

"No, I don't know anything else about it." She frowned. "You must ask Grandma or Flora."

"We'll take a look at that," he noted, "or else we'll just get the locks changed."

She winced at that. "You have no idea what you're saying. Some of these locks are very, very old."

"I'm sure they are," he agreed calmly, "but we don't want to give anybody easy access to you or your home."

"I think if it were that easy," she replied, "they would have already come in."

"How do you know they haven't?" he shot back.

She stared at him. He watched as fear remained on her expressive features. She added, "This house is so big, I wouldn't know. One time a cleaning person was working here, and I had no idea she was even here, and she'd been around for about six days. So, when I crossed paths with her in the kitchen about midnight, I was pretty freaked out about it. That's when we stopped having cleaning staff stay overnight."

"I can see that happening," Carson replied. "You have a

ton of space here. And, even for the person working here, it would have taken them weeks to get a real feel of the layout."

"Exactly. This happened years ago, when I was still dealing with the loss of my parents. So I didn't handle it very well. It was like the boogeyman jumped up and surprised me."

"That's understandable," he murmured, then turned and walked back to her door. With a final look around, he said, "Thank you for your time. I'll leave you to work," and he stepped out. Just then came a gong. When he looked back in at her, she smiled.

"That's the dinner bell."

"Oh, I guess that means I'll see you downstairs then."

At that, her phone buzzed. She groaned as she looked down.

"Problems?"

"No, I just asked Flora to text me whenever dinner was ready."

"You need a text after that gong?"

"Sometimes, yes," she murmured, "but I actually wanted the text in advance of the gong." She smirked. "So I'd be ready, but I guess I should be happy I got a text at all."

"How do you get on with Flora?"

"I guess that's another part of your job, isn't it?" she asked. "Do you really like to snoop into people's lives?"

"Nope, I sure don't," he admitted, "but I really like saving them."

At that, she shut up.

Chapter 3

EVA FOLLOWED CARSON downstairs, feeling like a heel yet again. "I don't mean to be so bad-tempered," she murmured.

"Good," he replied. "It's nice to know you have that skill. Sometimes, when things don't come naturally, I know it can be hard. So sometimes you must work at it."

At that, she stopped and glared at him, then relented. "How is it that you can find your way to the dining room on your own already?" she asked, as she hurried behind him.

"Because I've been studying the blueprints."

She wanted to argue how that made no sense because she'd had lots of people who had been here many times, and they still couldn't find their way around the house. But apparently he had already, and knew where to go. It was a little daunting to think of somebody so competent that, within an hour—possibly two, as she checked her watch—he had already figured out the layout here.

She got to the dining room right behind him, and he abruptly stopped, before stepping inside, and turned to her, clearly rattled. "I wasn't supposed to dress up for dinner, was I?"

"Not today"—she chuckled—"but there are days when that does happen."

As they walked inside, Aida was already seated at the

dinner table, waiting for them. She looked up, smiled at her granddaughter, and said, "Glad that you are here on time."

Eva murmured, "I'm really hungry."

"Thank goodness for the gong. I could have spent hours just looking around this beautiful home," Carson admitted warmly.

Eva looked over at him and realized that he was being sincere.

The fact was, her grandma's house *was* absolutely stunning. But it was also old, and not everybody appreciated the beauty of the times gone by. Eva sat down across from Carson, just the three of them at the end of the long formal dining table that could easily seat sixteen. "It's weird to have somebody else here."

"What about Flora?" Carson asked. "Does she join us for dinner?"

At that, Aida shrugged. "No, she prefers not to. I have told her that she's more than welcome, but she insists on eating in the kitchen."

"Some people are more comfortable alone," he murmured.

"Maybe, but you know the olden days of that kind of master-servant relationship have changed greatly," Eva added.

"But, for her, obviously not," he muttered, with a bright smile.

She nodded. "Very true."

As they were talking, Flora came in with a large trolley and placed several dishes on the table in front of them. He realized that they would serve themselves as well. Completely out of his element, he was trying to figure out how the system worked, so he wouldn't commit a faux pas. He watched as Flora took off the lids before departing.

He quickly offered to serve.

Her grandmother immediately handed over her plate with aplomb and said, "Yes, please, I do so hate standing up all the time, getting to all the dishes."

He smiled, adding some of each offering to Aida's plate. "Yet I'm sure that Flora would serve it, if you wanted it done that way."

"Now maybe," she replied, with another shrug. "Still, it's nice to honor some part of the old system too," she murmured.

When Carson returned Aida's plate to her, he looked to Eva, who nodded and handed him her plate. Quickly he scooped her up some of the same. The entrée for tonight was roast beef with gravy and grilled onions on the side, plus roasted potatoes—a mix of russet and sweet—together with sautéed mushrooms and steamed broccoli with cauliflower. A mixed green salad had already been dressed and scooped into separate bowls. Carson distributed one to each of them.

When he sat down with a hefty serving on his own plate, Aida stared at it and smiled. "You know something?" she began. "That is one thing I do miss, watching a man eat."

"I do like my groceries," Carson noted, with a smile.

"How are you doing getting around the house?" Aida asked.

"I've seen most of it," he replied cautiously. "I need to hit the basement, and I haven't yet made my way to the pool."

"Ah, the pool." Aida nodded. "I'll go for a swim after dinner myself."

He asked, "And is that something you do alone?"

"I do," she replied, looking at him. "I always have."

Eva watched the interaction between Carson and her grandmother from the sidelines. Eva hadn't really planned on keeping quiet during dinner, but something was interesting about watching him approach her grandmother with simplicity and what appeared to be pure sincerity. Eva hated to acknowledge the reality here, but something was very appealing about a man who could be tough as nails when it came to doing his job, yet still so gentle and kind with her grandmother.

When he turned to Eva and asked if she used the pool as well, she looked at him in surprise, realizing that she would be questioned about things like that as well. "I do. I quite often swim in the middle of the night."

He immediately frowned.

She shrugged. "Sometimes, after being deep into my painting, I suddenly look up and realize it's well past midnight, and I'm sore, stressed, and suddenly wiped out," she murmured. "It helps to ease some of the soreness if I get in the hot tub."

"Agreed," he noted immediately. "Nice for you both that it's there and available."

Eva nodded but grimaced. "Another reason why I like to use it is because it always seems like such a waste to have so much luxury here only to not use it."

At that, her grandma laughed. "As I've told you before, that's just foolish, my dear. It's here, so we might as well enjoy it, but, if you don't want to enjoy it or don't want to go for a swim, don't feel you must force yourself," she shared. "That kind of thing will only take the joy out of it."

"Maybe," Eva replied, as she smiled at her grandmother, "but you know how I work such strange hours."

"Which is also why I'm glad to see you here for dinner

tonight," Aida admitted. "I do hate eating alone."

"I'm trying to be available for dinner as much as I can," Eva explained. "It's just—you know—sometimes I get busy."

"You mean, you get lost," Aida stated, with an affectionate smile.

Eva had to agree with that. "I guess. It's not quite the way I intended to go through life."

"No, but, just because you don't intend something, it doesn't mean it won't work out that way." At that, Aida returned her attention to Carson. "Now, back to the house. Do you have any questions about the layout?"

"Not yet."

"You know that it would be hard for anybody to reach my suite on the second floor," she told him.

"I didn't yet find the access to the attic."

"Oh, that is through the studio," Eva said. "If it's absolutely necessary, I can show you after dinner."

"It is necessary," he stated. With a nod, he then added, "Thank you."

She winced at that because, of course, it would be necessary. He wanted to see every inch of the property. But given what he was trying to do, maybe that was okay. She didn't know anymore.

It seemed as if, in spite of her objections, this was going ahead and happening, so the only thing she could really do was try to get along with him as much as possible. For her grandmother's sake, if nothing else.

As soon as dinner was over, she suggested, "Let's go up to the studio, and I'll show you the attic. Then maybe you can go down to the pool with Grandma."

At that, her grandmother smiled. "I like that idea." She looked over at him. "Did you bring a swimsuit?"

"I did, even not knowing you had a pool. However, I normally pack for all contingencies."

"Well, as it turns out, I do have a pool. I know Ice would have loved it here."

"Oh, definitely." He smiled. "Use of your pool is a luxury I hadn't quite expected. Thank you."

"The pool is one of those things that you should enjoy because it's there, if you want to, that is," Eva said, mimicking her grandmother just a tad.

"Carson, you may go with my very amusing granddaughter. Then I will meet you down at the pool in a bit. If you so choose, that is," she added, with a nod to a smirking Eva. "I'll do a few lengths, and then I'll probably sit in the hot tub."

"Agreed. I could use some laps myself."

"Good. I do like to see people looking after their fitness." And, with that, she slowly rose from the table.

He stood to help her and pulled back the chair for her.

She smiled. "There is still a gentleman inside, isn't there?"

"There is always a need to have a gentleman inside," he murmured. "The world is mean enough without taking away a few of the niceties that make things more pleasant and a bit easier."

She looked at him and nodded. "I knew I liked you." With that, she slowly made her way from the formal dining room.

He watched her steady progress with a narrowed gaze. She was mobile and quite capable, but, at the end of the day, it looked like she was more fatigued than she wanted to let on. As he looked back at Eva, she was chewing on her bottom lip. "Is this normal for Aida?"

Eva gave him a reluctant nod. "It is. She seems to be aging in front of me, faster than I want to admit."

"And yet she's still doing pretty well for a woman in her eighties," he said. "I'm sure this distressing situation is taking quite a toll on her."

"I guess." Eva's shoulders slumped. "I really wish this wasn't happening. She'll just blame herself."

"I don't know that there's any blame to be assigned in a deal like this," he murmured, studying her face. As she got up, he reached over and started to stack up all the dishes from the table back onto the trolley. Noticing that, she did the same. "I presume Flora will come and take it away?" he asked.

"Yes. And, yes, I do this every night as well."

"Good."

"I don't think Flora's got all that many more years in her either," Eva noted.

"Health-wise or mobility-wise?" When Eva frowned, he added, "Well, it's one thing if you're feeding your own family, but she's working a lot. At what point in time does she get to retire?"

"I don't know," Eva admitted sadly. "It's like the passing of an era racing toward me, and honestly I'm not ready."

That explained some of her resistance to everything Carson did. She was probably fighting any change in her world at all. "And it'll happen whether you're ready or not," he murmured. "I'm sorry. That sucks."

"I know, and it just makes me so angry. And it terrifies me." Jerking out of her negative headspace, she shook her head and motioned to him. "Come on. Let's go take a look at that lovely attic."

"Have you been up there?"

"Not in ages. Honestly, I like to keep it locked up, so I don't think about what's up there."

"I'm surprised that, if it bothers you, why choose to stay on that floor?"

"Well, I have the whole third floor all to myself," she explained. "There's quite a benefit to that, particularly when I'm caught up in my work. As long as I keep it locked, I don't worry about it."

"Is there any other access up there?"

She shook her head. "Nope. No rooftop deck, helipad, or anything luxurious like that," she replied. "It's a very old home. Modernizing now would probably take way more money than even my grandmother has."

"Well, from what I've seen, it's been modernized several times over," he told her. "And I'm not sure anybody really needs a helicopter on their roof."

"My understanding is that Ice has one."

"Not on the roof," he corrected. "She has several in the compound though."

"Of course she does." Eva laughed. "She's quite the pilot, I hear."

"Ice has been close to your grandmother for quite a while, hasn't she?"

"Actually I've known Ice for a good decade myself," she shared. "It's been pretty amazing."

"She's an amazing person," he said, with a smile, as he followed Eva upstairs.

"Oh, by the way, there is an elevator."

"I saw a space where I thought it might be. Can you show me?"

She walked over and back down the stairs, to the corner at the back of them, then pressed what looked like a door knob. Instantly an elevator opened up.

He nodded. "Now this makes sense. Does it take your grandmother straight up to her room?"

"It takes her up to that portion of the second floor just outside her bedroom. It resembles a closet up there."

"Good to know. It's always a great place to hide, just in case."

"Right, I hadn't thought of that."

"Well, if you ever needed a place to hide," he explained, "this elevator accessway is not something that anybody will see immediately nor identify as an elevator."

"No, and I think that was part of the reason for it being so subtle. Nobody wanted to have the place modernized to the point that it looked modern."

"Got it."

"I'm just happy for Grandma's sake that an elevator is even here."

"Agreed."

And, with that, she led the way up the stairs.

"So, do you choose the stairs for health?"

"Yeah, it gives me a way to wear off some of those hefty dinners and snacks that I'm always eating," she said, with a sigh. "It's too easy to eat a lot of food, when it's presented to you like that."

"It's really good food too," he said, with a smile.

"It is."

Upstairs, he followed her to her studio, which she quickly unlocked, something that he noted with a raised eyebrow. "Do you always lock it?" he asked.

"Most of the time," she stated cheerfully, as she stepped through.

He followed her to a spot underneath one of the alcoves.

"It's up there?" he asked.

"Well, this is the access point," she explained, "and it heads on to the south side of the property."

He shook his head. "This should be fun."

She quickly reached up and pulled a lever, releasing a series of steps that came down.

"So, how do you lock that?" he asked.

"I keep a stick stuck through the lever, so nobody can bring it down on me from inside."

"Ah, that's also interesting," he murmured. "Yet it wasn't locked just now."

She stopped, staring at him. "I ... I must ..."

With the stairs down, he motioned ahead. "Do you want to lead the way?"

"I don't want to go at all." She wrapped her arms around her chest.

"It really bothers you, huh?"

"It does," she murmured.

"Any particular reason why?"

She shrugged. "Not really. It's not as if I've ever found any stranger up there. It just always gives me the creeps a little, thinking somebody could be hiding there."

And, with that, he headed up the steps, but, when he reached the top riser, the ceiling was really low, and he had to crouch to get inside the attic, but this was definitely a hallway that he headed down, moving toward the other side. There it widened into a series of storage rooms.

From the looks of it, they were all pretty full. He shook his head to think about what would be required to clean out just this attic someday.

It was massive. He quickly did a full check, locating another door on the other side, but, when he went to open it, it was sealed shut. Probably during one of the renovations. It wasn't just locked; it was actually cemented in. He frowned at that, but, since it didn't appear to pose a problem, there wasn't a whole lot to be worried about.

With that, he headed back down toward her, taking several photos as he went. When he came down the stairs, she sat near the bottom, waiting for him. "Thank you for letting me check out that attic space."

"You're welcome. And despite all the evidence to the contrary, I'm really not trying to be difficult."

"I know." He nodded. "You're just trying to ignore the fact that something's going on and that your grandmother might be taken from you. I get that, but I come from a world where sticking your head in the sand doesn't do any good."

"I come from a world where it's the only way I've ever managed to get through life," she confirmed. "Like losing my parents. I had my mother longer than my father, but she wasn't quite all there ever since the accident. So my grandmother and I became very close because we only had each other," she murmured, "and that makes you fearful of loss. Every time I think about losing someone, and remembering all the pain of what I've already lost," she explained, "it makes me just … Life is very difficult like that."

"And, when it's difficult, it's hard for you to work. Or is that when your best work comes through? Do you use your work as a way to release all those emotions?"

"No." She shook her head, grimacing. "I wish I could. It might be easier. Instead it seems like all I have is the fear and panic. Then I must ease all that away to begin to work."

"Maybe there's a way you could reverse that somehow," he suggested, "and give yourself permission to just paint away all that fear."

She smiled at him. "What are you, a therapist now?"

"No, but I've seen a lot of loss, and I've seen a lot of people deal with it," he murmured. "Yet everyone has to deal with it in their own way."

"And how do you deal with it?" she challenged.

"I go to the gym, and I destroy a ridiculous amount of reps—and sometimes my body in the process," he admitted. "We all must deal with loss in our own way, and none of it is ever easy."

"Now that's the truth," she agreed, as she walked him to the door of her suite.

He inclined his head as he stepped out and said, "Have a good night."

"You too."

As she went to close the studio, she hesitated. "Carson, ... do you ... do you really think she's in danger?"

"WHY DON'T YOU tell me why you *don't* think anything wrong is going on?" Carson asked Eva.

"Well, ... I don't want to believe it for one thing," she began. "In my mind, everybody loves my grandmother."

"Of course." He smiled, acknowledging their close relationship with a smile. "But the reality is ... what?"

"The reality is, my grandmother believes someone is trying to kill her," she stated, with a nod. "I just don't know whether it's something her imagination has come up with or what. I mean, that email was rather generic and another threat didn't come, except that one typewritten letter. I think more could be read into them than was really intended."

"Let me ask you this. Would anybody be trying to make it *look* like it was Aida's imagination? So that she appears to be losing it? Or do you think that really nobody is involved in this at all?"

"I don't know." She frowned. "I hadn't considered that *make her go crazy* idea, that somebody might be trying to make her look like she was losing her edge. She runs a lot of charities within her main charity, so, if she looks like she's not quite all there, it could have quite the impact."

"It would have an impact on her how?"

"I don't know that it would have an impact on her personal life, especially if she didn't believe that nonsense. I guess it would depend on whether anybody else involved in the charity business believed it or not."

"But you also know how touchy businesses can be."

"Absolutely," she murmured.

"So I presume she has lawyers and advisors and assistants and accountants and board members or whoever to deal with—on the business side of things?" Carson asked.

Eva frowned. "Yes, although I … I really don't know the details firsthand. I'm the main beneficiary of all her holdings, including life insurance. My name is on the businesses for ease of transference and access to operating capital after she goes, but other than that, … I have no idea. You have to remember that I'm mostly in my studio here on the third floor, missing meals, missing daylight. So while my grandmother could have tons of meetings in person in her office on the first floor, the only way I would be made aware of them would be if she brought me in. And she doesn't do that very often, only if she needs to. Otherwise she handles it herself."

Looking worried, yet at the same time doubtful, Carson smiled at Eva. "Honestly, I don't have all the answers yet, much less an opinion," he shared. "What she has told me so far involves the vaguely worded email and then a typewritten letter of the same kind, plus dead birds on the stoop, strange sounds at nighttime, being followed when she's out on a drive, that sense of being watched when she's out walking, and the few odd hang-up calls. And, while unnerving and bordering on stalking and threatening, none of that is enough to get the police to believe somebody is trying to kill her."

"Exactly," Eva agreed, with emphasis. "Which is why I struggle to find any validity in it myself. But, at the same time, I don't want to think that she's making it up or that she's so spooked that the death angle makes sense to her."

"Of course not, but sometimes people have an instinctive way of knowing that something is wrong."

"Wow." She stepped back. "My grandmother has always been that way," she replied immediately. "So, now I'm not sure what to say."

"Let me finish my investigation, and then hopefully we'll find out just what's going on."

"And your investigation amounts to what?" she asked, back to her testy tone again.

"Well, if Aida's hearing things, then I want to know more than what I can see with a cursory check of these rooms. I have some equipment arriving tomorrow," he added, "and I'll be coming back through here again."

She just glared at him.

Carson nodded and shrugged, all with a smile. "The last thing you want is to make the wrong decision."

And, with that, he turned and headed back downstairs.

Chapter 4

W HEN EVA WOKE the next morning, she felt an odd sense of disquiet. She checked her watch and realized it wasn't even six. She was never awake at this hour. Even if she worked all night or didn't work at all, she didn't wake up now.

Feeling strangely disturbed by it, she hopped out of bed and walked over to the window. The morning light was just coming up, and, despite the circumstances, something was seriously gorgeous about the whole look of the morning. She smiled at it, until she noted her grandmother, walking out the front door. Eva opened the window and called down to her, "Where are you going?"

Her grandmother looked up at her, waved, and asked, "What are you doing up so early?"

It was actually hard to hear her, since they were that far apart. "I don't know why, but I don't like the idea of you going out alone."

"Greta just called. She's having a bad time."

"Well, don't go alone, for crying out loud. Give me a minute, and I'll get dressed."

"No, no, no," her grandmother replied. "That's not what I intended at all."

"I know that," Eva called back, "but, if you've brought somebody here who's supposed to keep you safe, the least you can do is stick around so he can do his job."

At that, her grandmother looked at her in surprise. "I forgot he was here."

That comment made Eva worry even more. "What?"

Her grandmother quickly brushed away her grand-daughter's question. "If you're coming, hurry up. I told Greta I'd be right over."

"Maybe so, but you also must look after yourself, and this isn't the best time for you to be out running around." At that, Eva heard another sound and immediately saw Carson step out, watching her grandmother. "Are you going with her?" Eva asked.

He nodded. "I'm not letting her go anywhere alone. Not even when she tries to sneak out on me. He then turned to face Aida.

"Well, I most certainly wasn't trying to sneak out," she argued, "outside of the fact that I didn't want to wake anybody."

"And what's the point of my being here?" Carson asked. "Your granddaughter has a valid point, and, if I'm not to be told when you're planning to leave, my purpose for being here won't work very well."

"Well, I thought that, if nobody knew where I was going," she added, "it wouldn't be an issue."

"But chances are, it'll be an even bigger issue." He gave her a slight nod. "Because, if somebody *is* watching you, they'll find you completely alone."

She stared at him. "I keep forgetting how much I don't like this."

"That's because, now that you've made some progress, you don't really want to acknowledge what could actually be happening."

"Does anybody?" she asked crossly.

He gave Aida a bright smile.

Eva had joined them at the front door by now, having thrown a robe over her pajamas, and even she saw the humor in this. "If I'm not allowed to argue about his ... *intrusions*," she warned, "neither are you, Grandma."

At that, her grandmother raised both hands in mock surrender. "Fair play," she agreed. "Carson may come with me. We'll stop at the bakery on the way back, so get your shower, Eva, and we'll be home in an hour or so."

"Not if you're going to Greta's place," Eva replied.

At that, Aida winced. "Maybe not, but hopefully it won't be that bad."

"Well, if she's called you at this hour, how good can it be?" Eva asked.

"I don't know," Aida replied in frustration. "However, I must go see her. She is my friend." And, with that, she turned and looked at Carson. "So then I don't need to drive, is that it?"

"No, we'll take my car, if you don't mind."

Eva watched from the front door in great amusement as her grandmother was led to Carson's vehicle, a small sedan, which was a much different level of vehicle than Aida was used to.

When he opened the door for her, she got right in, as if to say she had absolutely no problem riding in something so beneath her. And, of course, her grandmother wasn't a snob at all. It was just funny to see her in a vehicle that she was so unaccustomed to.

She got in and settled without any problem, and it did make Eva feel better to know that Carson was going along. What did that say about what she actually believed was going on then? Because, if it were really true that she didn't believe any of this mess, then she wouldn't have given a crap. But it was her grandmother, so anything dangerous that went on in her world was something Eva cared about. It was just so ugly to think about what this problem could be, so she was definitely trying to hold off on even acknowledging that something so bizarre was really happening.

But ignoring it wouldn't help either.

Still, if Eva and her grandmother had a chance to talk, maybe her grandmother would open up a little bit more about the problems that she saw. Because, based on what Carson had told Eva earlier, her grandmother hadn't revealed some things. If that were the case, it would be up to Eva to tell Carson all of it.

No way to keep any of this hidden, nor should there be any reason to. As a matter of fact, chances were that her grandmother wouldn't open up at all.

Frowning, Eva sent her grandmother a text. **Tell him about Melody.**

And, with that, knowing she'd done all she could, Eva headed back to bed.

AS CARSON DROVE Aida through the gates, he heard her phone go off. "Is that Eva again?" he asked, with a note of amusement.

"Yes," she replied crossly. "But ..."

He looked over at her and frowned. "You know that you need to tell me everything because, the minute you try to hide something, that'll probably be the one thing I needed to know."

"It just doesn't make any sense," she argued, "but Eva's

reminding me to tell you about Melody."

"Well, I haven't heard that name before, so maybe it's a good suggestion, and there is no time like the present."

"Well, first, … you tell me. Did you find anything … *off* in the house?"

"I've only just begun, but, so far, I have found all kinds of places to hide, and that the security, particularly on the windows, is pathetic," he stated bluntly. "If somebody wanted to get in, they could certainly get in without any problem. More so, they could hide in this house for a very long time without being detected."

She winced at that. "While it hurts to hear that, you are quite right, I'm sure," she agreed. "Though it's not something I generally want to acknowledge, the house does need some work."

"The house needs an upgrade from a security perspective," he noted. "So, it's not even so much about the house needing work. It's really quite impressive, but there are definitely some tech issues that need to be attended to."

"Of course," she murmured. Then she turned to face him. "You really didn't have to come with me, you know?"

"Yes, I did, and, just so you know, I'll be going everywhere with you from here on out."

"Well, I guess I brought that on myself," she muttered. "I'm really not used to having somebody around me so protectively."

"You matter a lot to the people who sent me here," he stated calmly. "I won't do any less for them or for you."

She sighed. "I'm sure a nice young man like you has better things to do with his life."

He burst out laughing. "A nice young man like me would be doing this anyway, either for you or for another person, another group, or even another country," he explained. "So that's enough excuses. Now I realize you're accustomed to traveling in a bit more style, so we can switch to a different vehicle if you like, once I've had a chance to do a safety check on yours." She smirked, and her sense of humor made him realize just what a fascinating woman she was.

"Despite the fact that you just made me sound like a bit of a snob, I do like the fact that you have a sense of humor."

"Ditto," he replied. "I work with and for a lot of different people, many who don't see very much of the humor in life," he added. "I never know whether it's because of the circumstances or not, but it is very nice when I get to spend time with somebody who does."

She nodded. "Life is tough enough," she admitted, "and, if it's my time to go, well, it's my time to go, but I certainly don't want to leave my granddaughter with anything to make it even more painful."

"Whenever you go, it is bound to cause her great pain," he murmured quietly. "So let's not do anything to make it worse, much less sooner than it should be, huh?"

She reached over and patted his hand on the steering wheel. "You're a nice man."

He snorted. "I don't think your granddaughter agrees at the moment."

"That's just because she's being forced to do something she's not good at. Nobody likes that."

"No, that's very true," he murmured. "Nobody likes being forced to do something they don't want to do."

"So you must make it so she's happy to do it," she suggested firmly.

He burst out laughing. "I don't think it would be that

easy to force your granddaughter to do anything."

"No, you're certainly right there." She chuckled. "She's been a bit of a law unto herself."

"And probably with good reason. I'm sure she's very talented and has spent a lot of time developing the personality that allows her to be so creative."

"Did you see her artwork?" she asked eagerly.

"No, she wouldn't let me," he noted. "Sheets were thrown over all the canvases. But it is a stunning studio."

"It is, indeed. She claimed that space almost immediately."

He nodded. "Yet the attic bothers her."

Aida shook her head. "I tend to forget about the attic."

"And why would you do that?" he asked her.

"Because there have been some problems with it in the past. It's one of those places that I don't see, so I don't go there often. But, on the odd occasion when I've had to, it does bring back some bad memories."

"For you?"

"Yes. My granddaughter was caught up there for a couple hours once, and it frightened her pretty badly," she murmured.

"Of course it would," he stated. "It's a big space and quite confusing. It feels almost like a prison, particularly with the door that goes nowhere."

"That door goes nowhere on purpose because we had it walled up when I was just a child. That was after I was locked up there accidentally."

"Accidentally?"

"I wasn't so sure that it was an accident at the time."

"Tell me more," he invited.

She shrugged. "I wasn't sure that the people I was playing with at the time didn't do it on purpose. I mean, no harm came from it because, obviously, here I am, but it did give me a very horrible feeling about being imprisoned there."

"It would give anybody that kind of a feeling," he murmured. "And I presume that nobody from that era is still around?"

She looked at him, surprised, then chuckled. "That's a rather roundabout way of suggesting that I'm old."

He laughed out loud. "Well, I'm not sure there's any easy way to say things like that. However, whatever happened was a long time ago."

"It was, indeed," she murmured, "and you are right to suggest that those people aren't around anymore."

"That's what I assumed," he murmured, "but I can't ever make that type of assumption fully."

"No, of course not," she said, "but it was a long time ago. And it was a case where nobody got caught and no punishment was meted out. So it was one of those situations that no one could do very much about at the time."

"Of course not," he agreed. "And you have managed to leave me with a lot more questions and not many answers."

"Well, since it's been sealed, nobody else has been up there, except Eva. When she first got here and was busy exploring the place, she managed to get locked in there herself."

"And, after that, you changed all the outside locks?"

"Of course. I will never forget what happened to me, so I was desperate to make sure that she was okay too."

"Of course you were." Carson kept on driving, following her directions, until they pulled up in front of an interesting high-rise condo. He asked, "Is this where you're going?"

She nodded. "You can sit here and wait in the car."

"No, ma'am, I'm afraid I won't," he replied calmly, as he got out, came around, and opened the door for her.

She hopped out and glared at him. "My friend won't be happy if I come in with somebody."

"Levi and Ice won't be happy if I let you go anywhere without me."

She stared at him for a moment. "Oh no, that's quite true. They won't be, will they? And I certainly don't want to listen to them after you tattle on me either."

He burst out laughing. "I won't have to tattle on you if you just let me do my job. But, if you don't, then that is definitely happening."

She rolled her eyes at that. "Sometimes people just like to tattle."

"They do, indeed," he teased. "Yet I have better things to do with my time, and one of those things is to ensure that you're safe. And besides, I'm a little bit afraid of Ice, so let's go."

"Ha. That is an amusing image I have of Ice taking you to task."

Carson shook his head and led the way up to the door. "These are apartments?"

"Yes, they are. Rather interesting ones actually."

He nodded as he looked around. "Quite fascinating really." And it was. There was no easy way to determine just how many people were here and what the kind of security was in place. "Do you ring through for her?"

She nodded. "The doorman will let me in."

And, with that, after a moment's hesitation, the doorman strode to the door. As soon as he saw who it was, he smiled and opened it for her. But, when his gaze landed on

Carson, he shook his head. "You aren't going up, sir."

"In that case, neither is she," he replied.

"You're not cleared."

"Nope, I'm not. And, if you can't clear me, she doesn't go up either."

At that, the security guard turned and looked at Aida. "Are you in trouble?"

"Well, you could say that, but I've gone to great lengths to keep myself safe, and he is now part of my security detail."

"Ah." The doorman looked at him. "That explains it."

"It should," Carson agreed. "And honestly it is nice to know that you at least are trying to stop me."

"Trying?" he asked, with a note of challenge.

"I don't care if we're going up or not," Carson added, "but I think it matters a lot to Aida."

At that, the guard hesitated. "I was told to let Miss Aida right through."

"Well, then let me right through," she stated impatiently. "And I get that you two are busy with your pissing contest, but it's really got nothing to do with me."

At that, Carson burst out laughing, and the doorman, though irritated, couldn't help but chuckle.

"Well, you're supposed to get clearance *ahead* of time," the guard reiterated, "but let me see about getting you cleared."

"Better get to it fast. Otherwise I'll tell her that you won't let me in," Aida stated. "I can be a tattletale too," she murmured, looking at Carson. He just laughed.

But the guard glared at her. She threw up her hands and started to turn away. "Hang on," he said. "I'll call her."

"Well, do it fast because my legs can't keep me upright for much longer."

That was the first inkling Carson had that her legs were anything but great. So far, she'd been this pillar of strength, and it was interesting to see her show weakness—or at least use it to get what she wanted.

Almost immediately the doorman walked over, picked up a phone, and contacted her friend. As soon as the guard got an answer, he nodded and motioned them through. "You can both go on up." He glared at Carson as they walked past.

Carson didn't say anything because really the guard was just doing his job, and the fact that he was actually doing it so well was to be commended. Carson had seen way too many instances where that much effort was never expended.

He stepped out the elevator door at the second floor and looked at her. "How long do you think you'll be here?"

"Honestly, I have no way of knowing," Aida admitted. "Greta's not in very good health."

As they headed toward the apartment, he knocked, and it opened almost immediately.

The woman inside the apartment studied him closely. "Well, you're not exactly what I expected."

"I'm never what anybody expects. But never mind me, may Aida and I come in?"

"Of course *she* can," Greta snapped, "and I suppose it'll be useless to tell you that you can't."

"Absolutely," he agreed.

"Well, you *could* stay in the hallway."

"I *could*, but I won't," he stated, his tone completely inflexible. "Where she goes, I go."

Greta raised both hands in frustration and glared at him. And he just gave her a bland look back.

"Just forget about it, Greta," Aida declared. "We're here now. Otherwise I'm heading home and back to bed."

Immediately her friend turned to her. "No, no, no. Come on in." She let them in and way too quickly moved to the kitchen of the apartment. "Let me get some coffee." As they stepped inside, she called out to somebody behind the closed door down the hallway.

At that, Carson froze, then turned and looked at Aida. "Who else is here?"

"Her housekeeper companion," Aida said quietly. "No need to panic."

He just raised one eyebrow.

"You didn't ask," Aida explained, "so I didn't say anything."

He nodded. "Let's address that beforehand the next time."

She smiled at him. "It's such a strange feeling to have someone like you around all the time."

"Get used to it," he replied. "As long as we have a problem, I'm your solution."

With that, he shut Greta's front door and took a hard glance around the apartment and the one door that remained closed down Greta's hallway.

Chapter 5

EVA FELT STRANGE, knowing that her grandmother was out with Carson. But then, everything about Carson disturbed her. He was a force to be reckoned with, and she didn't have any experience with men like that.

It was all about power, but it radiated from the inside out, and her fingers were itching to sketch his face—which was also bizarre because she typically didn't do portraits. And certainly not for people she knew, but something was awfully striking about his features.

About the man himself, for that matter.

Not only striking but disturbing. Something was a little off about him—not off maybe, but different—yet so very bright. She didn't know why, but it was driving her crazy. She had absolutely no way of making any sense of it, at least not yet. Hopefully he would do a full analysis of her grandmother's case, determine that they had absolutely nothing to be worried about, then life would continue as it always had.

The last thing Eva wanted were more reminders that her grandmother's time grew short. Although Eva knew that was a possibility, she desperately wanted another ten years or longer with her, if she could get it. Her grandmother was a special person, and it was terribly hard to contemplate losing her at any point. Right now it was beyond impossible to consider losing her before her time.

Most people would say living to be eighty-plus was definitely not before her time, but, for Eva, it was a different story. She loved her grandmother, who had always been such a huge force in her life. Eva was in no way prepared to lose her. It would come, no doubt, but Eva hoped not until many years in the future, when there was no other option—or when Aida was in such pain or couldn't live a quality life anymore. Anything other than that would hurt Eva terribly. A hurt that would already be bad would then become impossible.

Determined to drive away the subject of death, Eva walked over and picked up her charcoals. For whatever reason, she studied the medium in her hand, wondering why on earth she would even choose charcoal when she had not worked with it for such a long time. Nonetheless, feeling something building inside her, she selected not a canvas but picked up one of the biggest sketch pads she had, turning to a clean page. She set it up on one of her empty easels and took slow deep breaths.

She closed her eyes and just let the power of whatever was bothering her come out. Such an odd thing for him to have suggested this very thing to her, and yet he was right. It was something she had done before the loss of her parents.

But she didn't really expect that reminder to come from this guy. But then it was just one more thing in a long line of things so very disturbing about him. Disturbing, and yet ... how could she ignore the fact that he was also fascinating?

She lifted her hand to the canvas, realizing that she was working basically without any kind of control, just letting her hand do what it wanted. She should have known when she had first picked up the charcoal just what she intended to do with it, but not until she stared at the drawing did she figure it out. Only after her hand dropped to her lap and relaxed did she realize how much of an impact this man had had on her.

His face stared back at her and absolutely no way could she *not* recognize him.

And the image was complete, including those deep magnetic eyes, the craggy forehead, the firm lines of his jaw, and those amazing cheekbones. But what stunned her most of all was the power that radiated off the page.

She never drew people—and for a very good reason. She never felt she could capture the essence of them. If that were the case, then what the hell had she done here and now? Yet the compulsion to continue drawing Carson from different angles was unavoidable and impossible to ignore. As her arm lifted once again to the next clean page in front of her, she stared in complete fascination, while her hand moved with a surety that she in no way felt herself.

It was so bizarre and yet fascinating, compelling, and quite frankly a little terrifying for her. When she was done again, she stepped back, feeling an ache in her arm that she hadn't experienced in a long time. But more than that, she sensed such awe and fascination at her creation on the page.

Something she had never, ever expected to see had come from her hand, and it glowed with a passion and a power, one she couldn't dream of experiencing. Just something about him, something about who he was, fascinated her. More than fascinated really, he had apparently struck the artistic side of her in a unique way. It was intriguing and detrimental to her senses, yet her body just wanted to pick up more charcoal and paper, to keep trying, to continue working on that face. She wanted to capture all the different essences of who he was. She knew the path was an uneasy one because he certainly wouldn't be up to sitting for her, so whatever she could do solo must happen in secret, without him noticing.

She wasn't even sure that what she was doing was fair. Whenever she had any living person in a photo or an image, she had always gotten permission from them. In this case, it wasn't even something that she wanted permission for because she didn't want him to know. She wanted to capture his essence without having anybody realize what she was doing. She knew that it sometimes changed people, and they looked at things differently, and that wasn't something she wanted to happen.

She didn't want him to know because then it wouldn't be the same. He wouldn't have the same look on his face, and yet this entire session still stunned her. It was all the more inspiring to see it. She wondered, considering her own words, had she become jaded with her work?

He was a fascinating man, a fascination that wouldn't leave her alone. Then she laughed because the last thing he would want to know was that he was a model for her latest artwork. More so, a model she was interested in working with again and again.

Somehow she didn't think that was part of his plan at all. Then again, seeing how she was stuck trying to deal with him, maybe this was a good thing.

Because it gave her something to work with, whether he liked it or not.

"SO NOW TELL me about Melody," Carson said to Aida, as they got back in the vehicle and headed toward home.

She groaned. "She worked for me a while back, ... an

unhappy soul."

"Dangerous?"

"I didn't think anybody in my world was dangerous. And, like the police told me, there wasn't anything concrete."

"And now?"

"I haven't been attacked, but I am still afraid it will happen," she stated.

"So you still think somebody is trying to kill you."

"Yes, and I know it all sounds stupid and like a fanciful old lady making things up," she muttered, "but the email and that letter, the phone calls, the unexplained noises, all just add up to something wrong."

"But that doesn't necessarily add up to somebody trying to kill you."

"No, no, it doesn't," she agreed, then hesitated.

"So, obviously something else is going on that you haven't told me. Something that is making you think like that."

She frowned. "I hadn't expected it to be this difficult."

"Everything that you've given Levi and Ice hasn't offered any leads, so what else have you got?"

"And if I haven't got anything else, you can leave. So will you?"

"No, of course not," he replied. "You have one week, and I will do my darndest to get to the bottom of it in that week."

"What if I'm ... What if I am just a lonely lost old lady?" she asked sadly.

"Then we'll find that out, and you'll know that you have no need to be worried. Because it's not you that you're worried about, is it?"

She looked over at him and slowly shook her head. "No.

How very astute of you."

"It doesn't take anybody very astute to understand that you love your granddaughter very much."

"And I wouldn't want anything to happen to her—or to me," she added firmly. "It's just so upsetting to think that something could be happening."

"There are no witnesses to the incidents, so why are you so adamant? With the police report I gathered there was nothing concrete, so why do you think you're being followed? You've had a couple hang-ups, and you got an uneasy email, which you turned over immediately, and you received a typed letter in the mail, right? So, what else are you hiding?"

"Dead birds on the front doorstep," she reminded him.

He nodded. "Right. And that isn't enough to make anybody raise an eyebrow, because, well, … birds hit windows and land on doorsteps all the time."

"Right." She sighed, her shoulders sagging. "And how do I explain that instinct? That need to turn around and look all the time because of that fear that I'm being followed?"

"I don't know," he said. "I just need one concrete thing to happen, and then believe me. I'll be all over it. I'm all over it now in terms of checking things out and seeing what's going on," he explained, "but, so far, there's absolutely nothing for me to tell Levi and Ice."

"I would never want to waste their time or yours." She then almost visibly appeared to pull herself together. "And that appears to be what I am doing, so you should probably go home."

"That's not happening," he told her cheerfully. "I'm here for the week."

"And what if I don't want you here?"

"Then you must tell Levi and Ice that."

She groaned. "They won't take that well."

Carson burst out laughing. "No, they won't. Just like your granddaughter, they love you dearly."

She smiled gently. "They are very good people. Just some people in this world you hit it off with, and they are prime examples."

"Exactly," he murmured. "And they don't want anything to happen to you."

"No, and I just feel foolish since nothing *is* happening. Yet, at the same time, I don't want anything to happen."

"Don't feel foolish," he said instantly. "We don't need a major confirmation that something's going on. That wouldn't make any of us happy. What we need is something that's less likely to have just happened *naturally*."

"You mean, more than a bird on the front steps?"

"Yes. If it were a dead cat, squirrel …" He stopped and thought about it. "Yeah, even a squirrel would be off. It would give me a little more ammunition to work with."

"Have you talked to Flora at all?"

"I have," he murmured. "And she doesn't know what to say either."

"No, of course not, because, like me, she doesn't appear to have seen or heard anything major."

"And yet she's worked with you for a very long time, right?"

"Yes, twenty-plus years."

"Is there any reason for her to knock you off?"

"Well, only if she's trying to retire," she teased, "but she doesn't want to quit."

He smiled at that because just enough wryness filled her tone for him to realize she was joking.

"Sometimes people can't quit because they're stuck in a scenario that won't give them enough money, or time, or purpose, or whatever it is that they need," he suggested. "Obviously you don't seem to think that's the problem here."

She shook her head. "No, I wouldn't think so. I have told her several times that, if she ever needs to quit, to just let me know, and I could hire someone else."

"And yet maybe she doesn't want to be replaced."

"Oh." Aida turned, looking at him. "I hadn't actually thought about it like that. Still, I can't see her as somebody who would kill me. And it would be way too easy to just put something in my food."

"Yet, at the same time," he muttered, "then it would be way too easy to pin her down as the guilty party."

"Right."

"So she must find another way to do it."

She groaned. "Let's just say that I hope all of this magically goes away. I'm kind of sorry I got you involved in this."

"Don't be sorry that you got me involved," he replied, shooting her a glance as he drove them home. "I hope I'm not the problem here."

"No, but I'm not exactly convinced that you are part of the solution either."

He smiled gently at her. "Why don't we just park that discussion and see how this goes along?"

"Not only do I not want to think about it"—she visibly shuddered—"but the consequences of being wrong are just so severe."

"Which is why we'll keep doing what we're doing," he noted calmly. "And I've only been here not even twenty-four hours, you know? At least let me get a chance to go through everything, and then, if I think you're making it up, I'll tell you."

She looked at him in surprise, as they pulled into the large gates, then paused for a few moments. "Would you?"

He looked at her and asked, "Would I what?"

"Would you tell me the truth?"

He smiled. "One way or another ... I would absolutely tell you the truth. I promise."

And, with that, she gave a sigh of relief. "Okay, in that case, do your worst. Sort out absolutely everything you need to, and, if I'm making it up in some form or fashion, please tell me."

"I will," he said solemnly. He decided right then and there that he would because, of all the things that she needed to know, first and foremost was that she wasn't crazy. Life had dealt her hard blows over the years, and he didn't want her thinking that somebody was out there trying to kill her, especially not when there was a good possibility that it was just her imagination.

At the same time, he was quite prepared to believe that she understood what was going on a little more than she was saying, and she was hoping that, when he wouldn't uncover anything, it would go down as nothing but her imagination.

"And that brings us back once again to Melody," he repeated, as he shut down the engine and turned to look at her. "And I won't let that subject go."

"Fine," she replied stiffly. "Then I'm heading for a cup of coffee poolside. If you care to join me, we can talk there."

"Fine by me," he agreed, as he got out. Then he hopped around and quickly opened the door for her. Giving her a hand to get out of the vehicle, he watched to see how she navigated in the early morning. "At least you know that your friend is okay."

"I do now," she stated. "Unfortunately she is somebody who tends to see the boogeyman everywhere."

"And that could be true for Greta," he suggested, "but you are a good friend for showing up to ease her fears."

She stopped, then looked at him and asked, "What if I'm actually doing her a disservice?"

He cocked an eyebrow in her direction. "Meaning?"

"Well, it's just …" She hesitated a moment, then stared and shrugged. "What if something *is* going on in her world. Maybe—"

"Are you thinking it's connected to yours?"

"I don't know," she admitted, "but what if somebody is out there, scaring old ladies around here?"

"Instinctively, I don't think that's what is happening." He thought about it and nodded. "Although if it's a concern I can take a closer look at that angle."

She smiled. "Just include Greta in your investigation, will you?"

"But she didn't have any similar kinds of problems," he reminded her.

"And yet they weren't all that unsimilar, if you think about it," she noted. "She just feels like somebody is always following her or looking in her windows."

"Her windows are on the second floor, and no high-rises face her apartment, so nobody will be looking in from that height," he noted.

"I know," she agreed, her shoulders sagging. "That does complicate matters."

He smiled. "It does, and yet, at the same time, it's perfectly fine. I will consider the problem from your angle and Greta's." As he thought about it, he asked, "How many people know that she's a friend of yours?"

She looked at him and shrugged. "I don't actually know. We've been school friends since, well, school," she murmured. "I've seen her through two husbands passing on, and she's always stood strong. So to see her now, she's definitely not the person she was before."

"None of us are though," he noted. "I'm not the same person I was twenty years ago."

She looked over at him. "I like that you don't mince words, young man. But I'll have you know that I am still a force to be reckoned with."

He chuckled. "Oh, believe me. I would never make the mistake of assuming otherwise."

She laughed. "Now, if I were only fifty years younger, then I would give my granddaughter a run for her money."

And, with that, she made her way into the front door, leaving him staring after her in shock.

Chapter 6

EVA WALKED INTO the pool area to see her grandmother bundled up, after completing her swim, now talking intently with Carson. Eva poured herself a cup of coffee from the service and then joined them. "You two appear to be in a heavy discussion."

"We kind of need to be," her grandmother shared.

"How was Greta?" Eva asked.

"Worried—and for similar reasons as me."

At that, Eva stopped dead in her tracks and looked at her grandmother. "What?"

Aida nodded. "I know it doesn't make any sense, but she's scared that she's being followed and that people are looking in her windows. It just makes me feel like I'm being more paranoid than normal myself. She's often that way, but now it's almost as if it's rubbing off on me."

"What are the chances of that happening to the two of you together?" Eva asked, puzzled.

"That's something Ice'll look into, checking street cams and facial recognition to see if you two have the same visitors. It's a long shot, but we'll do what we can," Carson replied. He hopped up. "Now that you're here, Eva, maybe you can persuade your grandmother to tell me about Melody. She keeps avoiding the topic."

At that, Eva looked over at her grandma and frowned.

"Come on. You need to tell him about her."

"She's nothing but a disgruntled employee," she snapped.

"More than disgruntled if you ask me," Eva added. "I think in some ways it's a sore spot for you that will never heal."

"Tell me, Aida. Eva has piqued my interest."

"Fine. Her father used to work here, and she did as well. Her father was here for quite a while actually." Then Aida went silent.

"And then Grandma fired him, and, at the time, Melody didn't appear to be too bothered. She wasn't at all close to her father, but, over time, it seemed to grate on her more and more. Finally it became something that she would bring up with sly little digs thrown out, about how her father had been fired and that nothing was ever good enough for Grandma, and things like that. It kept getting worse, didn't it, Grandma?"

"Oh, yes, the comments and the digs got quite nasty, far uglier than I would have liked."

He raised an eyebrow. "Why did you fire her father?"

"Because I thought he was stealing," Aida stated simply. "And I chose not to contact the police, so don't even ask me to do that."

"And why is that?"

"Because I didn't want the unpleasantness to come to my door," she murmured. "Anytime you have something like that, it can get quite nasty in the end."

"It absolutely can," he agreed, "but it also lets people know that you won't press charges, so oftentimes they come back for more."

"Well, it wasn't him getting nasty later. It was her. After

a while she just got ugly enough that I couldn't handle it anymore," she said. "It started with nothing, but it was almost like she convinced herself that she had some justifiable reason for getting mad at me over firing her father."

"Did you tell her why he was fired?"

Aida shook her head. "No, I didn't. Maybe I should have. But again I didn't want that kind of ugliness. I did tell her that I was fully justified in firing him, but that wasn't enough for her."

"No, for most people it's never enough," he murmured. "More often than not you must make it very clear and sometimes in a painfully blunt way."

"Maybe so," Aida agreed, "but again I just wanted the problem to go away."

He stared at her steadily. "Did it?"

She shook her head. "No, it did not."

Eva spoke up. "Melody made life very difficult around here for quite a while, until finally Grandma ended up having to fire her as well."

"And of course, that couldn't have been well received."

"No, of course not," she agreed.

"Again," Carson reminded them, "it's just my perspective, but, if you can't nip things like that in the bud, it becomes ugly right from the first go around."

Eva nodded as she listened. Her grandmother had struggled with Melody's rude insults, and Eva agreed with Carson in so many ways.

A FEW HOURS later, after lunch, Eva looked over at Carson, still sitting here by the pool, sipping coffee. Her grandmother had gone up to her room to lie down. "The whole thing with Melody was really hard on her."

"Sounds like it," he agreed, looking at her.

Eva thought for a moment. "Do you really think she would be involved in something like this?"

"There really is no way to know what somebody will do, but, if Melody felt like an injustice had been done, and those feelings just continued to compound, then, depending on where her headspace was at, a deep hatred may have festered and grown. In a case like that, someone like her could be unstable."

"*Unstable* is one word for it," Eva noted, as she smiled at him. "I mean, obviously we're not the easiest people to get along with. We certainly acknowledge that, but I also know that my grandmother pays her staff quite well and has always treated them fairly."

"Of course because that is how you keep good and loyal employees," he murmured.

"Exactly. Plus, she doesn't want any ugliness in her life at this stage."

"Does anybody, at any stage?" he asked, with a smile. "It just seems like sometimes in life there is more ugliness than we are really prepared for," he murmured, "and that's a problem."

She chuckled. "Agreed. I would be quite happy to never be caught up in any sort of mess like that again."

"How affected were you by it all?"

"Mostly in the sense that it was really distressing for Grandma. Every time she told me about Melody's latest verbal attack, Grandma became distraught over it. Finally, after I don't know how many times, she took my suggestion and fired her, knowing full well that ultimately it would cause other problems for a time."

"Exactly," he noted, "but sometimes there's just no way out of it. So she never gave Melody's name to the police? As in somebody potentially involved in all this? Because it's not in their file."

"No. I think, like so many other things in life, Grandma has just tried to forget about it all."

"And yet we know that doesn't work very well," he reminded her.

"No, but I can't really blame her for trying to go that route." Eva shook her head. "I'm not much better."

He stared out over the pool for a long moment. "You know what? Hiding your head in the sand won't make any of this go away."

"Are you sure?" she asked, with a bright smile. "We thought that maybe, if we left it long enough, it would."

"Keep in mind it could end up going away in a whole different manner than you had in mind," he reminded her.

At that, she winced. "That's not what we want."

"Of course not. So, let's see if we can get to the bottom of this and put a stop to it. Honestly, the little bits and pieces I've got so far point very well toward somebody like Melody."

"How do you figure?" she asked.

"Because there's nothing acute, and there's nothing particularly difficult either. She knows the layout of the house. She could easily come and go unseen."

"What about the security system?"

"That old thing needs to be updated. She could easily get in and out without setting that off."

"How?"

"She had access, right? And if you didn't change the password afterward, ... she would still have access."

She stared at him. "I think Grandma changed the passwords on the security system at one point."

"And how long ago was this?"

She frowned as she thought about it. "It wasn't all that long ago."

He waited patiently, as she was thinking hard. "A few weeks ago?"

"I don't know. Longer, I think."

"Before or after Melody was let go?"

"I want to say after, but maybe it was after her father was fired. I don't know."

"All right, we must track that down and definitely get it changed now. So back to Melody. Tell me more about her. How did she react to being fired?"

"She was more upset at her father being fired than anything."

"Which is why it should have been made very clear from the beginning what her father had done."

"And again, that's easy to say but not so easy to do. Plus, Ron had been living on the property, so he had to find a new place to live."

"Wow. So free room and board, I suppose. Those are nice perks. And did Melody live in too?"

Eva shook her head. "No. She didn't want that. She wasn't particularly close to her father."

"Yet she worked with him," Carson noted.

Eva laughed. "In a ten-thousand-square-foot house, where their duties didn't overlap, you would be surprised how little they saw of each other, even while both were working here for a little over the same year."

Carson shrugged. "Did your grandmother have anybody managing her affairs?"

"Yeah, that's what Melody's father did." She shrugged. "And that's one of the reasons he was fired. It was obvious that money was going missing."

"When was he let go?"

"Probably two years now."

"Yet you didn't bring in the cops to charge him with theft?"

She winced and shook her head. "No, we didn't, and I know you'll blame us for that again."

He shook his head. "I'm not trying to be on your case, but it's a little hard to understand when you're faced with an obvious crime, but then you do nothing about it."

"Right." Eva took a deep breath. "Do you really think that Ron would do something like this?"

"Well, he's gotten away with it so far, and, in his mind, for all you know, he's about to make a reappearance and try to save the day."

"I don't think so. It got pretty ugly when Grandma let him go."

"Did she call in anybody to remove him?"

"No, that's true," she replied thoughtfully. "When I came into her office, hearing their raised voices, they were arguing, and it was definitely bad, but he wasn't being physical. He didn't appear to be threatening her or anything like that."

"Well, that's good. If he had, would *you* have called the police?"

"Absolutely." Then she frowned. "I guess we should have called the police back then, shouldn't we?"

"Yes," he stated, "as you very well know. What we don't know is whether any of that is related to what's going on now. I'll need their names and any contact information you have. I'll have Ice do a full and detailed background check on them. Any chance your grandmother would have told Ice about Melody or her father?"

"Probably not."

"I won't be making that same mistake," he said.

"Right." She groaned, pulled out her phone, and searched her Contacts. "I'm not so sure if these are valid anymore," she murmured, "but this is what I have for the father and daughter."

"So, Ron Grogan and his daughter, Melody," he confirmed.

She nodded. "Yes."

"Fine. I'll send these two names to Ice, and we'll see if we can get some answers fairly quickly."

She took a deep breath. "And don't forget that no one seems to think there is anything to any of this."

"Let me ask you something," Carson added.

"Sure."

"Did Melody know about Aida's friend?"

"Which friend?"

"The one who we went to see today. Greta."

"Sure. I mean, Melody was with us for more than a year, I think. Her father had been here way longer."

"Ah, so, from your grandmother's point of view, the father's theft and all the nastiness from the daughter thereafter were two betrayals that were quite personal and very hard to deal with from two full-time employees."

"Yes. That's another reason why I think she didn't deal with it in the way you would have liked. It *was* personal."

He nodded slowly. "Yes, and yet some people would have been seriously angry and called the cops immediately."

"I think my grandmother was just very sad and hurt and

held off doing anything like that because she was so upset. And then, when enough time had passed, she didn't really have a reason to tell the cops and then just let it slide."

"There are enough indications that these two people are problematic, and we've got to make sure it doesn't happen again," he warned her. "Because, once you let something like that slide, you know ..." He left it at that.

She nodded. "And I can't really blame Grandma. I mean, a lot of things are going on in her life, and she's very busy, so to deal with the betrayal on top of it all? I just think it was something my grandmother wasn't up to at the time."

"As long as it doesn't have anything to do with what's going on now," he noted, "we can deal with Melody and Ron later. But, right now, if there is a connection, we must nip it in the bud quickly." He frowned at Eva. "How much money did he steal from your grandma?"

Eva's eyes widened, then she closed them, shaking her head. "You don't want to know." And she promptly left.

CARSON WAS NOW alone at the swimming pool and didn't waste any time sending out the information to Ice and Levi. When Ice phoned him back just a few minutes later, she asked, "Aida really didn't call the cops about this?"

"Nope." Then he told her what Eva had said.

"Well, it only makes sense. Melody didn't live here, as she and her father didn't get along that well, but she served the family for maybe a couple years, and you feel like you must justify your actions to yourself," she murmured.

"The best thing Aida could have done would have been to contact the cops the minute she suspected the father of theft. And with the kind of money that Aida seems to have, it could have been a large amount."

"Aida was probably hurt and embarrassed, had no idea it could grow into an even bigger problem with time."

"I'm not so sure she admits it yet," Carson suggested.

"Ron looks like a good suspect," Ice noted, "and I'm happy to investigate."

"If we can actually prove he embezzled money from Aida, I'd feel better."

"No details of that yet, is there?"

"No, not at the moment. Eva was helpful, but Aida is the one I need to talk to. She won't like it, but I can look into it. We also need to consider that this stalker activity could be a little more widespread than what we were initially thinking."

"Explain, please." And he quickly told her about the session he had with Aida at her friend Greta's house. "Interesting. So, the same kind of complaints, … she is afraid that somebody's watching her and afraid that she's being followed."

"But no dead birds or anything like that," he reminded her. "That may be due to her location though. Greta's in a place with good security thankfully. There was even a bit of a rub to allow me in to see Greta today. So, it's more secure than most buildings—and most certainly more than Aida's house. She needs to update this old system of hers."

"No, you're right about all that," she replied. "I'll look into the father-daughter duo." And, with that, she also signed off.

When Flora came to him a little bit later, she stated, "A parcel has arrived for you."

"Oh, good," he murmured, as he got up. "I've been waiting for that." He immediately grabbed the boxful of listening equipment that Ice had ordered for him. With that in hand, he headed to the ground floor. Starting here, he worked his way through this first floor, skipping Aida's office for now as she was in there working. However, he continued on to the second floor, checking every inch of it, so far finding everything was squeaky clean. It seemed like absolutely nothing was going on, until he got to Aida's bedroom, and the equipment chimed like hell. And, sure enough, he found a bug.

"Welcome to the party, sneaky little bastard," he murmured, after stepping outside of the room and shutting the door. Pulling out his cell phone, he immediately contacted Ice. "Hey, thanks for the equipment," he said the minute she answered. "I found a bug in Aida's bedroom."

"Shit," she murmured.

"I know, but it's only the bedroom I've checked so far. I have to go through the others yet."

"What else is there?"

"On the second floor is the suite for Flora, so one occupied bedroom and a couple empty guest rooms, plus the servants' quarter on the opposite side. On the third floor is Eva's studio and, yeah, her bedroom. I'll go through the attic again now too," he noted. "I already made a trip through the basement and the cellars, then through the whole first floor. This place is a bloody maze."

"It is, indeed," Ice agreed. "It's also worth millions, just for the land value alone."

"Right. Well, I think it ever being sold is pretty unlikely. Aida is totally committed to it, and even the granddaughter has made herself one hell of a studio upstairs."

"Good. A place like that should stay in the family anyway."

"Well, let's do our best to keep it in the family then," he murmured, "because, right now, a whole lot is not going their way."

"And yet nothing definable."

"Yeah, which speaks to more of a campaign of fear, doesn't it?"

"It does, indeed," she noted.

"It's beginning to piss me off, truth be told. Aida's a real sweet lady, and nobody has any right to do that to her."

"Well, we're always looking for people with a grudge, and I think you may have found one or two."

"Maybe, but why didn't Aida tell you about them?"

"I don't know," she admitted. "Aida was embarrassed maybe, plus she probably knew I would ream her out for not having called the cops right away." Ice laughed. "That will still happen, I assure you, but maybe not right now."

"I understand reaming her out, but she's a little fragile today, particularly after all the questions I put her through and the deal with her friend this morning."

"Right, so I'll hold off on that," she replied in a much gentler tone. "But it's still something that she needs to be aware of."

"Yeah, and I need to find out who is handling her business affairs now, if this Ron guy is out of the picture."

"You know what? I have the answer to that as we ran a full check on him before she hired him," Ice stated. "Give me a minute, and I'll text you his name although he's been cleared already."

"Okay." As long as Ice had done the check he was good with that. Still, it helped to have names if only to understand all the players in Aida's world.

When he disconnected, he waited a few minutes for Ice's

intel, using the time to continue scanning the rooms for electronic devices. It took about ten minutes before a text from Ice came in, with the information he needed.

And, with that in hand, he quickly made a phone call.

Chapter 7

EVA HAD BEEN working for hours in this impromptu creative frenzy. The only thing that made her happy about this diversion was the fact that everything for her art show was now already done and ready to go, so the sketches that she did right now had nothing to do with any of that. Thankfully, because this new affliction had stopped her from doing anything else. She was free to let her fingers race across the sketch pad with an abandon she didn't recognize.

She didn't know whether she was crazy or what. It was confusing, and she wasn't at all sure why she was constantly sketching this man's face—this man who roamed about her house and annoyed her so much ever since the first moment he had arrived. But every time she saw him, another angle of his face caught her attention—or something in his expression or in his eyes, which were so magnetic.

She found it hard to figure out what was going on in her world, now that he had unwittingly stepped in and had taken over as her muse. At the same time, she also saw a level to her art that she had never suspected. And that was pretty damn hard to be upset about.

He was powerful, and every time she put something on paper about him, it gave her exactly what she wanted. It made her more excited than she ever thought possible about her art. Something was incredibly compelling about this man. At the very same time she felt utterly stupid because she just couldn't stop drawing his face. Over and over and over again, one expression after another, she kept at it, until finally a knock came on the door. She dropped her arm, feeling both exhaustion and exhilaration.

She quickly stretched and then walked over to the door and flung it open. She stared at Carson in shock and then immediately slammed the door in his face. She had completely forgotten he was even here. Yet the only reason that she had forgotten was because she was so busy recreating his face.

God, was she losing her mind?

She quickly pulled extra sheets over her recent sketches. They were charcoals, but even more direct and starker than she had expected. Moments later, her art secured behind her, she returned to the door, opened it, and glared at him.

He gave her a benign smile. "Hey, I gather I'm supposed to give you a direct warning before I venture into your area?"

"Damn right," she murmured, and then she gave a heavy sigh. "What is it you want now?"

He laughed out loud. "It's hardly as if I'm bothering you every hour of the day. And I never bother you without good reason. The fact of the matter is that I need to run some equipment through your suite, and I want to check the attic again."

She stared at him. "And what if I want to work? You know you can't just interrupt me anytime."

"Maybe not," he agreed lightly. "But since I just found a listening device in your grandmother's bedroom, I'd like to make sure there isn't one in your bedroom as well."

She stared at him, feeling everything inside her go cold and clammy. "You found what?" she managed to squeak out.

She instantly stepped back and opened the door wider. "Are you serious?"

He nodded. "Unfortunately, I am."

"In her bedroom? Why? Dear God. In her bedroom?"

"I don't know much yet," he replied. "And I also don't know how long it's been there. Two more men from Ice's team are coming up to give me a hand. We'll run a more powerful bug detector over the place and check for listening devices a second time."

She shook her head. "But none of that makes any sense."

"No, not to us, but there it was. So it must make sense to somebody."

"But—"

"What I don't know is whether it made sense to somebody who's currently in her world or to the person who used to be in her world."

Eva winced at that. "You know what? I could almost see Ron setting up cameras, but that's just, like, ... *ugh*." She cringed at the idea. "That's seriously icky."

"*Icky*? Is that an actual word?" he asked, with interest.

She glared at him. "Of course it is."

She stepped back as he came into her studio, then turned on the small machine in this hand. He went through the place, carefully checking all the electronics, lighting, and everything that turned on, then smiled at her. "Looks like you're free and clear in here."

"Oh, thank God for that."

He nodded. "But I do still need to check the attic."

"What could the attic possibly tell you?" she asked, raising both hands.

"It's hard to say, but, just like I've done your studio," he explained, "I also need to check your bedroom."

She glared at him. "I haven't made the bed," she said stiffly.

He gave her a flat stare. "Like I care."

She groaned, then walked over to the far side of the room and tossed open the connecting door. He might not care, but she did. And that was stupid. Still, it bothered her that her room was messy, that the bedding remained tossed back, as she'd bolted straight from bed the second time, and headed for her artwork.

Eva hated to feel that sense of invasion. Then she frowned. The problem was, it didn't feel like he was invading her space; it felt like he was finally arriving in her space after a long absence.

God, she was getting sick of this. She had to stop drawing him if that created this kind of havoc in her mind. She stood stiffly by her door, as he went through her bedroom. When he got closer to the nightstand, the machine in his hand started to buzz and flash. "What does that mean?" she gasped.

"It means," he replied, his tone grim, "that we've found another one."

She stared at him. "You are saying that somebody has been listening in to my bedroom?" The violation was instant and almost crippling. She sagged onto the floor.

He immediately walked to her and squatted before her. "Look. That's why I'm here," he told her quietly. "We will get to the bottom of this."

"But ..." She stopped, then looked at him. "You have absolutely no way to know that this is even related, do you?"

"No, not yet."

"God, but to think ..." She shook her head.

"We don't really have a way to know how long these

have been here," he admitted, "and that's another thing we must figure out."

She took a slow deep breath. "My God." She felt tremors inside her. "Have you told Grandma?"

"No, not yet. I called Levi and Ice first."

"She needs to know."

"Well, I thought that we may need them to give Aida some support when she finds out," he murmured.

"She was always very paranoid about people knowing her business."

"Is there any particular reason for that?"

"She handles a lot of money," Eva murmured. "She gives it away, but she always tries to keep it quiet—where it goes. No one knows for sure, except she does of course, and I suppose her financial advisor and accountant." She was on the verge of tears. "I don't know why anybody would do this." And then she raised her palms. "Of course, of course I do. Because somebody is trying to manipulate her money."

"That brings me back to the security system around here. It is older, and I'm not sure it was properly cared for."

She stared at him in confusion. "Like what?" she asked him.

"Digital media, for example," he replied. "Do you have any idea where your grandmother's banking is being done? How secure her computer system is? Any of that?"

"You must talk to her manager about that. I just know that they installed some new system," she said cautiously, "but I don't really know what that is, whether computer or security or something else." She stared helplessly around her studio and her room. "Now I'm starting to feel like I should have had a bigger hand in all this myself," she murmured. "I know just how crazy this sounds, but I wasn't thinking *this* ... spying would be a problem."

"It's not a problem until it becomes one," he noted quietly. "And when it becomes a problem, it typically becomes a really bad one."

"Now I hear you," she murmured. "I'm just beside myself to think that somebody has been listening in on my private life."

"You told me that you never had your boyfriend stay overnight though, right?"

She slowly shook her head. "No, and I can't think of anything I am more grateful about right now. Jesus, could you imagine that?"

"So where did you meet instead?"

"At his place," she said instantly. "I used to spend some evenings there, occasionally the nights. And once we got engaged, Grandma told me it was totally fine to have him over, but it never really felt fine, if you know what I mean. It always seemed out of place. I just never really wanted to stay overnight under her roof with someone else."

He nodded slowly. "For some people that wouldn't matter."

"Well, it mattered to me," she declared. "I know that it was hard for her to be that modern, and I didn't want to make her uncomfortable. And why would I? He had a place of his own, so we didn't need to be here."

"Okay." He nodded calmly. "And I presume Levi and Ice have done a check on him?"

"I have no idea." She shook her head. "That is what I presumed, once Grandma told them about what's been going on here."

"Did he ever have anything to do with your grandmother's business?"

"No, not at all." She stopped, then frowned. "But I did meet him … Oh, Jesus. I met him through Ron, so I don't know if that's connected or not." She shuddered. "God, this is not something I want to even think about."

"No, of course not. Now, when you say *connected*, what do you mean, … *connected to Ron?*"

"Family," she replied, "as in cousins."

"And Ron, was he the one who introduced you two?"

She nodded. "Yes, but then he had introduced me to a lot of people over the years because he was always a mainstay of our lives."

"He was a mainstay, until he wasn't."

"Exactly," she agreed.

"And that's the problem. When you split apart like that, after so many years of being together, it's this huge wrench, and you don't know quite how bad things will get," he suggested. "It's a bit like a divorce, in that you find out who your real friends are, and who were friends of both of you when you were together. Often, after a divorce, both sides must remake friendships again."

"I guess," she murmured, not really seeing how that was relevant.

"Eva, I need you to understand this because it's really important, because Aida's friends go with her, and Ron's friends go with him. Like your ex-fiancé's friends and family go with him, and your friends stay with you. Sometimes you find out that you don't have any friends left at all."

She looked over at him, and her lips twitched. "Are you divorced by any chance?"

"No," he stated, with a smile. "However, my brother went through hell with his."

"I'm not sure there is anything but hell with a divorce,"

she shared. "After I split up with my fiancé, I swore I would never get married."

"And now?" he asked curiously.

She flushed. "Well, I'm not quite so against it anymore. And, as my grandmother gets older, I can see that being alone will be a really difficult thing."

"I hate to say it," he murmured, "but, as your grandmother ages, and that time of your being alone comes closer, you must take more precautions because people will find out just how much money you're about to inherit."

She stared at him and stated flatly, "That is the last thing I even want to think about when it comes to marriage."

"You may not want to think about it, but I'll be just as blunt with you as I am with your grandmother. You need to think about it, or you stand to have some serious trouble."

Eva snapped, "You think?"

"I'm not a great fan of a lot of societal norms in life— like knowing which fork to use when presented with five of them," he admitted, "but I am a big fan of making sure you know exactly who it is you are marrying, long before you get there."

"That's not very romantic."

"And neither is finding out that you've been married for your money," he noted. "I do believe in true love and all those good things," he added, "but I'm not a fool. Lots of things go wrong in this world, and I encounter enough shysters on a regular basis to confirm that. I would never want you to go through something like that."

"Thank you for that." She felt cold and clammy and like she might vomit. "Dear God, if that ever happened ..."

"If you ever feel the slightest bit serious about someone," he suggested, "be smart enough to get Ice to clear him first."

She looked at him. "Would she?"

"For you? Hell yes. Because she knows just what can go on in that world out there and how messed up things can get."

"I never even thought of doing a background check like that on someone I may date," she murmured. "It seems so, ... I don't even know the word."

"It doesn't matter how it seems. You must protect yourself," he said. "And, if you have any doubts, remember that somebody close to you, somebody who had access to your bedroom, put a bug in here."

She gasped at the stark reminder.

And, with that warning issued, he headed to the attic, leaving her staring at him in shock.

THANKFULLY CARSON FOUND no bugs or other electronics in the attic. He wanted some more sophisticated equipment, and he knew that Bonaparte and Tomas were bringing everything Carson needed for now. They would text him when they hit town later today. As he waited for them to arrive, he took one last look around the attic, then popped back down to her bedroom and did another full check, as she stood here, her arms wrapped around herself, still visibly pale.

He walked over and said, "I'd give you a hug, but I don't want you to deck me."

She gave him a shaky smile. "You know something? Right now? ... I'd probably take a hug and be grateful for it."

Instantly he opened his arms, and she stepped into them at once.

"There's such a sense of violation," she murmured.

"Indeed," he agreed. "And don't ever forget it."

"That will never happen. *Gawwwd.* To think that somebody was here."

"I just ..." He hesitated, then looked around sharply.

"What's the matter?" she asked. "What are you thinking?"

"I'm just trying to make sense of it all. These bugs are old, so I don't know just how long they've been here. I don't know who might have put them in place, and I don't have a clue if anybody is actively monitoring them."

She stared at him. "Christ, I never even thought of that part. I've been creeped out enough about someone being here to install it." She stepped back a bit and continued. "It doesn't matter now that you found them, right?"

"You would think it doesn't, but it actually does matter," he murmured. "What I don't know right now is ..."

"You don't know lots of things apparently."

"We're getting there."

"Honestly, I never expected you to find a thing," she admitted.

"Well, the good news is, so far, I haven't found anything suggesting somebody is actually trying to kill your grandmother," he clarified. "The bad news is that I am finding out that your place is definitely not secure, and there are problems," he murmured. "What I don't know ..." He paused, as he stepped back, giving her a moment to collect herself, "I will be finding out." With that, he smiled gently and said, "You can go back to your painting, or something that makes you happy, and I will let you know when the other guys arrive."

"What will they do?"

"We'll see if we can track the signal back." He watched her expressions, as she stared at him in shock. And then looked at the bug.

"Oh shit, you can do that?" she asked.

"It depends on how old the bug is," he shared, "so I can't guarantee that we'll have any luck in that department."

"I want it to be old, and yet, at the same time, I don't want to think that it's been here this whole time."

"Of course not. As I said, I don't know if anybody is monitoring them, and that is a concern."

She nodded slowly. "It's a huge concern, but we do need to find out."

"All right then, I'll check in with you later," he said and started to leave.

"Wait," she called out, moving after him. "I want to be there, you know, when you tell Grandma."

"Why don't you come with me now, and we'll do it together. I want to break it to her before the other guys get here."

She looked around and nodded. "I can't work at the moment anyway, and honestly I feel icky in here right now."

"Until we get this solved, you can always take a break, you know?"

"I won't do that."

"So, do you talk to yourself very much when you're here?"

She faced him, frowning. "What do you mean?"

"Talking to yourself. I mean, some people do that. I just wonder why your bedroom was bugged and not your studio?"

She shrugged. "I have no clue," she muttered. "I don't understand any of this. What would anybody hope to gain?"

"Well, that's part of the problem," he murmured, "and I don't know either. One step at a time." With a smile, he reached out for her hand. "Come on. Let's get you downstairs, maybe grab a hot cup of tea or something, and see what we can figure out with your grandma."

And, with that, Eva took his hand and followed him downstairs.

When they got to the first floor, Aida sat at her office desk, that huge imposing antique that made her look so tiny behind it.

Carson stepped forward and got her attention. "Hi. How about a cup of coffee and a chance to regroup?"

She looked up at him, her gaze intent. "Whatever is going on? Have you found something then?"

"Yes, I sure did. So let's have a conversation, but let's not do it here."

She looked over to see her granddaughter behind him. "Are you joining us, dear?" she asked in surprise, and her face split with a smile. "That would be lovely. I do miss seeing you during the day sometimes."

He looked over to see sorrow on Aida's face. "I think she gets caught up in her art and doesn't see what's going on around her," he murmured, trying to ease the awkwardness of the moment.

"I do understand. And seriously she is incredibly blessed. Hers is a gift that needs to be shared with the world, so I try not to disturb her."

"But you wouldn't disturb me, Grandma," Eva argued quietly. "To spend more time with you would be lovely for me, and I hope you know that."

"Perhaps not," she noted, "but, when you've *got* to spend more time with me, then it's not the same thing, is it?"

And, with that bombshell, Aida led the way to the small sitting area, and Carson moved to the far side that he had already checked and secured for private conversations.

Once there, she pointed at their coffee service being wheeled in and asked, "Would you pour coffee, sweetheart?"

Once everyone had coffee in hand, they all sat down. He waited until Flora left the room and said quite directly, "I found two bugs."

She stared at him. "Bugs?"

He smiled. "Listening devices."

She shook her head slowly. "What do you mean by listening devices?"

"It's a transmitter that can be used to listen in on everything said in its proximity."

"Well then ..."

"It's worse than that, Grandma," Eva explained. "He found them in our bedrooms."

She stared at her granddaughter in shock. "What on earth?"

"Grandma, somebody has been listening in on us in our bedrooms."

Carson sensed the impropriety registering, and it completely overwhelmed Aida.

As she understood exactly what that meant, she sagged back in her chair.

"So, we have a rather delicate situation. Please don't be insulted, but ..." Carson hesitated, glanced at Eva, and then turned to Aida. "I've already asked your granddaughter this, so I feel like I need to ask you too."

"Well, spit it out, young man. What is it you need to know?"

He cracked a smile. "Being the beautiful and brilliant

woman you are, I need to know if, … if you have been entertaining men in your bedroom recently."

She stared at him in shock, and then her incredibly sexy, full-throated laughter rang out. "Oh my, I would so love to say yes. However, I must admit that, over the last couple years, I've experienced a bit of a drought in that department."

She had put it so marvelously, even in a trying situation, that he couldn't do anything but grin like a fool. "Sorry for the intrusion, but I was trying to figure out how to say it nicely."

"You couldn't have put it better," Aida said. "Quite a nice compliment actually. If I were a little bit younger, I would definitely give you a run for your money."

"Grandma, enough with that," Eva chided.

"Oh, my dear, ever since you broke up with that horrible fiancé of yours, you've stuck yourself in that studio, and you've just hidden away, completely ignoring everything else in the world. I kept hoping you would find somebody else to put some love back into your life," she admitted, "but you haven't even given anyone a chance."

"That's because I haven't found anybody worthy of it." And then, with a glance over at Carson, she murmured, "And you don't need to be privy to all our personal woes, droughts included." Her impudent snicker followed.

"Not at all," he agreed, with a smooth response and a wink. "Only things that pertain to my investigation."

At that reminder, Aida's smile fell away, and she nodded. "And that's what this is really about, isn't it? Finding out why someone would possibly be interested enough to actually bug our bedrooms," she murmured. "I mean, I can't imagine anybody thought that they would find any pillow talk. And even then, what kind of pillow talk would they care about?"

"And it may not even be pillow talk, as much as"—he hesitated—"any chance you ladies talk in your sleep?"

Aida stared at him. "Not that I know of."

"Or how about ... do the two of you ever sit and have hot chocolate together before bed?" he asked them.

Aida smiled. "Oh, absolutely we do, particularly if we were both out swimming later in the evening. I'll get Flora to bring up a tray to my room, and we cozy up under the blankets. Don't we, dear?" She smiled over at Eva, only to see her granddaughter staring at her with *that look*.

"Oh my," Eva gasped. "That's exactly what we've done, isn't it?" She turned and looked at Carson. "But ..." And then she didn't know what to say. Eva got up and walked over to her grandmother's side and sat down beside her, reaching out to hold her hand. "What could they possibly want to find out?" she murmured.

"That'll be the question I need to figure out," Carson replied. "And I don't really have too much of an answer for you. So what kind of discussions would you have at that hour of the night together?"

Aida looked over at Eva and said instantly, "Men."

Her granddaughter nodded. "Yes, and kindling some old memories," Eva added. "Some of Grandmother's old flames and a few of my previous relationships, depending on how long the devices have been sitting in our rooms. I just don't think any of that could possibly matter to anybody."

"What about your ex-fiancé, Eva?" he asked. Looking back at Aida, he murmured, "And you are a force to contend with, so I'm sure you have had lots of interested men."

She nodded. "There have been some. I just haven't had

too much energy for it these last few years," she admitted, blushing beautifully.

He grinned at her. "No need to apologize, but it is definitely a shame for the men in this world."

She chuckled. "Again, nicely put. But my time of caring about whether men like me or not is long gone."

"And yet," Eva added, "you and Ron were very close."

She nodded. "Well, yes, we were, … until he betrayed me," she murmured.

Hesitating, Carson asked, "It was a while ago that you fired him, correct? Some two years ago, I believe."

"Yes." She nodded.

"So, I'll be blunt here. Did you have a romantic entanglement with him?"

She stared at him, frowning. "Oh my, you really do see me as a femme fatale, don't you?"

"I see an absolutely vibrant woman, who has the potential to make men very happy," he replied gently.

She stared at him with a twinkle in her gaze and smiled. "That's why Levi sent you, isn't it? So you could charm the socks off an old lady."

He chuckled. "No, not at all. And you're still not answering my question, by the way."

She winced. "Mostly I was trying to avoid letting my granddaughter know."

At that, Eva stared at her. "Did you?"

She nodded slowly. "I did."

"Wow." Then Eva started to chuckle. "You know something, Grandma? Carson's right. You are a force to contend with."

The older woman blushed again. "Remember now. That began quite a few years ago," she noted, "and I was trying to figure out if I really wanted to go in that direction again."

"And, of course," Carson noted, "then firing Ron, after stealing from you, would have been doubly tough on you, and it would have made the breakup, ugly as it was, all that much harder."

"Exactly," Aida agreed. "After that, I was done."

"I understand that perfectly," he murmured.

She groaned. "This foolish old woman fell for a man who was ten years younger," she shared. "And I paid the price when I found out he was cheating on me too."

"And that's why you didn't call the cops about his embezzlement, isn't it?" Carson asked gently, wishing he could meet that man in person.

She nodded. "Yes, because what do you say to that? How do you explain that you've been just an old fool?"

"I don't think loving someone is being an old fool," he corrected her quietly. "Presumably you cared, or you wouldn't have taken that step."

"I did care," she agreed, "enough to contemplate maybe changing things in a bigger way, but then it all blew up."

"So, how did you find out what was happening?"

She stared at him. "Oh boy." She winced. "I always had the bank make contact regarding checks of a larger amount. Normally they would have gone to him for confirmation, but, when they contacted me, I didn't understand what the check was for. When I challenged him about it, everything came tumbling out. I ended up contacting the bank to find out exactly what was going on, and the news wasn't good. Apparently he'd been writing his own checks and cashing them for some time. Not too much at one time but just enough to fly under the radar. Then when that one came through, it was larger than the regular occurrences. They contacted me about it, and that's the first I found out."

"God, I am sorry," he said.

"I am too." Aida shook her head. "Nothing like being a ridiculous old fool."

"No, ma'am. Not ridiculous and not an old fool. You tried to step back into life," he murmured. "I don't think anybody would want to miss out on a chance for love."

"I blame myself," she said, shrugging. "I was trying to live well past that point in time. I just thought my grand-daughter would leave one day, and I didn't think I wanted to be all alone anymore. Well, believe me. I'd rather be alone than be so betrayed."

Chapter 8

L ATE THAT NIGHT Eva stayed in bed, hating that sense of discomfort now that she knew a bug had been in here just a few hours ago and, matter of fact, was still here. She was hesitant to make any sound, and yet, just as Carson had warned her earlier, the absence of sound, if somebody *were* listening, would make them suspicious. That wasn't something she wanted to think about either. But her mind was completely locked on the betrayal from her grandmother's point of view.

How absolutely devastating to realize that—when her grandmother did get back into a relationship, spending so many years with Ron—he had been betraying her in two big ways, cheating on her and embezzling from her.

Eva hated Ron for that.

Even more than she had ever hated anyone. She realized just how big these betrayals were for her grandmother, who was such a wonderful woman, who had spent so many years helping people. To actually think some asshole out there had done that to Grandma was devastating on so many levels.

To think that a bug was also in Eva's bedroom just made her sick. She wanted to believe it was still there from Ron way back then, but that just made it worse in a way because of how much he may have listened to. That was intensely difficult.

Hearing an odd sound outside, and already as spooked as she was, she hopped up to her feet and walked over to the window, where she could stare out into the night.

It was almost impossible to see what was going on in the darkness. Even with a full moon, it was hidden behind clouds. If the clouds would separate, that would be great, but, in the meantime, she couldn't see a thing. Sighing, she slipped back into bed. Only when she heard another sound did she bolt to her feet again.

Finally she knew she wouldn't sleep at all, and she made her way downstairs to the kitchen. She wasn't in the least surprised to find Carson sitting at the table, drinking tea perhaps.

He looked up at her. "Can't sleep?"

She shook her head. "I keep hearing things outside," she murmured. "And then I keep thinking about the stupid bug in my bedroom, and it's almost impossible to sleep."

"We tried not to disturb you but once today," he said.

"I understand that, but, at the same time, now it feels like every time I breathe, somebody's listening."

"I'm sorry. I really am. We are tracking it, but, at the moment, it looks like your bug might be dead."

She stared at him. "Dead?" she asked hopefully. "What exactly does that mean?"

"Well, they do have a certain lifespan," he explained. "So, it's quite possible that it was working way back when, but, maybe once Ron got kicked out, he had no chance to replace it."

"Maybe," she murmured. "I haven't let anybody in my studio for a very long time. And that included his daughter, Melody."

"So, you never gave her access to your room?"

"No, the only one who has ever had access is Flora. She changes the bedding once a week."

"Right," he noted. "So, she most likely could have switched that, but odds are she isn't involved."

"I would hate to think that she is." Eva stared at him. "There's been enough betrayal here already."

"Unfortunately money attracts betrayal."

"It doesn't have to," she cried out. "Why must everybody be an asshole?"

He chuckled. "Again, not everybody is."

"Still, it's a lot of people." She winced. "Too many, if you ask me. How do you know if that bug is dead?"

"Well, Tomas has checked it, and he'll come back tomorrow with an expert for a second opinion. They didn't have some equipment they needed, so they are trying to hold off one more day for you."

"I know. I know." She sighed. "I just wish it was gone now."

He nodded. "Look. If you want, I can come up and remove it. I'd rather we waited a day, so that we can do this other testing. It's one extra step to see if we can find out anything else on that bug. And I would like to do that, but, if you really want me to pull it, then I can."

She raised both hands in frustration. "That just makes me feel like an idiot, who can't hang on a little bit longer."

"I wouldn't think that at all," he assured her. "The fact that you're even hanging on as you are is amazing."

She shrugged. "It doesn't feel like it. I feel like an idiot."

"And there goes that whole judgment thing again."

"Well, I'm sure my grandmother is feeling pretty idiotic at the moment. Did you leave the bug in her room?"

"Yes, she didn't have any problem with it. I was surprised at that, to tell you the truth."

"I'm not surprised at all."

"Maybe she just figured she would sleep and, if anybody wanted to listen to her snore, more power to them," he teased.

She chuckled at that. "You know what? That almost sounds like Grandma too."

He smiled. "She has a great attitude about life," he added warmly.

"She does," Eva murmured. "She's had a pretty interesting life."

"Good. Everybody should have an interesting life, and we shouldn't have it cut short or diminished because of assholes."

"I hear you, but wouldn't it be nice if we had a little more to go on than what we do now?"

"Hey, we're getting there," he noted cheerfully.

"Did you ever find out where it backtracked to?"

"Yeah, back to town," he replied immediately.

She gasped. "What?"

"You didn't expect that?" he asked. "Why?"

She frowned and shook her head. "I don't know why, but I just assumed, … but why would I, really? I guess I just thought that, maybe in a circumstance like that, they would get up and leave. Like escaping the scene of the crime."

"Maybe they had no place to go," he suggested. "Did you consider that?"

"No, I don't even want to consider that now," she admitted. "Honestly, I was just happy to put them out of my mind. Well, they were out, but, of course, now they're right back in."

"I understand."

"So you traced it to a person then?"

Carson shook his head. "No. It's not that pinpoint accurate. It's in about a ten-square-mile area that covers warehouses, homes, malls. So that's why we wanted our specialist to take another look at this end, at your two bugs. Once that is done, with no leads to follow, we'll just disable both bugs."

Eva sighed. "Why would they bug my bedroom?"

"Maybe to make sure you didn't have another lover?"

She stopped to stare. "You know what? That makes sense in a way. My ex was that kind of a person, very possessive."

"So, in this case, it's quite possible that he is involved."

"What a horrible thought," she murmured.

"I mean, think about all your grandmother's done, all that she's managed to do in all these years. Then here you find somebody who is close to both of you—Ron—who turns around and betrays you both. He was spending her money without her permission. Once he got away with it, I'm sure the checks increased on a regular basis, as he tried to find ways to get a little bit more out of her. He gets you to date your ex, meanwhile Ron may have planted the bugs, all to keep an eye on things."

She shook her head. "I hate him," she murmured. "I absolutely hate Ron, Melody, and my ex."

"Go ahead, hate away, but it won't help anything right now. What we really need is to see if any of this is connected to what Aida believes is going on now."

"And that would immediately make me think that it's them somehow," she murmured. "And how is she supposed to live with that additional betrayal too?"

"I don't know." He shook his head. "But what I do

know is that your grandmother is really very strong, and, as long as we keep her safe, we'll get through this."

Eva gripped his arm and said, "Please promise me that you'll keep her safe."

"I'll do my best," he replied.

She stared at him.

"Yes, I will keep her safe," he added.

She shuddered. "I almost believe you."

"Do believe me, and also don't forget. We have Levi and Ice a short drive away, if we ever need backup," he told her. "Everybody is doing their best to keep Aida safe. So far, it's gone from a non-investigation to something completely different," he noted. "I just don't know if any of this is connected."

HAVING MADE THAT promise, which Carson had no intention of breaking, had clearly given Eva a little more peace of mind. He didn't want her to become so complacent that she put herself in danger unnecessarily. That went against everything he was already dealing with because he still had no proof that anything was *currently* wrong.

However, a lot of little things were adding up to a whole lot of *wrong*, though maybe not at a deadly level yet. Aida still had yet to explain in what way she thought this situation amounted to murder.

There were all kinds of bits and pieces to fit together but absolutely nothing concrete.

The next morning, he woke to an odd chill in the house. Not liking the sensation at all, he got up and dressed quickly. He was a floor below Aida and two below Eva.

He didn't understand why they would want it that way,

but, from his point of view, it wasn't great. He needed to be as close as he could to all the action, regardless of what they liked. The trouble was, there just wasn't any convenient place for him to be up there on the second floor or the third, and that was disturbing in itself as well. But he would make the best of it, like he always did.

Roaming around the ground floor, he found that nobody else was up. It was six in the morning, as he walked out to the pool area, just to make sure that Aida wasn't already out swimming. And, sure enough, she was sitting there, wrapped up in a warm blanket, sipping a hot drink.

He sat down beside her, more than a little disturbed to see the look on her face.

"What happened?" he asked.

She looked over at him, still in shock. "You know that feeling when somebody walks over your grave?" She nodded. "That's how I woke up."

"Any particular reason?"

"Just ..." She stopped, then shook her head. "No. I mean, I don't have anything concrete, that's the problem. Every time I turn around, it seems like something's going on, but I have no way to prove it and nothing to show for it."

"So, it was just a feeling?"

She looked at him with a wry look. "Young man, when you get to be my age, just a feeling may be all you'll get."

His laugh was instant and full, evoking a big smile from the frightened woman.

"You're a nice man, Carson," she said. "Sometimes I think everybody is just honoring a foolish old woman."

"We're not going there," he stated instantly. "Even if that is what we're doing, it's still a worthy move." She pulled the blanket a little tighter around her. "Did you get any sleep at all?" He knew that older people often didn't sleep as much as they needed to, then made up for it during the day.

"No, I didn't get much sleep at all," she admitted, "between worrying that I'm actually losing it and the whole idea that someone has been listening in my bedroom and that of my granddaughter."

"Did anything else happen?"

"Just some weird sounds in the night," she noted. "That kind of kept me awake, thinking there might have been somebody coming."

"How? Any idea from what direction?"

She shrugged. "I don't know. It just seemed like it was all around me."

He stared at her for a long moment. "And what kind of sounds?"

"Just thumps and creaks, you know? Probably just this old house."

"So, in other words, nothing that's concrete that you could point to and say, 'Hey, this is the noise right here.'"

"Exactly," she agreed, with a wry look. "On the other hand, if somebody's trying to make me look like a batty old broad, they're succeeding."

"If somebody were to do that, what would be the consequence?"

"Outside of my pride, everything I've built probably would be looked at in a different way."

"Would it be though?" he asked. "I guess what I'm trying to discern is what the real damage would be if somebody was trying to do that?"

"You're back to seeking some motivation now on their part, aren't you?"

"Well, there has to be a reason for it," he stated. "People

generally don't play games like this, unless something is in it for them."

She stared at him. "Wow. I've seen a lot in my life, but I still maintain a more positive attitude than you do. I think maybe you should work on yours."

He smiled at her gently. "Maybe so. However, I do meet some really wonderful people."

She nodded. "But you've also seen a lot of the dark side of life, haven't you?"

"Way too much of it," he murmured.

"Sometimes there's just nothing for it but to try to understand the human condition. That we're here to learn, that we're here to make the best of it, and hopefully that we have something in our hand to leave behind as a gift to humankind," she shared, with a curious and mysterious voice.

"I like that," he said, "but it's not all that easy, is it?"

"No, it sure isn't. I stare back across the years and wonder how I've even made it this far. You know that we came close to poverty several times, but we always managed to recoup it. But those times were enough to keep me very aware of my spending habits, making sure that I don't go too far, too quickly."

"And that's a good thing," he agreed. "Too often people in wealthy circumstances are born with a silver spoon, then they die with a silver spoon, without ever understanding the plight of the rest of the world and what they go through."

"That was never me," she murmured. "It was never anything my father would have allowed. He was a stickler for making sure we understood where we came from and how much work it was to get here from there."

"I agree with that." He nodded.

"Me too," she replied, "though I didn't expect to be

alone at this stage of my life."

"Hence your foray with Ron."

She nodded. "Yes, and that just left me feeling like a very old fool—kind of the way I feel today." Then she gave a light laugh. "Listen to me bitching about everything. You'll think that I'm depressed."

"I don't think you're depressed," he stated. "I think you're wary of the world."

She studied his face. "Now that's an interesting word. *Wary.*"

"Well, you and I know that, at any point in time," he explained, "it could be our last moment. And that's the same for everyone, but sometimes the younger generation feels invincible and just doesn't realize it. So our respective ages have something to do with our perspectives as well. As we get older, we look at our lives more objectively. Look at what you've done, and look at what you still hope to accomplish."

"It does make you wonder if you've done the right thing." Aida smiled. "And that's exactly what I'm wondering, if I've done the right thing over the years."

"Is there anything that you think you've done wrong that might be coming back to bite you now?"

"I've been racking my brain about it," she admitted. "Outside of Ron and Melody, there really hasn't been much in the way of problems. The trouble is, it's very hard to remember bad employees because typically, once they're fired and gone, our minds do a great job of erasing them. Therefore, we don't keep remembering them, especially if it's painful."

She groaned at another thought. "My husband wasn't always the nicest," she added quietly. "And I guess the way he did business always bothered me."

"And he's been gone how long?"

"Almost fourteen years ago," she said. "Then not even two years later I lost my son, brought Eva here, and got lost in my charity work. That was a tough two to three years back there."

Carson nodded. "Enter, Ron then, soon thereafter."

She nodded. "I needed a manager to help out. Yet I was lonely and facing a lot of years ahead of me that looked like they would be pretty tough for someone my age," she explained, "and I just didn't want to be alone."

"Don't feel guilty about that," he stated, sensing that inner disquiet in Aida. "Your heart was in the right place."

"It's so foolish," she said sadly.

"No. You were operating out of love. Ron wasn't—or at least not the level of love where you come from. Remember. That isn't on you. That's on Ron," he murmured.

She looked over and laughed. "Wouldn't that be nice. My husband was basically a good man, but he was hard, and in business he was pretty ..." She hesitated. Finally she shrugged. "I guess it makes absolutely no difference at this point in time."

"Wait," Carson said, holding up a hand. "There is always a chance that it could be somehow connected to what's going on now, so it still would be good if I knew."

"It's just, if people crossed him, he'd cut them off at the knees," she explained. "I ... I'm pretty sure that was because we had come so close to hitting poverty a few times in life that he became quite the cutthroat businessman. He didn't use to be like that, but, after he'd been taken advantage of a few times, he learned that you had to be that way—or else. I just never could, and, sure, I probably got caught up in manipulation more often than he did. I still oversee a mean business, but he was the true essence of it, much more so than I would ever be."

"You're doing the best you can," he noted, "and I believe you did the best you could at a time that was very difficult for you. You also had your granddaughter, and you were dealing with the loss of your son and the loss of your husband, so come on. Cut yourself some slack."

She chuckled. "You see? ... That attitude wouldn't get you far in business. My husband would have found out about something like this much sooner, and he would have gone through any hoops or numerous rings of fire to put a stop to it, even before it started. He was the kind who would have made sure that, whatever he wanted out of the deal, he got it, and it may well have been an okay deal for them as well, but he definitely would have taken full advantage of their circumstances to make sure he would come out on top."

"Any case in particular that comes to mind?" Carson asked curiously. "Because that kind of stuff can affect people for a long time."

"I don't know," she said, with a frown. "I do have some files of real estate deals he was involved in, if you want to see them."

Carson nodded. "I do want to see them, and I'll let you know when we get a couple more of my guys here to do a deeper check on the two bugs. Plus, I'll also go talk to both Melody and Ron."

She winced at that. "Better you than me. I'll be happy to never see him again."

"Let's hope you won't have to. The fact that you didn't press charges may constantly be weighing on him."

"Or he's happily already off on another ill-gotten venture, trying to pull another poor woman into his clutches."

"If you actually had pressed charges," he pointed out, something that he doubted she wanted to consider, "that may have spared another woman from being taken in by Ron."

She looked over at him. "I can see that now. At the time, I couldn't have cared less. I'd been taken advantage of, and it wasn't in my heart at the time to even deal with it. I just wanted him gone. I wanted to recover and live as much of my life as I could in peace with my granddaughter, without having to deal with more slugs like him," she murmured. "*Now*, of course, I feel differently, and I realize that I should have done something to stop him."

"Well, you still can," Carson noted, but she shook her head at that.

"No, I just don't think I'm up for it. There are some times in life when you don't want to deal quite so brutally with people or to find out more truths that you really don't want to hear."

"Agreed. It's one of those things that life sometimes throws your way that you don't want to deal with."

"And I definitely don't want to deal with it now," she murmured. "And yet I'm very sorry if, by not doing something earlier about that, I ended up causing somebody else grief."

"And it's quite possible that you'll still face that, if and when that news comes out."

She stared at him for a long moment. "That's all part and parcel of me bringing this up now, isn't it?"

"It is," he murmured. "Unfortunately it very much is."

She groaned. "Damn. Just when you think that you can move past all this BS, you find that you don't get to move past any of it."

He chuckled. "You get to move past it, but maybe not the way you had hoped."

"Doesn't sound like I get to move past it at all," she moaned. "Sounds like it'll be all sitting there, staring me in the face, particularly if he's trying to swindle another person."

"Why don't we figure that out first?" he said. "Then we'll go from there."

"Meaning, if I feel like I can press charges at that time, I can decide?"

He shrugged. "Let's find out what he's up to, and who knows? Maybe you won't need to press charges. Maybe he'll be hanging himself by stealing from somebody else who will press charges."

"Still, I could have been nicer and protected them."

"Maybe. Let's save all the recriminations until we get more information."

She smiled. "See? You're definitely nicer than I am."

"In what way?" he asked. "I'm the one who's looking to get you to press charges."

"Yeah, but I didn't press charges because I was scared, and, … well, I didn't really want the world finding out how pathetic I was. I mean, looking for love at my age, even back then, was ridiculous."

"There's no age limit on love," he stated firmly.

She looked over at him. "Do you believe that?"

"I do. I really do. I have seen a lot of older people in relationships that do incredibly well."

"Maybe, but the older we get," she argued, "the more baggage we have, you know? It's hard to even imagine that we're functioning adults."

"And yet not everybody has bad baggage."

She laughed. "Is there any such thing as good baggage?"

"I don't know," he said, with a wide grin, "but we'll find out."

Chapter 9

WHEN EVA WOKE up, she felt a sense of disquiet rippling through her. Frowning, she bolted from bed and immediately checked on her paintings. With them safe, she settled back somewhat, but she still couldn't place what was wrong.

Thinking about her grandmother, she quickly dressed and headed downstairs. Not finding her or Carson in the kitchen, Eva moved on, then found the two of them sitting by the pool. She walked over and shared, "This is quite a habit you two are forming."

Carson looked over at her, then smiled. "Your grandmother leads an active life."

At that, Aida laughed. "And she's about ready to lead a much less active life," she added, with a smile.

Eva frowned. "In what way? Is there something you need me to take on to free up some of your time?"

"Oh no, I haven't wanted to bother you with any of that."

At that, her heart froze. "Grandma, if there is anything you need me to learn, or to do, you only have to ask."

"And yet your head is in your paintings, and that's where it should be," her grandmother stated firmly.

Eva stared at her for a long moment. "No, my head is not so full that I can't learn something else. Now, is there something you need me to do?" she asked. "Is there something you want me to learn or something I need to learn for your sake?"

Her grandmother shook her head, but almost immediately Carson replied, "Yes."

They both looked at him.

"If you don't know how to run this household, Eva, and you don't know how to run the charities and your grandmother's estate," he explained, "then all that would be a good thing for you to learn."

"Why? We have a manager for that."

"And you've been taken to the cleaners once already by some *manager*. Even if you have somebody who's loyal and honest, you still must oversee them. Don't you agree?" He looked at both women.

Aida nodded. "Well, yes, I do, but I don't want to bother Eva with that."

"Yet, soon enough," he noted, as a pointed reminder, "it is something that Eva must learn. It would be much easier for her to learn from you, instead of later, at a time when she's dealing with massive grief."

The two women stared at him. "We don't have to push something like that," Eva jumped in. "And it's not like she's dying."

But her grandma surprised her. "No, I'm not dying, but I do understand what he's saying, and he's right."

Eva looked at her in shock. "Seriously?" She collapsed into one of the chaises with a resounding *thump*.

"Yes. Of course I'm not dying yet, and have no intention to do so at any time in the near future," she added, "but an awful lot is going on with the charities, and, right now, Eva, you are not very involved in any of it. It wouldn't take much of your time and is something that you should probably start learning about now. That way I can explain my reasoning and my visions for this money."

"Well, I know some of it," she said hesitantly, "but I haven't wanted to intrude. It's your money. It's your business. Hell, it's your life."

Her grandmother looked at her. "Oh my. Well, it is my money, but it'll all become your money soon, and Carson's right. If you end up trusting the wrong people, you could lose everything."

Eva was frightened, and Carson saw that look for the first time.

"No, Carson is right," Aida repeated, "and we must fix that. Now, I know that your showing is really important to you, so we'll put our discussion on the back burner until after that, but then we need to sit down and go over everything."

Unsettled by everything her grandmother had just said, but knowing it wasn't the time to argue, Eva nodded slowly. "That's fine. Just know that I'm not trying to take over or to even do more of the business than you would want me to do."

"I have deliberately kept you out of the business," Aida replied, "only so you could focus on your art and not fill your head with all this boring stuff."

Eva smiled. "Of course you have," she murmured. "Anything to keep me happy."

"Exactly." Aida nodded and returned her granddaughter's smile with one of her own. "You are my only reason for continuing right now. I really would love to see you make it in the art world."

"There's no guarantee that anybody makes it in the art

world, but you've provided me a situation where I haven't needed to hold down a job, so I've been able to focus, and I thank you for that. Of course I would love to gain recognition for my art, but, if that doesn't happen, it doesn't happen. In the end, I paint for myself."

"What you do matters, dear, but, at the same time, I also know that you paint for your soul. However, I think the world needs to see it. It's a gift. And, whether you are managing my charity or your art, you need a head for business."

Touched, she looked over at Carson. "Well, I'm not quite sure what you expected today," she murmured, "but, if that's what my grandmother wants, then …"

"It's a good thing," he agreed quietly. "Already enough has been going on that we aren't sure just what's happening, and I would like very much to see that you're in a better position to take things over—or at least to help oversee them. I know that Aida's current manager has that role, and has been fully vetted by Ice, and that's fine for right now. In the future, Eva, hopefully you have somebody you can trust to help you make the best decisions."

"Will there be many decisions? I know what Grandma wants for her funeral and all," she noted, "but other than that—"

"Yes, there are a lot of decisions, a lot that you may be unaware of because it's become rote to me," her grandmother stated quietly, now frowning. "I actually do a fair bit of business in the mornings."

Eva sat back and stared at her grandmother. "I knew that, but I actually hadn't really considered what it all entailed."

"And that's because I've also never pushed it. It's just

day-to-day business, yet it must be dealt with. As far as immediate decisions after my demise, or perhaps earlier, I can't say that Flora will stay. In fact, I suspect she'll leave immediately."

"Right. Of course." Eva stared off in the distance. "Something else I hadn't really considered. Flora makes my world happen, but, other than that, well, I've been fairly blind, haven't I?"

"Blindness is fine when you are in good hands," Carson murmured. "You have a focus, and you're working on your art. But, at some point in time, these fundamental things must be at the forefront, and it would be best to have a plan of sorts."

She groaned. "I guess." Looking at her grandmother, she continued. "I really hope that this is years and years away."

Aida chuckled. "I do too, but we can't always count on getting what we want."

"No, that's very true." Eva got up and walked over to the sideboard, where she poured herself more coffee.

"I wonder if I should be talking to Flora about this too," Aida wondered.

"I wouldn't think so," Carson suggested, "because, as you say, hopefully it will be many years. Flora's plans could change in the meantime, as she is getting older herself. Although you do have part-time cleaning help around the place, too. That reminds me. I asked her for a list of those names and haven't gotten it yet." He turned to look at the doorway, where Flora should be coming through any time with breakfast. "I need to vet everybody who's coming through for cleaning."

"Really?" Eva looked at him and then shook her head. "Of course you do. You're vetting everything else, so why not that as well?"

He nodded. "Exactly. I am vetting everyone else, so why not that? But not only that, … there is always the possibility that somebody who comes in once a week could be checking on the bugs, does whatever else they've got to do, and then they are good to go."

At that moment, Flora pushed open the door with a trolley and brought in breakfast. They waited until she placed the sausages and eggs on the nearby table, then added a platter of hash browns and a fresh hot coffee server, before she quickly left.

"Just like this," Carson noted, as he pointed at breakfast. "I get that, in the world you live in, this is common, but in a lot of places it wouldn't be. This alone allows access to you and to your household." He watched, as the two women took very little of the food. "So, does Flora bring this big spread all the time, or is it only because I'm here?"

Aida looked at him. "I instructed her to bring more to accommodate you. You're an active male, and I've seen you eat." At that, she chuckled.

He hesitated, then replied, "I do, but I don't want to put more work on anybody here."

She laughed. "Flora is happy to finally have somebody to cook for. Between the two of us, we barely eat much anymore."

He looked over at Eva, who shrugged. "When I get into painting, I can lose track for days."

"Days?" he asked in horror.

"Sometimes, yeah. And I know it's not healthy, or whatever you're about to tell me, but it really doesn't make a whole lot of difference when I'm in the zone."

"No, of course not," he murmured. And then he nodded

with a slight smile. "I can see that might be troubling for the people around you."

She groaned. "The only reason I come to the surface is because of Grandma. She nags me to come back down and eat."

"Let me just say this. If you want to be a painter for long-term, … and not just a flash in the pan," he added, "you must really look after yourself."

She looked over at him. "So was there a bit of a warning in that, daddy-o?"

He shook his head. "No, but I have certainly seen people burn themselves out. And, just when you think there's nothing left that people can do to hurt themselves, they still find other ways."

She stared at him. "I'm not trying to hurt myself."

"No, you're not, but you aren't looking after yourself properly either." And, with that, he scooped up the rest of the hash browns and put them on his plate.

Eva turned to her grandmother, who had a big grin on her face. "Oh, and of course he's saying everything you'd like to hear."

"Well, you really don't look after yourself," Aida agreed, practically giddy. "You know that."

CARSON LEFT THE pool soon afterward, with Flynn appearing at the estate, coming from his nearby animal rescue to further check on the bugs. Carson quickly brought him up to speed, then explained what was going on and where he was going with his investigation to date.

"Dang, I wish I could come," Flynn replied.

"You do your thing here. I thought about asking for

backup, but honestly I'll just go talk to somebody."

"You are," Eva said, from beside Carson, "but not alone."

He turned to see Eva walking toward them. She wore jeans and a T-shirt, and yet something was so fresh and innocent about the whole look that it shocked him. Not to mention having an instant physical effect on his body. He shook his head, frowning. "You're not coming."

"Why not?" she asked.

"Well, for one thing, you might set off reactions in other people."

"Since when is that a bad thing?" she asked. "You've got one week here, and that time is quickly running out. We need to do something to find out if anything is seriously wrong here or not."

Flynn looked over at him and shrugged. "You know that it's not a bad idea."

"It's a terrible idea," Carson muttered. Then shook his head. "Fine."

At that, Aida came out of her office. "If you're taking Eva," she stated, "make sure you look after her."

"I will," Carson vowed, then turned to Eva and glared. "See? Now you're worrying Aida too."

Eva shrugged. "I don't think that's her problem at all. She's afraid of what you might find." And, with that, Eva walked over to her grandmother and gave her a quick hug. "We'll be back soon." Then she walked out the front door, as Carson rolled his eyes at Flynn and moved to catch up.

"You don't have to come, you know?" he stated quietly.

"And yet I feel like I do," she replied. "So let's just put that to rest and get on with it."

Without a whole lot else that he could say, he walked

around to the passenger's side of his car, then opened the door for her. As he got in the driver's seat, he murmured, "Sorry. It's hardly the kind of car that you're used to."

"We're not snobs, Carson," she stated, looking at him. "I'm just grateful it's a car, and we're not on a motorbike or something."

He burst out laughing. "Would you have hopped on?"

"Yes," she stated, "but the only accident I ever had was on a motorbike. I was sixteen and defied my beloved grandmother's wishes with a boy who was completely inappropriate," she explained, with a snicker. "And he had a motorcycle, the most exciting thing in my world at the time, and, when I paid the price, it involved a whole lot of tears and heartache."

"Were you badly hurt?"

"No, not really," she replied, "just enough that my grandmother was very strict with me for a very long time afterward."

"Well, you got the chance once," Carson said, "and you blew it, so what do you expect?"

She chuckled. "Yeah, that's one way to look at it. Of course I have come to see the trouble of my errant ways."

"I don't know that you were so terrible at all," he added. "It's natural to rebel against the restraints holding you back and trying to keep you safe. Especially at that age."

"I don't even think I would care to raise a child in this day and age," she shared, "so kudos to my grandmother for taking me in when she did."

"Are you kidding? It sounds to me like you were her saving grace," he noted. "Losing your only child can be one of the hardest things a person can go through."

"No, that's quite true," she agreed, looking over at him.

He grinned. "Once again, you think I come up with the weirdest things to say, don't you?"

"Well, you're very, ... I don't know. *Philosophical.* Or at least you know a lot about humanity."

"The latter," he agreed, "and it may have something to do with having seen some of the very worst humanity can do."

"I presume that you've had an illustrious career."

"Yep, absolutely." At that, he glanced at her and asked, "So, can I trust you not to make a scene?"

Eva shrugged. "I'm really not the scene-making type."

"Okay, I wasn't sure if you would be one of those divas or not."

"Wow." She sank deeper into the passenger seat. "Doesn't sound like I've made a very good impression then."

"Well, the impression you've made is of someone who is very serious about her art. Someone who has been very involved in getting this show ready. Chances are, you're very talented. You also use denial to deal with life and not always to your advantage."

He watched her composure crack slightly as he said, "I'm not saying any of this to be mean, you know?"

"Yet," she added, with a hard laugh, "it doesn't come across as being anything but. You think I'm a fool for the way I've stayed out of Grandma's business, don't you?"

"No, not at all," he disagreed, "but I think that time is over. It's not so much that she is ready to hand the reins over to you but I think she would sleep better if she knew that you understood what needed to be done in her absence."

"The truth is, I probably would feel better too. As you told me, I wasn't really aware that the time was coming as fast as it could be."

"And of course that timing is part of the problem," he noted quietly. "You have no way of knowing how quickly it's happening, and, while we'll do everything we can to make sure Aida goes out on her own time frame, that in itself could be anytime or years down the road."

"I know, and I've just been trying to avoid thinking about it."

"That is obvious," he said, with a smile, "but it won't serve either of you very well, ... will it?"

She shook her head. "You know that she's my only living relative, so the last thing I want to contemplate is her being gone."

"And, for a lot of other people, all they want to contemplate is the inheritance."

She shrugged. "I have money from my parents now," she murmured, "so I don't even need Grandma's."

"Which is another reason you must be aware of how business works."

"And I'm nowhere near ready."

"Yet you need to be."

"Got it." She stared out the window, as they continued to drive. "Did you ask these people if you could come and talk to them?"

"Nope," he replied cheerfully. "I generally find that shock tactics tend to get me more answers."

"Oh, this could be fun," she muttered.

"Stay in the car, if you want," he said, as he pulled in front of a small older-looking home.

"Who lives here?"

"Melody," he murmured.

Eva stiffened slightly and then sagged in place. "Remind me why I wanted to come?" she murmured.

"You tell me," he stated, "because I'd like to know the answer to that too."

She shrugged. "I don't know. I just have so many questions that I need answers to. To know who was involved in what," she shared. "It's been very distressing to find out that our bedrooms have been bugged and not know who's done it."

"Got it." Carson nodded. "And we're obviously working on that."

She smiled. "Working on it is one thing. Solving it is another thing completely."

He reached over, squeezed her fingers with his, and asked, "Ready?"

She shook her head, and a deep breath escaped her, then she nodded. "Might as well, but damn."

"Yep," he agreed. "Life puts us in these very interesting situations. But remember that we don't want to give up what we know."

"If you say so," she muttered. "I never liked this woman from the beginning."

"And why is that?" he asked curiously.

She looked over at him. "Maybe it's the artist in me," she admitted, "but I see things that not everybody else does."

"Good," Carson noted, "so let me know anything you see throughout today. I understand people better than a lot of others, but it's easy to miss something when I'm busy reading their body language or watching their facial expressions while asking questions or trying to get people to open up to me." He also needed her to be prepared, so he let her know sooner, than later. "In this case, she's likely to slam the door in our faces."

"That won't bother you?" she asked, as they got out of

his car and walked toward the front door.

"Nope, not in the least, and it certainly doesn't take her off my suspect list."

"Now, in that case, I would definitely be keeping this one on your list."

"And is that because of a personal dislike?'

"You'll see. She got really ugly at the end," she muttered. "She didn't treat my grandmother well at all."

"And, for that, there is little forgiveness, is there?"

"My grandmother was good to her and her father for many years. Grandma didn't deserve to be treated that way."

"No, of course not, but there are also two sides to every story. And I'm sure, from Melody's side, either your grandmother had too much money, or you had far too easy a life, or whatever. Something made Melody angry. Or maybe she thought you should have given her more. Everybody comes in with a certain amount of judgment, but learning to suspend it while you investigate is a whole different story."

At that, they stepped onto the low porch, and he knocked on the door. It opened almost immediately, and a woman came out, still struggling to put on her shoes.

"I'm ready. I'm ready," she said. Then she stopped and stared. "Who the hell are you?" she cried out, and then she took one look at Eva. "You!" she snorted. "What the hell do you want?"

At that, Eva turned and looked at Carson. "And this is where you take over." She stepped back ever-so-slightly, understanding that Melody was already feeling threatened by Eva's presence.

Melody turned to Carson. "I don't know why this bitch is here, but, if you're with her, I got nothing to say to you."

"Except we have a problem, so we're looking into everybody who had an issue with Aida."

"Who *didn't* have a problem with her?" Melody laughed at his words. "She's nothing but a batty old lady."

"In what way?" he asked quietly.

"Not with Eva around," she stated, with disgust. "I mean, why would you even bring her? She won't exactly open doors. Besides, I'm in a hurry."

"Not until your ride arrives," he noted. Then he looked at Eva and asked, "You want to wait in the car?"

She frowned at him, but he gave a head nod, which left her with no other option. "Love to," she said, shooting a hard look at Melody, then returned to the car.

Carson looked over at Melody, smiled, and asked, "Better?"

"Well, it's better, but, as long as she's still around, no. You can't trust anything she says, you know that, right?"

"Why is that?"

"Because the woman is a liar, and she'll do anything for her grandmother's money."

"Interesting, since she has plenty of her own."

"I don't think those people ever have enough," she muttered. "Unless you're a part of those same silver-spoon brats," she snapped, searching his gaze.

He shook his head. "Nope, just a working man."

"Right. Well, in that case, you should see what that group is like already."

"Your father worked for them too, didn't he?"

"He did, until he got fired. I came on a year or so before he was fired. I tried to stay on afterward because we didn't have any money, and it was pretty rough there for a while," she admitted.

"Why is it that there was no money? He was well paid

for many years," Carson noted.

"Sure, but he also was under the assumption that there would be a lot more money coming, so he spent it quite freely," she replied bitterly.

"And does your father live here with you?"

"No, he's got a new lady," she said, with an eye roll. "He really doesn't know how to pick them."

"Is the new one just as bad as the old one?"

"*Huh*, he's been through three or four since Aida," she replied, with a headshake. "The good news is, he seems to be getting better at picking them."

"So he's got somebody who you like this time?"

"Well, she's got money, and I like her just fine. She's generous, so that helps."

He nodded slowly. "Her generosity would suit your father."

"Yeah, you're not kidding. I told him not to make the same mistake again."

"Which part?"

"The spending part," she snapped, with an exaggeration of her eyes. "What did you think I meant?"

"Maybe stealing."

"He never stole anything," she said hotly. "That old bat just made up stories."

"Are you sure?" he asked, with a calm interest.

"Well, if she didn't make it up, why the hell didn't she charge him then?" she muttered, shaking her head. "You can't trust these people. All they think about is themselves and their money. When she got pissed off that he was looking around for another lady friend, she started to make up all kinds of stories. Really hurt his chances of getting another job too. You can bet he holds that against her."

"Is he holding anything else against her?"

She shrugged. "Why should he? He's moved on. He's got another partner, and this one's generous, and, so far, there's no sign that she'll accuse him of any other bullshit."

"Well, hopefully this time he also won't go looking for another partner before he's done with the current one."

She nodded. "I told him that he was a slug for that, and he shouldn't have gotten involved in something like that to begin with. I mean, any fool knows that's bound to go wrong. We just never expected it to go *so* wrong. But he had to have known he would have been laid off."

"Getting fired sounds like a different story than being laid off."

"I think, in that industry, getting fired is probably more common than getting laid off." She shrugged. "I don't know, but he told me how upset he was with all the accusations she made."

"Of course," he noted sympathetically, "particularly if he didn't understand where any of it was coming from."

"Well, you know when you double-cross a woman," she said, raising her hands in frustration, "what the hell was he expecting anyway? What does any of that got to do with us here and now?" she asked, looking back to where Eva sat in the car. "And why is *she* here?"

"There have been a series of threats made against her grandmother, and we're trying to sort it out."

She started, "Well, you don't have to look very far to find that out. People all around hate her."

"And yet, so far, everybody I've talked to absolutely loves her."

"That's only because she holds the purse strings. But, when she cut off a charity, when I was still working for her, they made all kinds of threats."

"Why did she cut them off?"

"Same bloody bullshit." She gave an airy wave of her hand. "She accused them of cheating. Saying they weren't really working on what they were supposed to be working on. She probably just decided one of her friends should have the money instead."

He didn't even know what to say to that, but he nodded quietly. "So, you have no idea. Do you have anybody else in mind who might have done her wrong or would want to hurt her?"

"A lot of people," she stated. "Not my father, if that's what you're thinking. He might be a fool, but he's not that stupid. Although anybody sleeping with their boss and then choosing to change that arrangement, but thought they would keep their job, wasn't thinking clearly anyway. That just didn't make sense."

"Have you heard any rumors since you worked there?"

"I deliberately don't have anything to do with them," she stated. "I found that it was much harder on my peace of mind. If I kept myself all twisted up with the latest news in their world, what would it matter? I don't walk in their world. I don't understand their world, and I don't want to. Liars and cheaters, all of them."

"And yet your own father was doing the cheating, in more ways than one."

She nodded. "I didn't know about the affair at first. And I gave him shit for that," she told Carson. "The longer I was there, it was just like … everything soured. I knew I had to get out because it was just a bad deal, but every time I saw Aida, I wanted to accuse her of something. I did at the time too," she admitted, crossing her arms over her chest. "But then Dad told me that he had been cheating on her at the time. Boy, you should have heard *that* conversation when I found out."

She frowned, crossed her arms, and continued. "My ex did the same thing to me. So, when I found out what Dad had done to Aida, I mean, ... I get it, you know? It's still a shitty thing, but then she probably was justified in being angry enough to try and screw his life over by passing around all those lies, but really did he think she would do anything less? God, I hated Dad for that."

"Well, personal experience really jacks up that response too, doesn't it?"

She looked at him funny.

"Meaning that you went through it yourself you said, with your ex? So, you understand what it feels like to be cheated on."

"Oh, I do," she said, with a shake of her head. "And he's just an idiot too, like my dad." At that, another vehicle drove up. "This is my ride, and I've got to go."

"I have to check in with your father."

"Good luck with that." She snorted. "You probably won't get in the door."

"Why not?"

"Doesn't want anything else to screw up his life. His new lady has been really good to him, and he's very protective."

"I'm sure he is, but it still doesn't change the facts."

"Why are you even involved?" she asked, as she turned to lock the front door. "I don't even know who the hell you are."

"I work for a security company," he replied.

"Aida didn't go to the cops?"

"No."

"Ah, did you ever wonder why not? I mean, if this is for real, then why not go to the cops? She didn't go to the cops about my father either, so the same thing applies here. My guess is she's just making up all this shit."

"Why?"

"Probably for attention, or maybe she's finally crossed that line and needs to head to the loony bin."

"Maybe," he said.

"I've got to go." She waved goodbye. "Make sure you lose my number. I don't need to talk to you again."

"And what about your father?"

She called out an address over her shoulder. "Talk to him. Knock yourself out," she said. "When he calls the cops on you, that'll be fun."

And, with that, she was gone.

Chapter 10

A S CARSON PULLED away from the driveway, Eva asked him, "So, how did that go?"

"It was interesting," he said. "She has no love lost for either you or your grandmother, but, after trashing both of you, she did acknowledge that her father admitted to having an affair on your grandmother, though she didn't admit to him stealing. She still defends him and probably believes him all too much. She also says she had nothing to do with either of you and wouldn't want her life to go down that pathway."

They were out on the road, when he continued. "When she realized her father had lied about the affair, it brought up all kinds of stuff for Melody because she had a boyfriend who cheated on her at some point. Apparently she chastised her father pretty badly for his actions, and it's made her a little more forgiving to your grandmother."

He was thinking hard. "On the other hand, I don't think she has necessarily dealt with everything, and she has a lot of issues unresolved, when it comes to Aida."

"So, are you saying she is completely stable and normal?"

"Maybe not. The bottom line is, I'm not sure she's involved."

"And what about her father?" Eva asked, still trying to process everything he had just shared.

"Well, that's part of the problem," he noted. "According

to Melody, he's got a new lady friend, and it's a good deal for him. This woman is very generous to her and her dad, and Melody has warned him many times about not doing anything to screw it up."

"Well, that should be fun," Eva noted, "because that would just mean he has another person on the string."

"Maybe," Carson stated, "but we can't judge him for that, and you know that everybody thinks they are entitled to another chance."

"Maybe, but yet they aren't extending that second chance to my grandmother."

"Exactly. Melody also brought up that, because your grandmother didn't go to the cops, it was all just made up to get back at Melody's dad for screwing around on Aida."

"Of course Melody would say that, and honestly we've all seen women who do that too many times," she replied, as Carson interrupted her thoughts.

"Yes, we have," he murmured. "It still sucks though. Because your grandmother didn't do anything official, then it *does* look like she's just trying to make things up to get back at him."

"So it is what it is?" she asked him.

"Well, we're off to see him now."

"*Great*," she muttered.

"And, this time, maybe you should stay in the car."

"Yeah, I probably should." She groaned. "I didn't realize how hard it would be to see her again."

"Melody really disturbed you before she was fired, didn't she?"

"Yeah, it's like, … I don't know. If she were on medication, I would have recommended that the dose be raised because she was just getting weirder."

"Well, *weird* doesn't necessarily mean dangerous or that she had an ulterior motive in any of her actions."

"I know," she agreed.

"And that's just what investigative work is all about. You think that it could be Melody, so you're excited to find out that you may have a legitimate suspect, but then you find out that maybe it's not that way after all," he explained calmly. "We can't make assumptions. We must find proof and hopefully get a confession in the end."

"And yet confessions aren't all that easy to get either," she murmured.

"No, they're definitely not. In more cases than not they retract them anyway. Especially once they get a lawyer."

"Which is just BS," she muttered.

He chuckled. "Well, that's the law, as we have it now."

"And that's just BS too," she said stoutly. As they continued to drive farther, she noted, "This is definitely a wealthier area."

"Yes, Melody must be right about her dad's rich lady friend."

"Well, *at least this one is generous*," Eva repeated snidely. "Can you believe Melody even said that? Maybe he won't steal from this one then," she muttered.

"Maybe not," Carson replied, "but leopards don't change their spots."

"No, I don't imagine they do." An odd disquiet filled Eva's tone.

"Maybe you shouldn't have come."

"No doubt," she snapped, "but I'm here now. So, let's finish this." He looked over at her, and she shrugged. "I'm fine. Just keep driving."

He didn't say anything for a few minutes, and, for that,

she was grateful.

"It doesn't all have to be bad news, you know?"

"Maybe not, but it sure seems that way lately. Until we get answers, and that seems like something we're not getting very quickly," she muttered. "I mean, look at us. ... Your days are running out, and I'm sitting here, not even working on my art."

"Are you ready for the show?"

"Yes," she confirmed, "but that doesn't mean that there isn't paperwork or other things I should be doing."

"Of course not," he agreed. "Being an artist isn't just about putting paintings on canvases that are for sale. There's a lot of business besides."

She looked at him in surprise. "Most people don't understand that."

"No, I'm sure they don't. But that doesn't mean that I don't. Honestly, you're a little bit jumpy when it comes to people finding out about your art. I get the sense that you feel you're being judged for not doing more."

"Well, you know, just that conversation with Grandma this morning reminded me that I probably should be doing more for her, and I haven't been. That makes me feel really bad," she murmured.

He pulled through a large gate and headed to an attractive estate.

"This is something somewhere in between Melody's house and Grandma's place."

"Yeah, so Ron's landed in the middle of the fiscal road. But obviously this woman has enough money to keep him happy," he said. "Now, stay here, and I'll go talk to him."

She watched as he walked up to the front door and rang the doorbell. A moment later, a well-presented older lady opened the door and smiled up at him and stood aside to let him in.

Eva frowned at that because she'd been hoping they would just stand there on the front steps, and maybe she could actually hear parts of the conversation, but that wasn't to be.

And, if Carson was being invited inside, did that mean Ron was there too? Again Eva wasn't sure and didn't think that the chances of finding out anytime soon were likely.

As she waited and then waited and waited some more, she used her phone and dealt with emails, plus some text messages from friends and the gallery owner. Seemed like everything was fine, but she was getting more and more nervous as time went by and as there was still no sign of Carson.

Finally she started getting frustrated, wondering if they had done something to keep him inside. Just when she was plotting a rescue, the door opened suddenly, and he stepped out. She sighed with relief, something she needed to disguise before he got back in the vehicle.

But, even as she watched, another vehicle drove up behind her and out came a man. As he hopped out, she studied him through the rearview mirror and realized it was Ron. She winced at that, wanting to race out and scream at him, still filled with anger for what he'd done to her grandmother. And that wouldn't help them at all right now.

Ron stepped up onto the front porch beside the woman and kissed her gently on the cheek, as he looked over at Carson. Now Eva really wished she could hear the conversation because almost immediately Ron started getting angry.

She rolled down her window, hoping to hear something, but no such luck. Almost immediately the woman tried to placate Ron by placing a hand on his arm and talking to him in a lower voice. But he wasn't having any of it. Ron even went to jump Carson, but, with one hand, Carson reached out and nailed Ron against the pillar for even trying it.

She smiled at that. "That should do Ron some good."

Carson hadn't even done anything to Ron. It was just Ron's nasty mood showing up, but, as Eva remembered, Ron had one hell of a temper. And it wasn't something she remembered fondly. When there was no sign of Ron's yelling abating, Eva got out of the vehicle and walked up to stand beside Carson. Ron's attention was immediately diverted to her. He took one look at her and really blew up.

"You!" he screamed at the top of his lungs. "You've caused me enough trouble. How dare you come here!"

"*I* came here," Carson stated, stepping ever-so-slightly in front of her, "because we have somebody who's been threatening and stalking Aida."

At that, he stared at him, nonplussed. "What?"

"You heard me," he snapped. "So I'm checking on your whereabouts."

"Well, unless you're a cop," Ron yelled, "you can get the hell off my property."

At that, Carson turned and looked at the woman beside Ron. "Whose property is this?"

"It's mine," she declared, her voice clear and distinct. "And that's enough out of you, Ron," she continued, looking over at him. "I've never seen you like this, and it's not anything I ever want to see again."

"Look. They're part of a very bad period of my life," he said. "I tried really hard to put it behind me, and they're just bringing it all back up."

"Maybe they should," the woman stated, "because I

don't know anything about this, and he had some pretty disturbing things to share."

"Like what?" Ron asked wearily.

"He told me that you stole from Aida," she murmured. "Oddly enough, that's the first I ever even heard that you knew her."

"You know her?" Ron asked.

"Yes, we've worked on several charities together." She stopped and stared at him. "That woman is at least fifteen years older than I am."

"We were just friends," he replied in a calm tone.

"Oh, please, Ron, you were lovers," Eva stated hotly. "How dare you deny that relationship now? Just because you don't want to be seen as somebody who had an older lover?" She snorted in disgust. "You were happy enough to be her lover when her money was good for you too. But then you wanted more."

"She never even went to the cops," Ron snapped. "You're just lying."

"Listen." Carson stepped in. "We are not trying to cause more trouble for you."

Then Eva spoke again. "Would you prefer that we dragged your name through the mud and threw you in jail now?" she asked with interest. "You know that the statute of limitations on a theft of this magnitude, a federal crime, has not run out yet. I'm actually still trying to convince Aida to call the cops. She's just afraid of the humiliation of having people find out that any lover of hers would do something like that. Of course she takes it as a sign of poor judgment on her part. But really you caught her when she was still grieving the loss of her husband and of her son," she murmured.

Eva wanted to let it all out, and she didn't hold back. "And yet here you are, very quickly with yet another woman of means, after a few others in-between." Eva looked over at the woman in question and asked, "Does he look after any of your financials?"

She nodded slowly.

"That's how it started with Grandma. He worked her financials for ten years, and, as far as we can tell, he managed to steal about half a million dollars over that time period," she shared.

The woman paled, and the way she caved forward was like a punch to the gut. "Oh my." She turned toward Ron. "Please tell me that you didn't do this."

"I didn't do it," he said instantly.

"I suggest you talk to my grandmother," Eva murmured. "She has phone call recordings from the bank. She has the checks written with no invoices—and for ever-increasing amounts, payable always to him, deposited into his personal account." She glared at Ron. "And all of that is backed up. She has a hard copy and a digital copy as well, just in case you thought you could come and steal it all, *Ron*," she murmured.

The woman looked very confused, and Eva felt sorry for her. "I'm so sorry," she told the woman. "I don't know that this guy has done anything to you at all. I just know what he's done in the past—which included finding his next lady friend before leaving Grandma—and, now that we have a current set of threats against my grandmother, we're trying to figure out who's behind it all."

At that, Ron turned and glared at Eva. "You've done enough damage to my reputation and my relationship already. You're not laying something like that against me."

"Maybe not," she admitted. "But, if you're behind this latest mess, believe me, nobody will be saving your ass from going to jail this time." With that, she turned and stormed back to the car.

She heard a conversation behind her, but then Carson raced to catch up. He got to the car in time to open the door for her. She slid into the passenger seat and sat here, and that's the first she realized how much she was trembling.

EVEN AFTER THEY got back home again, as Carson and Eva walked up to the front door, she seemed oddly upset. He told her, "You did really well back there."

"Bullshit! I should have stayed in the car." She held out her hands, and they were still shaking. "Honestly, I'm not much of a touchy-feely person, but there are times … when human comfort is the only answer."

"There absolutely are," he agreed, turning to face her and opening his arms.

"Well, this is definitely one of them," she murmured.

"Good to know." Gently he wrapped her up in his arms and held her close. He didn't think she wasn't touchy-feely as much as she'd spent a good decade learning to push everyone away to keep herself safe from hurt, from being abandoned and betrayed. Yet it had happened—was happening—even right now. Maybe she instinctively understood that, hence her prickliness when he'd first arrived. She'd dropped it now, but some defensive mannerisms remained, … almost as if she were hiding something.

When the door opened, Flora stood there with a goofy grin on her face.

Eva rolled her eyes at her. "He's just making me feel better."

"Of course," Flora said. "We should all be so lucky." Then she went off, chortling, a broad smile on her face.

Eva groaned. "You can bet she'll tell my grandmother about it."

"Is that a problem?" he asked.

"No, it's just ... I was trying not to have anything like this go on in my world."

"*Like this*? What does that mean?"

"I don't know," she began, "but right now I don't need anything, definitely not distractions."

"You already said that you were done with everything for your show."

"Yes, but I've been saying things like that for a long time, so now I wonder if I'm even just using that as a way to avoid everything."

"Maybe," he agreed, "and you also have an awful lot going on in your world with your grandmother."

"Not to mention, I just met you," she stated, with an eye roll.

He chuckled and then gave her an extra hug, kissed her on the temple, and declared, "Okay, now you should definitely be feeling better."

"Maybe," she muttered. "I still don't understand this impulse though."

"What impulse?" he asked, as they stepped inside.

"To get hugs from you all the time," she muttered. "It's not me at all."

"It hasn't been that many hugs, as I recall. Besides, you're upset, and you've had a very upsetting day," he reminded her.

"And that would be my next question," Aida called from

the hallway. "How did it go?"

"Oh, it's just …" Eva looked at her grandmother. "I saw both Melody and Ron."

"Well, I guess that's a good thing in a way," she replied in a quiet voice. Aida looked from one to the other. "Did you get any helpful information though?"

"No, not necessarily," Carson admitted. "I don't trust Ron at all, but he may have just been given the heave-ho or at least may now have another reason to hate you."

"We don't know for sure," Eva added.

"It probably depends if he's been doing anything underhanded with his new relationship," Carson added.

"He has another partner?" Aida asked, her gaze wide.

He nodded. "Yes. As a matter of fact, according to Melody, several came after you. This lady didn't know anything about what happened with you, and yet she actually knows you."

When he mentioned her name, Aida gasped. "Yes, I do know her, and she has been talking about somebody new in her life. I was really happy for her. But now, oh my." Aida stared at him in horror.

He nodded. "Remember? When you take action or don't take action, there are consequences."

"Right," Eva agreed. "Now she may very well call you to confirm what we talked to her about."

"Yes, of course," Aida replied, looking shaky. "I definitely must talk to her. Oh dear, that's terrible."

"And yet it's to be expected, isn't it?" Carson asked Aida.

"Yes, yes, of course it is," she murmured. "It just … It makes me feel even worse because I know this woman."

"Of course," Carson agreed. "Other than that, I'm not sure we have much to go on."

She nodded. "Right, and that makes it even harder." And, with that, Aida said, "I'll go back to my office." And very stiffly, she headed there, leaving the two of them to stare at each other.

"What will you do now?" Eva asked Carson.

"I'll—" His words were cut off when Flynn strode purposefully into the room.

"We need to talk."

"Yep, absolutely." Carson excused himself, and the two men quickly walked away from Eva. On instinct, he turned and saw her heading after her grandmother. Nodding to himself, he breathed a sigh of relief, knowing that was what the both of them needed.

As he walked over, Flynn sighed, and Carson was all over him. "What's up?"

"So the bugs? … Both are old," he stated. "It looks like somebody was trying to fix them over time."

"So you mean they've been tampered with a couple times?"

"Yes, but nobody has put new ones in yet."

"That's interesting. I wonder why. Like what's the whole point of this?"

"It's hard to say," Flynn replied, "but somebody was trying to keep the bugs functional, trying to keep these running, but maybe now they've given up."

"Right, and it depends whether they still need whatever it was that they were after or whether it was just Ron literally keeping track of what was going on, from his lover's point of view."

At that, Flynn nodded. "Neither of which is a great idea."

"No, we don't have anything new to go on, and it is imperative that we find something soon. There has to be some clue as to what's going on here. The only people who would have had access," he murmured, "would be people working here, whether temp help or the live-in variety."

"But why would whoever it is be bugging their bedrooms? Aida doesn't have internet wired in up there on the second floor at all, and, with this old estate and its thick concrete walls, she'd need it up there for it to work. A simple signal booster won't do it either, in my opinion, not in this mansion. Otherwise nothing electrical is showing up as a problem."

"And nobody was either electronically monitoring the bugs or physically checking them?"

"Maybe the cleaning woman appears to vacuum their bedrooms, and somebody else accompanies her, specifically to check on the bugs in the bedrooms, maybe to switch them out or something. Only I don't think that would happen easily. Aren't these service people bonded and vetted on both ends, by their employer and by people like Aida?"

"It's hard to say. Even if they advertise as all their people are fully bonded, I'd be inclined to check regardless. I'm afraid it would widely differ between these service corporations, not to mention between the people who hire them. Probably one side thinks the other is running background checks on these temporary hires."

At the same time, Flora walked by.

Carson stopped her. "Flora, have you had any repairmen in here lately?"

"No, not at all," she replied curiously. "Why?"

"Just wondering who would have had access to the house."

She shrugged. "Only the people who live here," she

murmured. "And me of course. Then on cleaning days, we have the extra people come in."

"Do you vet them?"

"No, I don't," she murmured. "I can't possibly do that, but we have used the company that sends them for a long time."

"And, if you did have a repairman, what would it likely be for?"

She frowned. "We had somebody in the kitchen not too long ago because I was having trouble with the stove, and we've had a plumber in a couple times."

"Any idea where the plumber was working?"

"The main bathroom downstairs. I don't recall the last time anybody would have had a reason to go upstairs."

He nodded. "Good enough. And what about Eva's ex-fiancé?"

Flora shook her head. "I don't know about that one," she replied. "I certainly wasn't keeping track of him. And young people, being who they are, I'm sure he was all over the house."

"Good point. Have you seen him since they broke up?"

She frowned, shook her head again. "No, I haven't."

"No contact with him?"

"No, not at all," she confirmed.

"I understand that he was a distant relative of Ron's."

"Yes," she agreed, "that's what I understand."

"And when the relationship with Ron broke off, it didn't affect the ex-fiancé?"

"How?"

"I'm considering the timeline of those events," Carson replied.

"I think Ron broke off first. His daughter was already

here working, and that broke up next. I think Eva had met her ex-fiancé before all that."

"Right." Then Carson asked, "So afterward? Was her fiancé still with her after Ron was gone?"

"Yes, the fiancé was here."

"Anybody else around after she broke up with her fiancé?" he asked.

She shrugged. "Not that I know of. You must ask Eva."

"Oh, I will," Carson said, as Flora left for the kitchen.

Flynn turned to Carson and asked, "What are you thinking?"

"Access to this place has been pretty limited, and we also don't know that the bugs had anything to do with this current mess."

"No, we don't, and that is another concern," Flynn noted. "One thing that I am wondering is if the bugs are being used for something else entirely."

Carson stared at him. "Like what?'

"Well, modifications were made to them. I wondered initially if it were repairs, but what if it wasn't for that but to utilize them for something different?"

"Like what?"

He lowered his voice. "Voices in the night?"

Carson stopped, then stared at him and asked, "Is that possible?"

"Absolutely."

"Easily enough?"

"Hell no, but a hacker plus somebody who knew electronics could absolutely trigger a signal that would turn on a recording in those rooms."

"In which case we need to go back through those rooms. I was only scanning for bugs. You were only searching for plugged in electronics or internet, so that leaves battery-operated devices or solar or even an old-school antenna or whatever. Regardless we are now thinking out of the box and need to do another manual sweep." Carson hesitated and then added, "I already have full access to the house, so let's check it out." And, with that, he led the way.

Flynn asked, "Do you really think that's possible?"

"Well, it would make sense. Eva mentioned something waking her just last night. Plus, Aida told me that she's regularly hearing sounds in the night, and she's bothered by ghosts of her past. Her husband was apparently quite a cutthroat businessman."

"Yeah, you mentioned the dead husband to me, and his business practices. I know Ice is working on it."

At that, Carson got a phone call. He pulled his cell from his back pocket to see who it was. *Ice.* "Hey, what's up?"

"Well, we have more suspects for you guys to look at," she began.

"Locally?" Carson asked.

"Yes, local. One of them was roadkill at the hand of Aida's husband's business practices. He's number one on my list."

"How bad?"

"The family lost everything basically, and then the father committed suicide. That left the mother, who ended up taking cleaning jobs because she wasn't skilled or trained for anything else, and they had one son, who apparently grew up with a chip on his shoulder."

"Well, that could make for all good suspects," Carson agreed.

"It does," she agreed. "It's a sad story. Let me just state here that I don't believe for one moment that Aida had any idea that these shenanigans were going on or that she would have helped her husband in any way with these mob-like transactions. So, anyway, Aida's hubby was trying to get a building, a series of them. So this family got squeezed out of their mom-and-pop business, a small bakery. Basically a power play got them pinched out. They didn't get anywhere near what they should have for the value of it, and the baker, the husband, tried to be a handyman but couldn't support his family. His son was actually a better handyman than he ever was."

"Of course. When it comes to property, developers can get pretty ugly sometimes."

"Yeah, you're not kidding," she muttered. "Anyway it's quite possible that Aida's husband's mistakes are coming after her right now."

"But why wait?"

"That's one of the things I was looking at," she noted. "In this case, one reason for waiting is potentially that the son was just released from jail."

"Oh, now that's looking better all the time. What was he in for?"

"B&E and he got caught. He did six months, then he was out for a while, soon got caught again and did another six months. He was charged a third time, did his third sentence, and was out in time to start this current mess with Aida."

"And that's all that you've found on the son?"

"The crimes were pretty small-fry. Everybody was bending over backward to give this guy a break."

"What about his mother?"

"She died about a month ago."

"There's your trigger," Carson said in excitement.

"That's what I was wondering," she noted. "Of course it's all conjecture at this point in time."

"Maybe, but it fits. It's also a motive that would make a lot more sense than some of what's going on here."

"I'll check on the son's whereabouts and see what I can find. I understand you contacted Aida's old manager, Ron."

"Yep, I did, and of course everybody keeps bringing up the fact that Aida didn't go to the cops about Ron's theft."

"I can understand that too," Ice said. "It's hard to have the world know what a dupe you were. We can only do so much to protect ourselves, and, when we get caught by somebody like this, it's hard to have the whole world know."

"I guess," Carson replied. "Also, because of that, Ron's daughter, Melody, doesn't really believe any of the claims against Ron."

"Well, that's because they weren't actual claims filed with the police and because Ron *had* cheated on Aida to begin with."

"Melody thinks the theft was all trumped-up."

"Of course. I actually just got off the phone with Aida. She mentioned that you've found another woman now possibly affected."

"Possibly. At this point, we don't know if Ron's changed his ways or not. We can't just ruin this guy's life on the assumption that he's doing the same thing again, but I did let the current woman know what happened to Aida."

"And yet, how often does a tiger change its stripes?"

"I know. I know," Carson admitted. "I just don't want to turn around and be responsible for him getting kicked out if there's no reason for it."

"Well, Aida asked me if I would speak to this woman myself, should the need arise."

"Good enough," Carson noted. "That makes me feel better too."

"Good, so what are you doing right now?"

"We're checking out her bedroom because Flynn is wondering about something. The bugs look modified, and he initially thought it was a repair, but now it occurred to him that maybe the bugs are being used to send a signal."

"Well, they can certainly go both ways, so, yes, that's possible. What kind of a signal are you thinking?"

"Well, how about one to make noises in the night?"

"Ah, you know what? That's possible too. It would definitely make Aida feel like she's hearing things, wouldn't it?"

"It would, and it would also make her seem to be a liar. When nobody else is hearing them—other than Eva last night—then Aida might feel like maybe she's going a little crazy," he added quietly.

"She's worried about that already."

"She is, indeed. Although I'm not sure anything's behind it. Yet."

"Her mother had dementia," Ice shared, "and, in the last few years of her life, she didn't make a whole lot of sense."

"So Aida's worried about that being genetic."

"Anybody would be," Ice stated loyally.

"Yes, so now it's just a matter of trying to figure out who's behind whatever's going on."

"Well, we'll check out this guy, the baker-turned-handyman," she murmured. "From the sounds of it, the son's got an ax to grind, and he's pretty unhappy about everything that went on in his world. You can't really blame him if the family business went under and ultimately their lives fell apart, leaving him all alone now. Yet the couple did get paid for the property, but I don't know what happened to that money."

"So, that's another question," Carson noted.

"Well, if the mother is recently gone, maybe the son only just found out that really no money is there," Ice suggested.

"It's possible, but those bugs found here would have been here for a long time. And we also don't know when they were placed here."

"Seems the father may have done that," Ice guessed.

"Why the father?" Carson asked.

"Because he became the handyman, right? Apparently later on he was actually hired by Aida's husband to do some odd jobs around the house."

"Interesting theory," Carson muttered. "So what would be the purpose of bugs at that point?"

"Maybe he was trying to find something to blackmail Aida's husband with—the proverbial pillow talk. Maybe something to legally put him away. I don't know yet," Ice stated, "but, according to some of the intel, he wasn't exactly the brightest, but he was somebody with plans, and then he became very vindictive. Revenge is a strong motive."

"At that point in time, his entire life would have been a mess. The whole family was probably in chaos."

"Exactly. He couldn't take the pressure and didn't last much longer after that, taking his own life, but maybe he let on to his son about what to do about it."

"Again, it's all conjecture."

"We're missing the pieces that will make it all make sense," she admitted, "but we'll work on it from this end."

"We're heading up to Aida's bedroom right now to see if we can figure out what's going on."

"If you find a frequency on it," she noted, "we could

possibly figure out if any signal is going through the place."

"That's what we'll do," he stated. "We might end up needing Stone here."

"Yeah, he's got some new toys, and nothing he loves more than playing with this stuff."

"Good. Send him on over then." And, with that, he hung up. "Stone's coming too," he told Flynn and then quickly relayed the rest of the intel from Ice.

"Now that would be an interesting motivation," Flynn murmured. "When you think about it, there's all kinds of reasons why somebody in that baker's family would go after the guy who swindled them out of their livelihood."

"But why come after Aida? Why now?"

"Timing. … Either the kid didn't know before or he didn't have an opportunity. Or maybe he didn't know what to do with the information. Who knows, but it appears that somebody has obviously triggered something for him."

"More than just triggered—and his mother recently died too. I suspect that we'll find out that he and somebody else in his world came together with both the know-how and the wherewithal to figure it out and to actually do something about it."

"I wouldn't be at all surprised to find that he has had this burning desire to get back at the family who ruined his life, and we understand that avenging motivation too," Flynn noted. "That becomes the primary driving factor."

"Yeah, I get it," Carson muttered, as they walked into the master bedroom. He turned and looked around. "If a bug is here that's sending a signal—not just receiving or is no longer receiving—how do we figure out where it's sending to?"

"Well, let me ask Stone. Maybe he's coming already, but

we can do the basic legwork first. He's really good with this kind of stuff." And, with that, Flynn made a quick phone call and put it on Speaker. "Is there anything we can do from here?"

Stone replied, "No, but I took off while Carson was still on the phone with Ice. I'll be there in ten."

"Okay, we're looking for anything odd while we wait on you."

"Sounds interesting," Stone said. "This is a completely new idea on this matter with Aida."

"Yeah, and we needed to figure it out now more than ever because we don't have anywhere else to go," Carson added. "Plus, Ice only gave us a week. *Ticktock*."

"Yeah, not a problem. I'm coming. I don't take kindly to anybody messing with Aida."

"Do you know her yourself then?"

"Sure do," he said, "and, if something unauthorized is there, we'll damn well find it. This is not cool, and trust me. If we do find something, I won't be a happy camper." And, with that, Stone hung up.

Flynn grinned widely. "Yeah, that's Stone for you. God help anybody who's crossing him."

"I think it's like that with everybody on the team," Carson murmured. "One for all and all for one."

"Exactly." With that, Flynn turned and asked him, "So, what's going on with you and Eva?"

He looked at him in surprise. "What do you mean?"

"Don't give me that coy BS," Flynn replied. "I also remember what Levi said."

Carson shook his head. "Oh no. No, no, no. I don't know anything about that matchmaking thing."

"Says you." Flynn gave him a big grin. "I saw the hug at

the doorway."

Carson winced. "She's been pretty upset all morning."

"Of course she was," Flynn agreed, "but that still doesn't explain what's going on with you two."

"Nothing," he said immediately, "absolutely nothing." He knew he'd spoken too fast for it to come across as a legit denial. "I don't know what's going on, let me put it that way," he added. "It's a very strange scenario."

"It is. But it sounds to me like you may be the next one to go down."

"No, I'm not," he argued. "I'm definitely not."

Then Flynn got a text from Stone.

I'm here. Just coming through the gates.

Chuckling, they wrangled all the way back down to the front door. As they got there, Aida stood at her office door, staring at them. "Now what are you talking about?" she asked curiously.

Carson grinned. "Honestly, we were talking about your granddaughter and what a beautiful woman she is," he said graciously.

She laughed in delight. "Now, if only she could hear you."

"Did she go out?" Carson asked suddenly.

"Yes, a friend of hers called, and she just bolted."

"In a bad way?"

She looked at him and shook her head. "I don't know. She just had to go because a friend was in need."

He frowned, not liking anything about it.

"I don't think she's driven out quite yet, if you want to go with her."

Carson glanced at Flynn, who immediately said, "Go!"

Carson bolted out the front door, running down the

driveway, hoping that she'd see him. She immediately hit the brakes, and he ran up beside the Lexus. He leaned through the window. "I'm coming."

"No way in hell you're coming," she cried out. "This is private and personal."

"Yeah, and that means I need to know about it."

She glared at him and then finally her shoulders sagged. She hit the door release button.

"Thank you," he said.

"Don't thank me. As far as I know this is all about a busted-up relationship, and you'll probably listen to hours of bawling."

"*Great*," he muttered.

She laughed out loud. "Don't be a such a wuss. I told you not to come."

"You didn't tell me anything, I only heard from Aida that you were running out. And given the situation," Carson added, "I didn't want you to run alone."

She looked over at him and smiled. "Thank you for that, but I still think you'll regret it."

"Maybe, maybe not," he noted. "I guess only time will tell."

Chapter 11

E VA KNOCKED ON her girlfriend's door and, hearing a muffled cry from inside, immediately opened it. Carson stepped into the entranceway alongside her. Eva glared at him. "You can't really think any danger's here?" she hissed.

"I'm not exactly sure where the danger is," he noted.

"Remember? The jury is still out on that."

"Right, so we don't even know anything yet," Eva argued.

He nodded. "All the more reason to take precautions as necessary."

"This is about Alison, not me," she whispered to Carson, shaking her head. Eva took a left and her girlfriend looked up at her, stood, opened her arms, and they held each other close.

Almost immediately her girlfriend took one look at the man behind Eva and stepped back, frowning. "Who is he?" Alison asked.

"I'm her bodyguard."

She stared at him in shock, then turned to Eva. "What? Why do you need a bodyguard?"

"It's a long story," Eva replied, "and I'm not sure I even need a bodyguard. He may be making a bigger deal out of this than it proves to be."

"And until we know," he stated, "I'll be here at her side."

He held out a hand. "The name is Carson."

"Alison," she mumbled, without shaking his hand. She looked over at Eva. "Seriously, you had to bring him now?"

"Believe me. If I could have left home without him, I would have." She raised both hands. "Really, there's no getting around him."

"No, I guess not. He looks to be a little bit more of a tank than your normal kind of man."

At that, Eva glared at her friend. "He's not mine."

"Sure," Alison replied too quickly, "yet there's a real protectiveness to him."

And knowing that Carson heard all this had Eva flushing. "Anyway, if you don't want us to stay, I understand."

"I don't know if I want you to stay or not," she replied, disgruntled. She glared at him. "Can you sit in the corner and be quiet at least?"

He raised an eyebrow slowly. "I can certainly stay out of the way and not get involved in your conversation," he stated, with a nod. "But I'm hardly a dog to be put in place with an order to *stay*."

At that, she flushed. "Fine. I have some things to talk about, and I really didn't want anybody listening in."

"I understand. Believe me, domestic disputes are not exactly a topic I would choose to listen in on."

She snorted. "Of course not, being a male specimen and all," she snapped in a wrathful tone.

Carson just gave Alison that same flat look that Eva got every time she said something he didn't like. Eva groaned. "Look, Alison. Maybe this won't work."

"It'll be fine," Alison declared. "I can put up with him. Hey, at least he's your problem, not mine."

At that, Eva laughed. "True enough," she agreed. "Now

what's going on?"

Alison grabbed her arm and pulled them over to the couch, farther away from Carson. "Well, he walked out. *Better prospects elsewhere*, he said."

"Ah." Eva went silent, as she thought about it. "That's kind of on-target for him anyway, isn't it?"

"Of course," she snapped.

"You do know how I felt about him in the first place."

At that, Alison looked at her. "Right. You never did like him, did you?" she asked, puzzled. "Why was that?"

"Because he seemed"—she hesitated and then shrugged—"*dodgy* to me."

"Dodgy?" Alison rolled the word around on her lips. "That's not exactly a word I'm used to hearing."

"No, it's not a word I'm used to *using* either." Eva chuckled. "When did this happen?"

"Last night," Alison replied. "And without any explanation either. I don't get it. I mean, it's just like he went from, ... well, we were talking marriage ..." she mumbled, in tears again, "to suddenly it was over."

"Did he get cold feet, you think?"

"I don't know. Yet he had *better prospects*, like, ... like he'd already found somebody else."

"Were you pushing for marriage?"

Alison nodded. "You know how I want to get married. It's awkward being this age and not being married."

"Well, I know how your mother feels about it," Eva noted. "I guess I didn't really expect you to feel the same way."

"Well, I do," she wailed, "badly. So I don't know. Maybe I did scare him off." She sagged onto the couch, tears in her eyes.

"Why don't I make a pot of tea, and we'll sit and talk."

"I was hoping for a lot more than a pot of tea," she snapped in an ominous tone.

At that, Eva chuckled. "Right. Of course you were." She smiled at her distraught friend. "I won't be drinking right now though, considering all the craziness in my life."

"You're no fun then," Alison complained, glaring at her. "I thought you'd come and have a pity party with me."

She smiled at her friend. "You know that I'd rather have a celebration party instead. He wasn't right for you."

"Yeah, says you. But you know how long it'll take to get somebody else up to snuff and ready to get married?"

"So, maybe you need to let go of the whole marriage thing. Especially if you're making it out to be so urgent. I'm sure it's probably a turnoff for most guys." Eva wanted to glance at Carson, not even sure he should be here listening to this conversation, knowing she would probably hear about it afterward.

"Maybe," Alison noted sadly. "But every time we talked about it, he didn't say anything."

"No, and maybe he didn't say anything because he didn't know what to say," she murmured. "You can be a little strong at times."

"A little?" she asked, with a look in her direction. "I assume you mean *a lot*."

"Maybe," Eva said cheerfully. "But remember. Not everybody looks at relationships the same way you do."

"Why not?" she asked, with a petulant tone of voice. "My sister is married and has three kids already."

"Well, if you're mentioning kids, and he wasn't at all ready for marriage," she explained, "that progression might have spooked him."

Alison pouted on the couch. "Well, I just don't understand it. He was quite … almost angry."

"He didn't give you any further explanation?" Eva asked.

"No, just kind of angry. He did say something weird about me."

"What do you mean, *weird?*"

"I don't know exactly." She pulled out her phone and read from it. "Here is what he wrote. *Not sure what's going on, but you're too much work.* And, with that, he then goes on to say he found somebody else, who was a *much better prospect.*"

"Now that's interesting." Eva frowned at her friend. "Did you ask him what that part meant?"

"No, I haven't talked to him at all. How am I supposed to even open a conversation when the guy ditched me?"

"*Hmm.*" Something was so odd about this. This time, she did look over at Carson, who raised an eyebrow.

"You think it's connected?" he asked quietly.

"I don't know," Eva said. "I don't know why it would be."

At that, her friend looked at her. "What are you two talking about?"

He asked, "Eva, how many people know about your friendship with Alison?"

She shrugged. "We've been friends since grade school. We show up at a lot of the same charity events and all."

"Even though I don't have the same kind of money that she does," Alison added, "I *am* a trust fund baby. But, if they marry me, they still can't access it, outside of monthly money."

"Ah," Carson said. "So maybe that's partly what he was looking at. Maybe he checked into it a little further, and he couldn't get any more money from you without your permission, and that's not quite what he wanted."

She stared at him, disgruntled. "Why is it men want to get their money through women instead of working for it?"

"Why is that women want to get their money through men without working for it?" he came back instantly.

She gasped in outrage.

Immediately Eva held up a hand. "Time out. We're not getting into that. That'll be a downer for sure and not productive. It would certainly help us if we knew this was connected to some things going on in my world," she explained. "It would be great if you could ask him about it."

"I'm not talking to him," Alison declared defiantly. "You want to talk to him, you do it. He likes you far more than you like him, by the way."

"Doesn't matter if he likes me or not," she replied. "He was your partner."

"Well, apparently now he's somebody else's," she stated flatly. "And I don't want anything to do with it. And honestly this won't work today." Alison now openly glared at Eva. "If you hadn't brought him along, it would have been nice to see you. But now that he's here ..." She eyed Carson, who sat nearby, calmly trying not to aggravate the scenario.

"Fine," Eva replied. "I'll take him away right now, and you and I will talk later."

"Yeah, you do that," Alison snapped heatedly, then turned to send yet another glare in his direction.

He slowly stood, waiting on her to make a decision. She groaned and said to Alison, "Fine, but don't do anything stupid, okay?"

"I won't do anything stupid," she muttered. "He's not worth doing anything stupid over."

It struck Eva as an odd thing for Alison to say, even at

the moment. Eva just nodded, since nothing was more unstable than a recent breakup. Particularly with this friend, who was well-known for her histrionics.

As Eva walked toward the front door, she turned to her friend. "I'm sorry about the breakup."

She sat there morosely. "Yeah, me too. Next time you come over, lose the escort, will you?"

Eva nodded. Carson was already at the door and held it open for her.

As they walked to her car, he said, "Sorry about that. My presence was apparently more of a negative influence than I thought it would be."

"I don't know why you thought your presence would be welcome," she replied. "I can't decide if this ties into Grandma's problems."

"Why would it though?" he asked quietly.

"Well, it's hard to say. I mean, I didn't like him for one, so I'm sure my personal opinion will be affecting anything I say."

"Why didn't you like him?"

"I always felt like he was after her trust fund. She's lost a lot of guys once they realized her trust fund was never something they could inherit or control, and, even if she passes on, they don't have any access."

"Isn't that fairly common?"

"They're not all set up that way," she murmured. "In some cases, it does pay out to the husband."

"That's not a great way to go forward, focusing on a trust fund," he noted.

"No, it really isn't, and it causes all kinds of headaches."

"Sure does," he murmured. "I was thinking more like all kinds of murders."

She nodded. "But I wonder how we know for sure and if that would make any difference or have any effect on what's going on in my world."

"How much did you have to do with her?"

"Not a whole lot," she noted cautiously. "I mean, at least not lately. I've been working on my show, so I've been out of the mix for a while. It's one of the reasons I came when she called because I haven't spent any time with her recently, and I was feeling a bit guilty." She winced.

"Ah, but obviously her life hasn't been as easy as you had hoped it would be."

"This is not an unusual occasion though," she noted drily. "As much as I don't want to make it sound like she's somebody who's always getting dumped, well, she always seems to be."

"How do you see the situation?"

"Well, because of that trust fund, she's had multiple boyfriends dive into a relationship wholeheartedly, until she starts talking up the whole marriage thing. Then a little investigation on their part shows them that they won't do so well if anything happens, and they'll just end up out in the cold, without any access to her money."

"So, you think most of her relationships are based on people wanting her money?"

"She certainly has attracted more people like that than I would have thought was normal."

"It could also be that she's using the money as a way to attract people," he suggested quietly. "And that'll always draw a certain type of person. I mean, look back on what she said to me, a total stranger. *I am a trust fund baby.* She's quick to throw that into the mix with anybody she's just met, it seems."

Eva looked over at him, then frowned. "You know what? I do remember her in a pub talking to somebody about how much money she had. He did look quite interested."

"Money will always attract a taker, and, with that mindset, it's just as easy to fall in love with somebody who has money than somebody who doesn't. But, if upon further investigation you find out that she'll hold the purse strings and that she may or may not be very generous about doling it out," he added, "feelings could change. If you think about your grandmother and Ron, and the dynamic with his new lady friend, you can understand having doubts."

They were in her vehicle now, and she was driving toward home. "So, a wasted trip."

"Unless you want Ice to dig into his background, or we could just find the boyfriend and talk to him."

"No," she replied, "because I don't really want anybody else to know what's going on with Grandma. Plus, the more I think about Alison and her trust fund luring in her boyfriends, it doesn't feel like it's connected."

"Good," he noted. "Just keep that intuition running."

"Maybe," she muttered. "The only one who really sends up a red flag is Ron. Yet I know it might not have anything to do with him either and could just be more about my personal reaction to him treating Grandma that way. And that's disturbing in itself," she muttered.

"So, I have a question for you, and you don't get to shoot the messenger. What about your own ex-fiancé?"

She stiffened and glared at him. "I don't want to talk about him."

"You might not want to," he noted, "but I think we're past the time of doing so. Did he talk about your inheritance?"

"Well, anybody who knows anything about my family knows that there is just me and Grandma," she murmured. "So, if you are asking if he knew that I would inherit, I'm sure he did. Is that why he was courting me? Who knows? Maybe. But do I really want to go down that road? Hell no."

"Maybe not, but I'm not sure there's a choice anymore."

"Why? Why do we even have to go there?"

"Because somebody has been threatening and scaring the crap out of your grandmother, and, if she were to die, who is in a position to inherit?"

"Me," she stated starkly.

"And therefore, a boyfriend would also be likely to benefit—and, in your case, a fiancé is right here."

"*Ex.*" She shot him a shuttered look.

"An ex who could sweep in to console you." When she turned that glare on him, he nodded. "I get it. You don't want to think about that. Your breakup was recent, correct?"

"Not all that recent," she protested. "Like, not that recent at all."

"And he's also connected to Ron, isn't he?"

At that, she pulled into the front driveway, turned off the engine, and stared at him. "Yes," she murmured. "And that is something that I hadn't really considered."

"That's why we have a problem," Carson murmured. "We do need to consider it, and we do need to know where your ex is at and what he's doing."

"I gave Ice his name."

"Yet you've avoided telling me about him."

"Remember why my grandmother didn't press charges?"

"Yes, of course," he said. "She didn't want anybody to see her as someone being duped into falling in love with the wrong man."

"Exactly," Eva agreed, "and I find that I'm in the same boat."

He stared at her. "You do realize that men have been running this con for a very long time?" he murmured. "You're not responsible for the actions of everybody else in this world."

"Maybe not," she murmured, "but it still feels very much like it's all bad news for me. I just don't want to talk about it, and I don't want people to know about it."

"I'm not sure that'll be an option at this point in time," he stated.

She glared at him. "Well, it could be."

"No," he argued, "it can't. This is no longer something that you get to walk away from. This is about Aida and you, the safety of both of you. So I want to meet this guy, and I want to know what's going on in his world."

She glared at him. "Well, that means you're going alone then," she snapped. "I want nothing to do with him."

"How ugly was the breakup?"

She shrugged. "It was ugly."

"Why did it break up?"

"He was cheating on me," she cried out painfully. "So see? It had nothing to do with money." She frowned. "Well, he was looking for support for a project he was working on, but he wasn't looking for that when we first met."

"Or maybe he held off asking for the money until later," Carson suggested.

"I really don't like the way you think," she muttered.

He smiled at her gently. "You might not, but generally we try to keep people safe by asking the hard questions."

"But those questions aren't nice, and they're actually quite painful," she murmured.

"Painful, yes. Not nice, maybe. Necessary? … Absolutely." As they approached the front step, he repeated, "I need that information, so I can go visit with him."

She hesitated. "Well, I thought I didn't want to go," she began.

"But?" He looked at her steadily, with no judgment in his gaze.

"I'm thinking it might be easier on me if I do go."

"In what way?"

"Because …"

He grabbed her arm and pulled her gently inside the house, then suggested, "Obviously we need to talk about this."

"Yeah, well, I was supposed to have a bawling session with my girlfriend," she snapped, "not you."

"And you were the one who'd cry?" he asked, with interest.

"No, now I'm likely to get furiously angry."

"That's probably better," he stated, "but you need to tell me why."

"Because I don't think I gave a shit about him right from the beginning, and I feel really crappy about that."

He stared at her. "You want to explain that a little more?"

"No, I really don't," she snapped. "This is very difficult for me, in case you hadn't figured it out. This isn't a topic I want to deal with."

"Look, Eva. I'm sorry you don't want to deal with this now," he explained. "If there wasn't something wrong in your world, I wouldn't press you on this. However, the fact is, something *is* wrong, … and I do care."

She glared at him. "I think you're enjoying this too

much."

"To know that somebody in your life wants to hurt you? No, I'm not happy about that at all. I would do a lot to stop things like this from happening to people," he stated. "And more so for you. You're a really special woman, Eva, and I think all this has affected you in ways that you aren't even aware of yet. I would just as soon it never happened in the first place, but, now that it did, the sooner you get over it, the better."

"And why is that?" she asked bluntly.

"So you're ready to move on to another relationship," he replied, equally bluntly.

She stared at him in shock and then slowly shook her head. "I'm not sure where you're going with that," she said tentatively. "But, if it's where I think you're going, I can assure you that it would be an absolute disaster."

He gave her a ghost of a smile. "Why is that?"

But she didn't have an answer. In fact, her heart and all her nerve endings had jumped alive at even the thought of having a relationship with Carson. And all she could do was stand here and stare like a fool at the goofy grin on his face.

CARSON HAD NO idea whatever had possessed him to bring *that* up, but maybe it was the fact that she was so against moving on with her life that had him pushing. It was probably suicidal to even bring it up, since she obviously wasn't ready, but, at the same time, she would never make any progress as long as she continuously found excuses to avoid dealing with it.

He wasn't even sure how much she had to deal with, as much as guilt over the fact that she wasn't terribly upset about the breakup with her fiancé. It had also been interesting to watch Eva with her friend Alison. Eva wanted to cheer up Alison, but the fact that Alison's relationship had broken up was something both Eva and Carson were in full agreement with and clearly was for the best for all.

Surely Eva saw the same parallels in her own relationship, now severed, with her ex-fiancé.

Carson would still follow up with the guy to see if he had any involvement in what was going on with Eva's family, but, as far as Carson was concerned, he didn't want to say that Alison got what she deserved, but a part of him felt—if she were using the trust fund money to attract a boyfriend—that chances were she would get somebody who was attracted by the money that she dangled in front of these guys.

Maybe Eva had helped Alison along over the years, but it was an odd thing to be privy to the female conversation, which had come across in a way that he didn't really care for. But it wasn't for him to judge, and he did appreciate the fact that Eva was at least trying to cheer her friend on regarding the breakup, yet remain truthful and honest in her perceptions of their relationship. In Carson's mind, the breakup with Alison definitely needed to happen, even if the woman didn't appreciate the timing or the way it occurred.

Carson wasn't asked his opinion by either woman. Even if he had been, he didn't really know that sharing what he thought would do any good. However, now with Eva dashing off to her room to avoid any further conversation with Carson about any future relationship between them, it just made him smile, since she could run, but she couldn't hide. Not in the house where he was literally staying.

But it also meant that he had very little time to work on

her. While he was here, chances were she would close down immediately and try to put even more distance between them. So he had to make sure that he made an impression, well and truly made, before she really closed him out. For that, he needed some insider info. From Aida. That is, if Carson passed muster with Aida first.

He walked to Aida's office and tapped on the open door.

She looked up, smiled, and asked, "Anything new?"

"Not particularly," he replied. "I will contact Alison's boyfriend, who just broke up with her, to see if any particular threats were involved."

She shook her head. "Not likely. That girl has had far more breakups over the last few years than anybody ought to ever have."

"She's on some expedited timetable to get married *and* have kids. But worse is that she's using her trust fund to dangle in front of men, as a means to get a boyfriend," he murmured.

She stared at him and then laughed. "Of course she is." Aida shook her head. "And then she's wondering what's wrong when they find out they won't have access to any of that."

"Yet, if money is their only goal, their lifestyle could still be enhanced in many ways by having a relationship with her," he noted.

"Yes, but once people enjoy a slice of the pie, they want more. Then they also tend to realize that somebody will control the purse strings, but it won't be them. Most guys that I know of," Aida added, "aren't terribly happy about having somebody else determine whether they can spend money or not."

He nodded. "I don't understand that mind-set. Money-grubbing is certainly not my cup of tea," he stated.

"But then none of that would ever be an issue for you in the first place, whether she had a trust fund or not, would it?" she asked, with confidence.

He shook his head. "No. I fully plan on working my own way through life," he declared. "Good for her if there's money, and she can put it to good use somewhere, but it wouldn't bother me in the least to have it disappear. I can always make more money. However, you can't instantly replace someone you love."

"Are we talking about my granddaughter now?" she asked, with a twinkle in her eyes.

He rolled his eyes at that. "Only if I want to get shot," he declared, and Aida burst out laughing at that.

"Oh, don't think I haven't seen the way she reacts to you," she murmured. "I mean, if anybody can set her off, it's likely to be you."

"That's not necessarily a good thing though, is it?" he asked.

"But not a bad one either. She has always chosen men who didn't cause any stress or strife in her life at all. They were dull and boring, and there was no excitement. No spark. I always wondered if she was doing that on purpose."

He stared at Aida. "Why would Eva do that?"

"Because it's easy," Aida stated bluntly. "In that scenario, she doesn't have to feel things too deeply, which may well be what she is after, specifically because of all the losses in her life."

"That's an interesting take," he murmured.

"It is, but it's also something people do to protect themselves, and she has spent a lot of time keeping herself safe. Regarding the breakup with her fiancé, outside of her pride,

I'm not sure there was a whole lot else to it. He probably found that out himself and may well have been why he moved on. She wasn't 100 percent engaged in the relationship."

"Also interesting," he murmured, wondering if that was directed at him specifically. It most likely was because the lady in front of him was shrewd and had gained wisdom over the years in ways that he couldn't even imagine.

She added, "So, if you're looking to try, keeping her unsettled is risky."

"Maybe." He nodded. "But she's also hiding. And if a relationship will go anywhere, hiding can't be a part of it."

She chuckled. "Exactly. ... And don't misunderstand. I'm definitely not warning you off. I'm just warning you that she tends to keep herself hidden."

He gave her a gentle smile. "Thanks for the tip."

"And, if she knew that we were even having this conversation—"

"What conversation?" he teased. "I understand completely and utterly."

She nodded. "Ever since I met you, I've wondered. But as soon as I saw her reaction to you, I knew." She cocked her head, studying him. "It will be most interesting to see the fireworks begin."

He laughed. "Well, fireworks can be both good and bad," he noted. "I definitely wouldn't want to upset her to the extent that she goes running."

"And yet that may well be all you can do," she stated seriously.

"We'll see. ... And since you obviously aren't telling me to avoid Eva, then presumably you don't have any objection, should I move down this path?"

"None at all," she said, "but, if you don't realize that I've already thoroughly cleared you with Levi and Ice, you're not as smart as I think you are."

He burst out laughing. "Believe me. They would be thrilled. They warned me before I came that I would be *next*. The whole crew has been pairing up, one by one."

She nodded, with a note of satisfaction. "Those two are brilliant in ways that I couldn't ever hope to learn," she admitted, with a smile.

"They're smart. They're sneaky. And they're definitely seasoned old hands at this apparently." He chuckled. "I told them flat-out that I wasn't interested, but then the minute I saw Eva, well, … everything changed."

"Oh, I noticed." Aida smirked. "But I don't think my granddaughter did."

"That's because she keeps herself behind those walls of safety," he murmured. "Not realizing that the wolf is already in the chicken house." He gave Aida a broad smile.

She burst out laughing, the delighted sound ringing through the room. "Oh my." And then the laughter faded, and she looked at him seriously. "Just treat her right. That's all I ask."

"I have never treated a woman poorly in my life," he stated, with a firm tone. "I sure as heck wouldn't start now. In my mind, that would be like pulling the wings off a butterfly. I could never do that to Eva."

She smiled. "No, I don't think you could, and that makes me feel all the better. If you wanted to speed up this process, I wouldn't feel so bad about leaving."

"Leaving?" he asked, with a raised eyebrow.

"You know as well as I do that I could just not wake up any morning," she admitted. "Just because I'm strong and healthy, it doesn't mean that other human plans aren't being made about me not waking up one day or even just along the natural cycle of life. And I would so love to see my grand-daughter settled before that."

"Don't ever let her hear you say that," he muttered. "She'll think you're matchmaking."

She smiled at him. "She would, indeed. But she's also smart enough to know that the only matchmaking I would do would be something I believed to be in her own best interests."

"That's also not what she'll want to hear," he replied, with a smile. "I'm pretty sure she is confident about knowing what she needs."

At that, Aida looked at him and nodded. "You do understand her, don't you?"

"I do, at least at this point and to this level. I hope to get to know her much better, but that'll take some time."

"Well, you've only got a few more days here," she noted, with a twinkle in her gaze. "At least to cement what you've begun."

"I'm working on it," he said, giving her that same rakish grin he'd given her earlier. "It won't be a walk in the park though."

"And it shouldn't be," she stated firmly. "There should be all kinds of challenges in order to make it work the right way. When it comes easily, it's not a good thing either."

"No argument here," he replied. "As far as I'm concerned, anticipation of the journey itself should be a major part of it," he added quietly. "Eva is special, and I don't want her to ever feel coerced or put on the spot in any way."

"Good," Aida agreed. "But I suspect she has no clue what's even happening to her because it's the first time."

"First time for what?"

"To really love somebody, ... other than me of course. Everybody else she's ever loved up until now, she's lost, so take that as a word of warning."

"Got it," he murmured. "I will."

And, with that, she waved him off and said, "Go do something useful now. I'm busy."

Taking his leave as instructed, he smiled and quickly left. He found Aida to be an interesting, dangerous, and equally stunning woman in her own right. He stopped in the doorway, looked back at her, and added, "Your husband was a lucky man."

She looked up, smiled, and nodded. "He was, indeed." Staring at him, she continued. "We did have a great time together," she murmured. "That's what I was hoping to recapture when I tried again—but wrong person, wrong time. Wrong lifetime perhaps." She made an airy wave of her hand. "Don't make the same mistake."

With that, she returned to her work.

Chapter 12

EVA BURIED HERSELF in her art upstairs, and, only after she pulled herself back from her crazy frenzy of painting, did she note she'd been painting Carson yet again.

She groaned as she stared at it. The problem was, the painting itself was brilliant. It captured so much about him that was absolutely stunning, but it was so not what she wanted to show anyone.

She knew the gallery was looking for recent pieces, and this one would show her current skill in this new mode. She realized that she was continuously changing, and she'd been excited when she had first discovered this growth in her work because that also could mean more gallery showings down the road.

But how was she supposed to do that when the only thing she was painting was him, over and over again? She stared at the picture, distressed and unnerved, yet excited at the power exuding off the canvas. It was an absolutely brilliant piece, her very own masterpiece.

A knock came on her door, and she bolted to her feet, then crashed into her couch. Immediately ignoring the pain in her toe, she threw sheets atop her paintings. When the door opened before she was done, she turned around glaring, only to see Flynn. She raised both hands in frustration. "What's the point of knocking if you don't wait for a response?"

"Well, you didn't answer, so I figured you weren't here," he replied, stepping inside. Then he stopped dead in his tracks. "Wow."

"Wow what?" she asked, as she threw a sheet over the huge sketch she'd just been working on.

"That's phenomenal," he said.

So much sincerity filled his voice that she stopped and frowned, surprised by his reaction.

He looked at her quizzically. "But you already know that, right?"

"No, I don't. I don't usually do people." She stared at the canvas she was about to cover up. "I especially don't do faces."

"Well, you sure did this one," he noted quietly, "and you did an incredible job. You've captured him in a way I didn't think anybody ever could." As he spoke, he pulled back the sheet that had only partially covered another painting. "Jesus, you are really talented."

She looked over at him, still frowning.

He shrugged. "I've known Carson for a long time. He's always been kind of happy go-lucky on the outside, but there's also something intensely magnetic about his personality. He's very determined to do what is right all the damn time, and it can get him in a lot of trouble. In that way, he is too damn annoying sometimes."

"Seriously?" she asked. "I was wondering how much of his persona was just a flippant act."

"Not at all," Flynn said, "but I think you know that, just by looking at these paintings."

"Well, I wondered about that," she admitted. "But, of course, I'm coming at it from a very different perspective."

"Has he seen these?"

She shook her head. "God no, and I didn't even ask his permission." She winced.

Flynn nodded but didn't say anything and just stared, completely enthralled.

"Do you really think they're okay?" she asked, hating that pathetic tone in her voice.

He faced her and pointed. "They are beyond okay. These really are awesome."

She felt something inside her relax. "I'm having my first show soon, but it won't include anything like this."

"The team told me that you were busy getting ready for an art show," he shared, "but I had no idea that you were this talented."

She shrugged it off. "The trouble is, I'm not sure that I am. Of course I've spent a lifetime being told by my grandmother how absolutely wonderful I am. But that doesn't inspire confidence in me because—"

"She's your grandma, and, in her world, you're amazing no matter what. Plus, she's supposed to be supportive."

"Exactly," she agreed.

"You know that, should she hear you say that, it would also make her angry because it meant you didn't honor her opinion?"

She gave a stilted laugh. "Funny how we get all twisted up over things like that, isn't it?"

"That's because you don't have that same confidence in your own work yet," he noted. "That's really too bad because this is freaking amazing."

At the sound of somebody coming up the stairs, she immediately threw the sheets atop her work and said, "Don't tell him, … please?"

He looked at her. "Well, I won't right now, but I think he should know."

"Why?" she asked. "It's nothing. I mean, it's just me with an artistic impulse."

"Maybe," he replied, staring at her intently. "But these paintings show something else too."

"What?" she asked, frowning.

Just then Carson walked in, with a bright smile. "Hey. Did you ask about getting up in the attic?"

"No, not yet," Flynn admitted. "I was just doing that now."

Carson looked apologetically at her. "We need access again."

"Fine," she snapped. "What for now?"

"We're running extra lines for the new security upgrade," he told her. "Regardless of what we end up finding or not finding, your security here is pretty bad."

"*Great*," she muttered. "Just more to worry about."

"Well, it'll be less to worry about by the time we're done," he noted. "We'll set it up to be monitored at Ice and Levi's compound."

"You can do that?" she asked.

He nodded. "That's one of the fields that we're doing now, home security, but not just any homes," he added, "because, well, it's an expensive system."

"Of course it is," she said in a dry tone. She looked over at them. "How long will you need?"

"Well, you can always close the stairs behind us," Carson suggested helpfully. "Particularly if you need to work."

"I do need to work," she stated, itching to get back to the painting. "I just don't know that I want you guys up there while I work, for fear of you coming down any minute."

"I can text you when we're done," Carson offered.

"Can you give me an idea of how much time we're looking at?"

"An hour maybe."

"Well, in that case, yes, please text me," she said. "If it would just be a few minutes, I could go get myself a cup of coffee."

"No, it won't be that fast. I wish it were, but it's more involved than that."

She nodded and watched as they pulled down the stairs and headed up. She hoped that Flynn would turn so Eva could warn him again. But that didn't happen.

Flynn headed up the stairs first, and Carson looked back at her and smiled. "I promise we're trying not to disrupt you."

"Yeah, but you just being here is disrupting," she replied crossly.

"In that case, it's good enough for me."

She gasped in outrage, as he bounded up the stairs. She was beyond frustrated. "Now you're just testing my patience."

"Not really," he told her. "I'm not against having you be affected every time I come around."

"Maybe it isn't you that is affecting me. Maybe you're just disturbing my work."

"Maybe," he said, with a cheerful grin. "And maybe it's something else entirely."

She groaned. "Your ego is amazingly huge," she called out after him.

"Thank you," he said instantly.

That was not the reaction she wanted. But it also had

her smiling. She groaned at that and headed down to get a cup of coffee.

As she walked downstairs, Aida came out of her office. "Hey, dear. How has your morning been?"

"Well, it would have been fine, but the men are up in my studio."

"I'm sorry," she said apologetically, "but we decided to install a full security system now. I should have done it a long time ago. The world is changing, and this is just a reminder that we must keep everything precious to us safe."

Eva stopped and looked over at her grandmother with a gentle smile. "You are the most precious thing to me, so, if it's necessary, then we'll do it. As you said, we probably should have done it a long time ago."

"We should have," she murmured. "It's just one of those things that I pushed off because I didn't know who could be trusted."

"And you trust Levi and Ice?" she asked, for the umpteenth time.

"I do, and you should too."

Eva hesitated and then asked, "And what about their men?"

"Meaning?" But a twinkle was in her grandmother's eye.

Not sure what she was even asking, or why the amusement was there in her grandmother's gaze, but Eva shrugged and added, "Two of them are in my studio right now."

"Ah," she murmured. "Yes, I would trust all of them. I can't imagine that they would have anybody less than 100 percent trustworthy working for them."

"But people can be deceptive," she pointed out.

"They can, indeed," Aida agreed, walking over and giving her granddaughter a hug. "Not everybody out there is set to betray us."

Eva walked ahead into the kitchen. "I didn't mean it that way," she said hesitantly.

"Didn't you? Or are you more worried about people leaving us again?"

"That just brings us back to a place I don't want to go," Eva muttered.

"Of course not, neither do I. We've had a lot of losses in our lives, and they've affected us in ways we couldn't imagine. But there is just no way to prevent yourself from ever being hurt again," Aida offered.

"No, I'm not trying to …" Eva protested. "I mean, I was engaged. Remember? I was fully prepared to get married and to move on."

"You were," she said, "but I wonder, as it got closer, if you wouldn't have called it off yourself."

She stared at a grandmother. "Well, I would hope not." Then she frowned. "Why would you say that?"

"Because I'm not sure your heart was engaged as much as it should have been," Aida stated. Eva stared at her in shock, as Aida continued. "Think about it, dear. I mean, he could do almost anything he wanted and still you would blow it off."

"And here I thought I was just being agreeable."

"That wasn't being agreeable, Eva. That was not caring," she stated. "And, if he did find somebody else, it's quite possible it's because he felt like there just wasn't enough interest on your part."

She shook her head. "Really? Is that how you saw it?"

"Yes," her grandmother replied. "It seemed like somehow you'd made the decision that you should get married, so, when he proposed, it probably sounded like a good idea.

Then all of a sudden, well …" Aida stopped. "Maybe you were just trying to detach yourself from the fear that he would leave you or the fear that it wouldn't work out?"

Eva frowned. "And here I thought it was the fear that I wasn't good enough."

Her grandmother looked at her and then rushed over, her arms open wide, and hugged Eva. "Sweetheart, your parents didn't leave you because you weren't good enough. They died. They couldn't help it."

"I feel like an idiot for even thinking like that," she admitted, staring at Aida, tears filling her eyes. "How foolish to blame them for being killed."

"It's not foolish, especially considering how young you were when you lost your father. I think it's probably a fairly common reaction because you are the one who suffered from their loss."

"And yet I didn't suffer in many ways," she said, "because I had you, and that gave me a life that I could never have had without you."

"The best thing would have been if you'd had your parents. That would have been the best for all of us," Aida noted gently. "But it wasn't to be, and I know that is something they would have regretted themselves, if only they knew."

"Well, I like to think they're still hanging around, and they do know," she shared, feeling teary-eyed at the reminder of the tragic losses they both experienced. "Even after all this time it still has the power to bring me to tears."

"And that, my dear, is called love," Aida claimed. "I think that's why I felt like you didn't love your fiancé, even though you were prepared to marry him. I didn't feel like that level of emotion was there for you."

She shrugged. "I'm not sure it was," she murmured. "And that didn't really occur to me until after he left. A part of me felt more relief than anything else."

"Exactly," Aida agreed, smiling at her. "And nobody is happier to hear that coming from you than I am," she declared. "I didn't want you to misunderstand why all this was going on or how you were reacting to it. And I especially didn't want you to head into the next relationship just dragging that same kind of baggage."

"I think that's why I wasn't planning on getting into another relationship either," she admitted, "because I didn't trust myself. I couldn't trust that I would make a decision for the right reasons."

"What would it take for you to make such a decision now?"

"I don't know. If he was easy to get along with, and he was ... easy to be with."

"But that kinda sounds like your fiancé again. The thing is love isn't necessarily easy. There should be some excitement. There should be some ... I don't want to say fights, but there should certainly be an understanding that spirited disagreements are part of a healthy relationship. Communication is key. At times you yell at each other, and at times you make up too," she murmured. "I don't want you to inhibit your world out of a misguided fear that, if you yell or scream or say something harsh, they'll walk all over you ... or will walk away."

At that, she winced. "God, now I feel like I owe him an apology."

"I wouldn't do that. Your ex has his part in this too," she said, with a smile. "But understanding yourself and who you are is what makes that experience worthwhile."

"If you say so," she muttered. "I just know that I can't go through that kind of rejection again."

"Even though you rejected him first?" she asked quietly.

"Ouch, you're not pulling any punches, are you?" Eva murmured.

"Not on something like this. I love you too much to see you enter a marriage that is so much less than what it could be just because you're afraid of getting hurt, or you're afraid of doing something that would make them leave."

"God." Eva ran a hand over her face. "I feel like I'm just waking up from a long sleep."

"Well, you're waking up all right, but it's not from a long sleep. It's from avoiding feeling those emotions that allowed you to feel—which has been, in this case, more of a safety net than anything. You were stopping the pain, but you also stopped the love."

"I never even thought of it that way," she admitted, "and it's pretty lame to think that you saw it and that I didn't."

"I think it's always easier to see things like that when it's not about us," she noted. "And now you need to be easy on yourself and understand why it happened, so that you don't repeat it."

She laughed. "Well, what I'll do is not repeat it, and, in order to avoid repeating it, I'm just not getting involved."

"Getting involved will happen whether you like it or not," her grandmother noted gently. "You'll meet somebody who stirs up something inside you, that makes you confused, makes you feel things that you don't understand. It will make you look at life a little bit differently, and you'll end up going to sleep with that person on your mind, and waking up with thoughts of them first thing in the morning," she murmured. "And that's the way it's supposed to be. It's supposed to be confusing. It's supposed to be terrifying, but it's also supposed to make your heart swell with joy when you see him, and just the thought of him is supposed to make you feel something inside that's good, that's positive, and that's wholesome. Not someone who just checks the boxes on some list."

"Ouch." She winced at her grandmother. "That sounds terrible."

"And that, my dear, is why your ex found somebody else, somebody who could appreciate him for himself."

"So, it had nothing to do with my trust fund?" she murmured.

"It might have. Maybe he thought you'd be easy. Maybe like your lovely friend Alison and her beaus, he thought the money would be worth it. I'm happy for his sake and for yours that he moved on from that thought process to find something else. Something better for himself, which helps you to find something better for you."

"Wow," she muttered, as she collapsed into the closest chair at the kitchen table. "I'll have to think about this for a while."

"You do that," Aida agreed, with a smile. "Just don't take too long." And, with that, her grandmother sailed on out of the kitchen.

Eva wasn't even sure what that last comment meant. Since when was there a rush? But her grandmother had managed to escape any further questions by disappearing on her.

Eva got up, poured a cup of coffee, and slowly made her way back up to the studio. With the men that close by, she didn't want to work. Besides, it was just too disruptive to have Carson nearby. She didn't want him to find out what was under the sheets covering her paintings. It's not that she felt guilty about them. It was intimate; it was personal, just like the rest of her work. And also something else was in there. But, with all the shit that her grandmother had just slammed her with, she wasn't prepared to look at any of it right now.

CARSON LOOKED OVER at Flynn at the dinner table. "I need to run out for a bit. Are you okay to stick around, or do you need to head home?"

"I can stay," he said. "How long do you need?"

"A couple hours."

Flynn nodded. "No problem."

"Good enough," Carson replied, and, with that, he excused himself from the dinner table and headed to the front door. He didn't make it far, when he heard somebody moving behind him. He turned to see Eva heading his way.

"What are you doing?" she called out. "Why are you going out at this hour?"

He shrugged. "To check on a few things."

She frowned. "Like what?"

"Like Alison's former boyfriend, for one. Your ex-fiancé for another. And I also want to talk again to Ron and his daughter."

"Oh." She hesitated.

"Do you want to come with me?" he asked.

"Yes and no. ... I kind of want to come but not to see those people."

"That is what I need to do right now," he noted, as he continued to the door.

"What do you expect to find out?"

"I don't know. Nothing maybe. Hopefully I can start knocking people off my suspect list."

She rubbed her forehead. "Right. And, until we can, they are still suspects."

"Exactly." He smiled. "You are welcome to come along. Otherwise, head on up to your studio, and I'll check in with you when I get back. I'll let you know what I found out."

She looked at him. "What?"

"Unless you don't want me to," he said instantly.

"No, actually I'd really like that," she replied warmly.

He gave her a bright grin. "Good. Wait up for me then." And, with that, he walked out the front door.

He knew that he had no business heading in this direction tonight with Eva, yet he also couldn't help himself. Just something was so unique and compelling about her, and, at the same time, she wasn't so much broken but guarded, as if she'd come up against something that she'd never seen before, ... and *he* was it.

It was an odd feeling. He'd had plenty of relationships in his life, but never anything that struck him the way she had. It's like she kept herself away from everything in order to stay protected, which went along with what her grandmother had described. Carson just didn't understand how somebody who had gotten to be her age could manage that. Maybe it was all about living here with her grandmother that afforded her this extra shield from others.

The world wasn't an easy place all the time, and, as much as Carson didn't want to think about it, there would always be people out there ready to hurt others. Eva seemed to have walked away from most of it though.

With that thought, Carson headed to her ex-fiancé's place first. Just as he got there, Carson found him arriving home from work, tired and fatigued. Carson hopped out of his car and called to him.

The man stopped at the doorway. "Do I know you?" he asked politely.

"No," Carson replied, "but I need to ask you about your relationship with Eva."

"You mean, my ex?" he asked. "I haven't even seen her in months."

"No, maybe that's true, yet you were with her for quite a while."

"I was. I tried to make it work, but it just wasn't something I could accomplish."

"I understand that you had an affair while you were engaged."

"Yeah, and maybe that was out of desperation to make Eva actually see me," he admitted, with a bitter laugh. "All it did was break us up."

"Maybe that was part of it too," he murmured. "I mean, when the relationship isn't going anywhere, we often do things to get ourselves in trouble, so we have an easy way out."

The guy looked at him and smiled. "Yeah, I thought about that. Actually, my uncle thought it would be a good idea for the two of us to hook up in the first place. And I was pretty excited about it in the beginning, but eventually it became obvious that she wasn't really into the relationship. And I, ... you know, while it may sound good in theory, being with somebody with a lot of money can get old pretty fast. I mean, you want to be wanted for who you are, not because you're just a convenience."

At that, Carson nodded, hearing something that confirmed his suspicions. Smiling, he said, "I'm surprised your uncle would have thought that you guys would make a good pair."

"I think he just thought I could make my life work, you know, with the money, like he always seems to." Then the guy stopped, looked at him, and frowned. "And now I've got to ask what the hell you're doing, coming here and asking me about my relationship with her?" He must have just now realized how strange this was.

"Well, my purpose is twofold," Carson replied. "One is that I'm interested in pursuing a relationship with her myself," he admitted.

The other guy snorted. "Yeah, good luck with that. It's a pretty cushy position if you can get it and if you don't give a shit about where it takes you."

"Well, I do care about where it takes me," Carson admitted. "That's for sure."

"In that case you better be careful," he murmured, "because I'm not sure that she's necessarily ready to really give herself to a relationship. With me, it felt more like I was a convenience. You know? Like she had progressively checked off the boyfriend and fiancé boxes on her checklist for life and could move on."

Having heard that once before, Carson nodded. "Right. The other reason I'm here is because of your uncle's involvement with Aida and the way they ended up parting ways. We're currently having a problem with making threats against Aida. So we're trying to figure out who might be involved. Do you have any ideas?" Carson asked him, having already discarded this guy as being part of the problem. "Like anybody you may have seen around the place or who was there at the time that would have any issues with Aida herself?"

He stared at him for a long moment. "Seriously?"

Carson nodded. "Yes, I'm serious. We've been hired to get to the bottom of it."

"God, that's another part of that relationship I'm very okay to be away from."

"What part is that?" Carson asked curiously.

"I personally never got along with her grandmother. Whether that was because the grandmother didn't approve of me or maybe she saw something I didn't, but she didn't seem to be invested in the whole idea of us ever getting married."

"Interesting," Carson noted. "So, she didn't give you any advice on how to have a relationship with her? How to treat Eva?"

"God no, she barely gave me the time of day."

Carson nodded at that. "Did you ever hear any conversations or anything that, looking back, might suggest that somebody had a problem with them?"

"Not really," he replied. "It just reminds me of how detached I was from the whole family unit. You know that you could always ask Flora, but then you probably have."

"I have, indeed," he murmured. "But I can go back and ask her some specifics again if you have anything in mind."

He looked at him strangely. "And did you like, *ask her*, ask her?"

"Sure," he confirmed. "We've had direct conversations about it all, but she seems to be holding back something. Am I missing something here?"

"I don't know if you're missing anything or not because I don't know what she told you," he stated. "But I know that Aida's had some problems with other people."

"Right, like your other family members."

He winced. "Yeah, my cousin. Melody is trouble, although I must admit that, since she started doing therapy, she seems to have straightened out quite a bit."

"That's good to know," Carson noted.

"Yeah, it is. She was really off there for a while. Something was driving her crazy in life, and she needed help. She totally ignored the signs and was lashing out at everyone. Later on she took some responsibility, a little at least, and now she's doing better."

"Good," he murmured. "We're also looking at, you know, any business acquaintances from Aida's late husband. You know anything about that?"

"I don't know anything about that," he said rather instantly. "Believe me. Her family didn't let me in on much. Which, in hindsight, should have been a huge warning, I guess."

"I think hindsight is like that," Carson murmured. "It's easy to see what went wrong when you're not on the spot anymore."

"That's very true," he agreed. "I don't even know why I thought it would be a good idea to begin with."

"Possibly because of the money?" he asked. "Your uncle sure thought it was a good deal."

"He's a fool," he replied.

"He's got his own problems again now, it seems."

"It's like he just never learns," he said.

"What do you mean?" Carson asked.

"He's screwing around on his current lady friend, and they just had a major fight. That woman was one of the sweetest you could ever meet, but it's almost like he's got to self-sabotage everything in his world."

"Did they break up?" Carson asked.

"Yep, she kicked him out. Honestly, between you and me, I think he was dipping his fingers into the pot again. I know there was some talk about something going wrong and that she wouldn't tolerate it."

"I can't really blame her," Carson replied.

"No, I can't either," he agreed, with a sadness that looked genuine.

"If he didn't learn his lesson by now," Carson noted, "chances are he won't learn it ever."

"No, he'll just turn up with some other rich broad," he guessed, with a shake of his head. "I think that's what he was hoping that I would do, you know? Hook up with Eva and have access to money, but I have more self-respect than that. I actually thought I loved her."

"Maybe you did," Carson noted.

"Sure, but how much love can you actually have when you didn't really know someone? I think that's the way she preferred to keep it." And, with that, he looked around at his house and said, "I'm getting out of here. I need to go shower and get on with my life. Good luck with yours." And, with that, he stepped into the house and closed the door.

Carson had pretty well gotten all the information he needed to take this guy off his suspect list.

Now the Eva mentions were interesting. Obviously she didn't talk much to her former fiancé, and that pleased Carson to think that he and Eva were communicating well. Yet Carson still thought she was holding something back from him. Did she know more than she was telling, or did she just know more and didn't think it was of any value? Or didn't know what she even knew? He'd come across that time or two.

As he headed back to his car, he thought of stopping by

Ron's lady friend's house to talk to Ron, but that probably wouldn't be of much help if they had just broken up. Carson could talk to the lady friend instead, but she probably wasn't in any mood to have that discussion tonight either.

As he drove toward the estate again, a vehicle came up fast behind him. He moved out of the way to let it pass, but instead it just stayed with him, right beside him. Instantly Carson stared at the smoked windows, not able to see the driver. "Oh, interesting. Do you want to play games?" he asked out loud in the car. "I'm totally okay to play games."

Yet it would be foolish for anybody to even try to take him out, unless they didn't know what his background was, or unless they were feeling desperate.

Like Ron, perhaps.

Carson frowned at that and realized, instead of driving home and taking whoever this was toward the women, he should go somewhere else. He carefully exited, as if heading off to another location. He deliberately chose the stretch of highway close by, where he could open up and see what this guy would really do.

At the same time, he had his phone out and contacted Levi, letting him know what was happening.

"What's your plan?" Levi asked.

"I'm heading down the highway to a couple bad corners up ahead," he noted. "If that's on this guy's agenda, that will be where he tries to take me out."

"Good enough." Levi hesitated. "Be careful."

Carson smiled. "Yeah, I'll be fine."

And, with that, he hung up and focused on the road ahead of them. The question was, was this guy just trying to follow him, or was he actually looking to do some damage?

Carson knew that this corner up ahead would be the

place where he'd find out. Sure enough, as he approached the corner, the vehicle behind him sped up, coming faster and faster, and Carson stayed at a steady pace until the vehicle was right on his tail. And then it started honking the horn at him.

Which was also an interesting tactic. Not too many people would do it that way, but then, if they were untrained, unlike himself, then maybe it made sense. This was more of an off-the-cuff approach than Carson would have expected. He deliberately slowed down coming into the corner, and then slowed some more so that this guy could pass.

The vehicle started to drive into him, trying to push him off the road. But instead of falling for that, he hit the brakes hard, until his vehicle dropped back. Then he came up behind this guy, so that now he was in the following position.

At that, the driver seemed to panic and raced forward even faster. Now it appeared he was trying to get away. Carson just kept up with his speed. He knew how to drive on corners like this, and he certainly knew how to drive when he was pursuing an asshole. But he wasn't sure that this driver was actually that skilled.

As soon as they came up to the second rough hairpin corner, the car in front fishtailed wildly at a speed that was beyond the driver's ability. As they went around the corner, Carson knew the driver ahead was in trouble. He backed way off, waiting to see what would happen, and soon it began. He watched the vehicle skitter wildly and head over the drop-off.

He quickly punched in Levi's number. "The tail vehicle went over the hill. Send help. I'll head down."

He pulled up, parked out of the way of oncoming traffic,

then raced to the bottom of the canyon. He didn't have a clue who was in there, until he got to the bottom and got up to the driver's seat to find Ron, half dazed and glaring at him. "Come on. Let's get you out of here," Carson said. "This thing could blow."

At that, something came alive in Ron's face, and almost a hatred twisted his form. "What differences does it make? You've ruined my life!"

"I didn't do anything. That's all on you and your bad choices," he snapped, undoing the seat belt and pulling the man free. "How injured are you?"

"I don't know." He tried to take several steps and collapsed.

Swearing, Carson lifted him up and over his shoulder and carried him several steps away from the vehicle. He'd seen too many of these vehicles blow up, and, with the gasoline dripping slowly, it could go at any moment. He didn't want to be anywhere close when that happened, and unfortunately he saw no flat ground out of the danger zone where he could lay the man, to wait until the paramedics arrived.

Moving as quickly as he could, and sorry for any pain inflicted on Ron, Carson slowly made his way up the side of the embankment. When he got there, another Good Samaritan reached over to help.

"Hey, man," he said. "That was a hell of a climb."

"Yeah," Carson huffed. He carefully lowered his victim, now dead weight, to the ground. Thankfully he heard sirens in the distance.

Just then came a massive explosion, and the car erupted into a ball of flames. Carson hollered at the bystanders to cover their heads and then sheltered Ron from any falling debris.

Chapter 13

EVA SAT BESIDE Flynn, having a discussion with her grandmother about the new security system and about how they must regularly change passwords, when he received a phone call. She watched his face when he answered.

"Hey, Carson, what's up?" He immediately bolted to his feet. "Are you okay?" He paused, listening intently. "Okay. No, no, it's fine here. ... Yes. Yeah, go ahead and fill me in."

He listened for a few minutes, without commenting, as Eva grew increasingly frustrated, only hearing Flynn's side of the conversation.

"Wow, okay. ... Oh, good, so Levi already knows. ... Yeah, okay then, we'll wait for you." With that, he turned to see both women staring at him.

"What the hell happened?" Eva cried out, jumping to her feet.

He looked at her and explained, "Somebody tried to run him off the road."

"Oh my God. Is he okay?"

"He is fine, but the other driver—the person who tried to run him off the road—went off the road and down the hill himself." Eva stared in shock, and he shrugged. "We're used to dealing with things like that," he noted. "In this case, it didn't go so well for the other driver."

"Who was it?" Aida cried out.

He faced Aida and cringed. "Ron. He's in the hospital, and he's badly hurt, but it sounds like he'll be okay."

"Carson actually saw him?"

"Not only that, Carson pulled him from the wrecked car and carried him up the hill, before the car exploded and burned," he added. "When you have a wreck like that, fires and explosions happen really fast. Carson hustled down to get Ron out and away before any explosion. Otherwise Ron would have been a goner for sure."

"Well, thank heavens for that," Aida said, with a nod. "I knew Carson had the right stuff."

At that, Flynn grinned at her. "He's definitely got the right stuff." He turned toward Eva, who stared at him, stricken. "He'll be fine," Flynn offered gently.

"Oh my God." She sagged to her chair. "Ron really went after Carson?"

"Apparently your earlier visit rattled him and his lady friend, who dumped him," he explained, as he looked at Aida. "Did she contact you?" he asked.

"She did, and I also told her to contact Ice," Aida murmured. "I didn't want her to just take my word for it, and I thought Ice might instruct her on what to check for in her finances."

"Of course." Flynn nodded. "The end result, according to what Carson just told me, was that, while they were waiting on the ambulance, Ron said he'd been kicked out of the relationship because she accused him of dipping his fingers into the money pot."

"It's likely true," Aida agreed.

"Well, apparently Carson also spoke to your ex-fiancé," he said, turning to look at Eva again. "He mentioned something about being encouraged by Ron to start the relationship and how Ron had hoped that the relationship between the two of you would end up better because of that exact same thing—access to money. Your ex also admitted that he'd chosen to be unfaithful, hoping you would call off the engagement, so he would then be free to find somebody who gave a damn about him. His words, not mine, sorry."

She winced at that. "Wow, apparently I wasn't a very good partner."

He chuckled. "Until you find the right guy," he noted, with a smile. "And, hey, maybe you've found him now."

She stared at him, dazed, then shook her head. "No. … I don't know what you're talking about."

"Oh, I think you do," he stated. "Believe me. Those paintings spoke volumes."

She shook her head immediately. "No, they didn't," she argued, sounding almost panicked. "You don't understand."

"I understand just fine." He gave her a gentle smile. "I'm just not sure you're there yet." He looked over at Aida.

Eva followed his gaze to see her grandmother staring at her with a brilliant smile. "She hasn't quite picked up on it yet," her grandmother murmured.

Eva stared at her grandmother and then Flynn. He nodded. "I agree."

"Oh God, I'm so not ready for a relationship," Eva whispered.

"You'll never be ready for a relationship," he stated. "That's not why they happen. This is happening because it's the next good thing in your life, and you are lucky enough to have found a great guy. Now go toward it with joy."

"Sure, maybe when you've already passed all the awkward stages," she noted bitterly. "We haven't even gotten started on anything like that, and, besides, even if I am interested, that doesn't mean he is."

"He is," Flynn replied instantly. "Why do you think he's working so hard to make sure you stay safe?"

"Because it's his job."

"Yeah, it's absolutely his job," he agreed, with a smile. "And he always works hard to keep people safe. But this time it has the added benefit of keeping safe the people he cares about very much."

"And that brings up another point—not to change the subject because, believe me, this one is fascinating," Aida murmured, prompting a glare from Eva. Then Aida just chuckled. "So, do we think that Ron is involved in what's been going on here? Or is the car accident today just because Ron was angry at Carson for ruining his latest scam and decided to try to take him out?"

"Hard to say at this point. Carson didn't clarify that on the phone," Flynn noted. "However, it is something that we'll take a serious look at now."

"Was there any motivation for Ron to do something before now?" Eva asked Flynn.

"Well, tonight kind of stands alone. He's angry because he's just lost his rich lady friend, maybe even this woman mattered to him."

"Maybe, I don't know," Eva said, showing her palms. "How and why does somebody continually take advantage of women just to get to their money? Obviously Ron likes an easy lifestyle of affluence and thinks that's the only way he can get it, but, I mean, if he really cared about this woman, why would he continue to do stuff like that?"

Aida listened to both of them intently.

"Some people can't help themselves," Flynn admitted. "It's quite possible that he falls into that category. I don't know what to say because I don't know the whole story."

"No, of course not," Aida agreed, "but this is certainly an interesting turn of events."

"And hopefully it's enough to shake something loose," Eva added, wishing they could get to the bottom of it all.

"It's shaken something loose, all right," Flynn said quietly, "but we must make sure it shakes the right thing."

Unnerved by the news of Ron's actions and Carson's close call, Aida excused herself and headed to bed soon afterward.

Flynn looked at Eva. "If you want to go off to bed, feel free."

She shook her head. "I'll wait up," she murmured.

He smirked. "Hey, don't be so scared. It's a good thing, you and Carson."

"Is it?" she asked. "I feel a fool because, as usual, I didn't even really see it myself."

"You saw it," he stated. "You just weren't ready to acknowledge it."

"Is there a difference?" she asked, with a wry look at him. "It still feels like, … you know, that whole head-in-the-sand thing."

"Sometimes that is what's needed, giving you some time to adjust," he murmured. "Don't be so hard on yourself."

She laughed. "It seems like that's always my out, and I'm always harder on myself than anybody else."

"And I understand," Flynn agreed. "I think a lot of people are like that. You expect something from yourself, and then, when you don't actually see it happen, but other people do, it makes you wonder just if you're in tune with yourself at all."

"Apparently I'm not," she said bluntly. "I'm in tune with

my artwork."

"And that"—he nodded—"is a good thing, and maybe you should trust that more."

"I was absolutely struck by the need to paint him," she explained, "but I just chalked it up to being an artist."

"Maybe while you wait for him," Flynn suggested, "you should go up and take another look at those paintings. Look with a fresh eye and see what I saw—and what other people would see too."

"If it's that obvious, they can never go on display in a show," she stated in exasperation.

"Oh, I don't know about that. I think once you get your relationship settled, what you'll do is create a ton of envy from everybody else who sees them."

She stared at him, nonplussed.

He nodded. "Go. Really. Take a look before he gets back," he said, with a smile. Flynn hesitated and then urged her on. "I promise. It will help to clarify things in your own mind."

She shook her head but obediently got up and walked upstairs to her studio. The whole time her mind churned with everything she'd learned.

Was it even possible?

Was this even doable?

Am I reading it wrong?

How has this happened?

She couldn't even imagine, yet something was so right about it. All the while she wondered if it was even possible. After she stepped into her studio, she headed to the covered paintings, took off all the sheets, and then stepped back.

She stared at the charcoal sketches that she had done first and then at the painting that she was working on now, and she winced, knowing she'd never put these in a show.

Then she thought about what Flynn had said, and she realized that he was right too. The reason she couldn't show these was because her emotions and feelings were naked in front of her.

These portraits were just so powerful, so intimate a look at this person who she didn't even know. That was the thing that blew her away. She hardly knew this man.

Yet everything that she felt was there on that canvas in front of her. The fact that she respected him and saw him as the honorable man that he was. That curve of his mouth, that look in his eye, that steadfast expression but with a hint of amusement there. Almost as if to say, *Well, this is where we're at. Now let's take this path and see.*

She sighed as she saw it for herself, just the same as Flynn had. "God," she murmured. "I'm such a fool."

"You are, at that," a woman said from the doorway.

Eva turned around, surprised to see Flora standing at her door. "Hey. What's the matter?"

"Nothing," Flora said, as she stepped into the room. "I took a look at your canvases earlier."

Eva frowned at that. "You did what?"

"I know. I know." Flora had a distinct sneer on her face. "Who knew that the mighty had fallen so fast for a buff body in a macho alpha-male outfit."

Eva's back bristled at the implications and at the tone of Flora's voice.

"Sorry," Flora stated simply, with no sincerity involved.

"What are you doing in my studio?" Eva asked, frowning. She glanced around because this was not normal behavior for Flora. It was not normal to have anybody even here on this floor.

"Oh, don't worry about it," Flora replied. "I have the run of the house. You two just like to think you're in control." She snorted.

As Eva stared at her intruder, Eva realized something was seriously wrong here. "Maybe you've always had the run of the house," Eva noted quietly, "but that doesn't give you the right to come into my studio whenever you want."

Flora just waved that off. "Whatever."

Still not sure what was going on, Eva walked closer and said, "I'd like you to leave now."

"That's nice," Flora quipped. "I'll leave when I'm ready and not a moment sooner."

Something was hard and edgy to the woman's voice. "Flora?" Eva asked, puzzled. "What's the matter?"

"*You*. You and that damn grandmother of yours."

Eva stiffened, now noting that Flora held one hand behind her back. "I don't understand." Out of the corner of her eye, she saw a glimpse out of her window, the headlights coming up the driveway and knew who it would be. Relief and something akin to joy flushed through her.

"Move closer to the window," Flora barked.

"Why should I move?" Eva asked, using a regal tone of voice. Not at all sure what the hell was going on here but not liking it one bit. "Since when do you tell me what to do?"

"Well, somebody should have, or you wouldn't have ended up such a brat."

She stiffened at that. "Wow, I'm not sure what got into you tonight," she murmured, "but this is not acceptable behavior."

"You're damn right it's not," she muttered to herself, as she glared at Eva. "Twenty years I've slaved away here. Twenty years I've looked after your grandmother and then you were brought here too. So I had double the work."

"And," Eva murmured, "it's called a *job*."

"Yeah, it's a job, but it's supposed to be more than a job. It's supposed to be something that helps get me through in my old age, with a pension, so that I'm okay when I can't look after you two anymore. So I'm not just shuffled off, and somebody else brought in instead."

"I'm sure Grandma made arrangements for you," Eva stated, frowning. "You know that's something she would see to."

"I don't know that at all," Flora cried out. "What I do know is that she changed her will recently."

"She did?" Eva asked. "How would you know something like that?"

"Because I hunted for it," she snapped. "I had to search long and hard, but finally I found it."

Eva stiffened. "Oh God, you're the one who's been stalking and threatening Grandma? You're the one sending the email, the letter, the dead birds and all?" Eva stared at her in horror. "Not to mention everything else going on. Making her seem like either she's losing it or she's afraid that somebody's after her. It was you the whole time, wasn't it?" Eva asked.

"Of course it was," Flora admitted. "And the thing is, nobody even knew. That's because nobody ever looks at the help." She sneered again. "We're invisible, then just kicked out whenever we're done. Nobody gives a shit."

"That's not true, Flora," Eva argued. "I don't know what you think you read in Grandma's will, or whether that's even the current legal document," she noted, "but I sincerely doubt she would have done anything *but* looked after you. Not to mention the fact that she's always paid you a very decent wage."

Flora snorted. "A very decent wage?" She laughed. "Compared to the money you have? What is decent?"

"Compared to the money we have?" Eva asked in astonishment. "So, are you thinking she was supposed to pay you more than what every other cleaning lady would earn?" She was surprised, yet a part of her figured it all made sense.

"You know that we vouched for you time and time again as the men kept asking us more and more questions about you. But we kept saying, *No, it wouldn't be you. It would never be you. You were like family,*" she repeated, as reality started to sink in further and further. "My God, Flora."

"Oh, stop with the theatrics," she snapped. "They only go so far, and I've had enough of it. You don't realize that it's not just the wages," she cried out, her voice getting louder and louder. "I have a budget that I operate the kitchen from, and your grandmother hasn't looked at that closely for ages." Flora laughed. "So, don't worry. I've padded the expenses a little in order to get myself a bit of a pension plan."

"And even that wasn't enough?" Eva stared at Flora, yet seeing someone she'd never seen before. "So, even with all that, you still had to go cause all these other problems?"

"Yes!" she declared. "I was hoping to be left in a position of trust in order to help you out, but instead Aida decided my job should terminate when she goes."

"But then it wouldn't be her decision. It would be mine," Eva argued. "And I had no intention of getting rid of you."

"Sure, but you probably would have wanted to know about things. About all the accounts and you would have been in there trying to change things."

"Well, I would certainly learn more about them." She stopped and nodded. "Oh, but wait. You probably overheard that conversation, didn't you?"

"Oh, yeah. Not a whole lot happens in this place that I don't hear. God, you guys just don't get it, do you? My brother put those listening devices into your bedrooms and then had me following his instructions, hopefully turning your grandmother his way, whenever she got scared in the night. He was trying to cement the deal and to get her to marry him, figuring, once they were married, he would have control over her money. But somehow it didn't seem to work out."

"Ron is your brother?" she asked, feeling sick, as she stared at her.

Flora openly smirked now.

"Do you realize that Ron tried to run Carson off the road tonight?"

"I heard that conversation too," she snapped. "He's always been a hotheaded idiot."

"An idiot maybe but he's also now in the hospital, and he is sure to face charges."

She nodded. "He probably will at that. He has skated so many times, but he just can't ever settle into a good scenario and leave it alone. He could have been happy as hell here, but no. … He's greedy and had to start dabbling where he didn't belong," she stated in disgust.

"He couldn't keep it in his pants either," Eva stated. "It's hardly fair that my grandmother—or anyone else—should endure that kind of behavior."

"Who gives a shit about your grandmother? She's old."

"She's hardly old," Eva noted gently, "considering you're hitting sixty yourself."

"Which is precisely why I'm doing what I'm doing," she declared bitterly. "Because I don't want to end up with nothing, while your grandmother leaves everything to you."

"I think it would be quite normal to leave everything to me, outside of her charities," Eva noted. "But I still don't believe there isn't a provision in Aida's will for you."

"But it won't be the same," she complained. "It won't be me having my own accounts to tend to the house and to feed you from, then keep the rest for myself."

"Wow, is that really what you've been doing?" She shook her head. "And Grandma never suspected, did she?"

"Nope." Flora chuckled. "When you spend this long with somebody, they learn to trust you. Then it becomes easy for somebody like me to betray that trust, and it's much harder for Aida to figure it out … because nobody ever wants to see themselves as being duped."

"Christ, Flora."

"It's pretty funny actually because we got to her twice. My bloody brother, who was an idiot for blowing it, for accessing the accounts, draining them faster, whenever he wanted to," she explained. "Then me with the household money, which was automatically put into a joint account, so I could take care of everything. You can bet I sure as hell didn't pay the cleaning people very well for coming in." She laughed.

"You guys never even noticed if things were clean. You're not even looking, and that's how much it doesn't matter to you, just as long as you have your cleaning staff. You don't even seem to care how well the job is done. It hasn't been done right in this place for a very long time." Flora snorted. "I'm certainly not getting up on ladders and cleaning off cobwebs or the upper windows or anything else like that," she stated. "It's just how foolish you guys are. You don't even see what's happening under your noses."

"Well, thanks for the warning," Eva said in a snide tone. "What is it you expect to do now?"

"Not a whole lot." She shrugged. "Except that you're still despondent over your fiancé breaking up with you, yet you never even slept with him."

"Oh my God. So you were listening in my bedroom too?"

"Yeah, I was. I was hoping to figure out what was going on when Ron installed the bugs in the first place. We put one in yours, but never had any use for it, until you started seeing my nephew," she noted, "but then even he couldn't make it happen. I actually believe he chose *not* to make it happen." She shook her head. "He wanted something more than just an empty relationship," she said quietly.

Eva was horrified as Flora kept talking.

"What a fool. Love won't keep you warm at night when there are bills to pay."

"Maybe not, but at least he can look himself in the mirror in the morning and not cringe at what he sees."

"Believe me. I won't be cringing," Flora replied in a threatening voice. Then she pulled her hand from behind her back to reveal a snub-nosed revolver.

Eva sucked in her breath. "God. How could I be so wrong. I always thought of you as a motherly type. Part of the family."

"Bully for you," she stated brutally. "Not everybody leaves you, but everybody wants to."

At that, Eva went ballistic when she realized just how much the evil woman had heard. "You're really a piece of work, aren't you? When this is over, I definitely won't want hired help again."

"Well, if you ever do," she suggested, "you might want to make sure they're confined to the certain parts of the house all the time. Having the run of the house just gave me all kinds of opportunities to figure out what else in life I could aspire to steal."

"*Great*, not at all what I want to hear."

"Of course not." Flora laughed. "Yet it's probably what you needed to hear."

"Maybe so, but, if you have your way, I won't have a chance to use anything I've learned tonight, will I?"

"No, you sure won't. Glad to have that cleared up. The window is already wide open and ready for you."

Eva realized that the window she had been looking out of was actually open, something she never did. She clenched her fists, trying to calm the panic building inside. "And just what do you expect me to do with that?"

"I want you to walk over there."

Frowning, Eva stood frozen in place. With this residence being such an old building, these floor-to-ceiling windows were no longer allowed in newer constructions. It would be a very long way to the ground from the third floor, especially with these twelve-foot-tall ceilings found on each level.

She would not survive that fall.

Eva finally realized that this woman—who spent years with Eva as she had grown up here, sharing laughter, tears, even rejoicing at times with her—actually intended to kill her tonight. Eva stared at the woman in shock. "You really expect me to jump?"

"Oh, yeah," Flora declared, "and you will."

"No," Eva argued defiantly. "I won't. You'll have to shoot me, and then they'll know it was you."

"Well, right now, nobody knows anything. So, it won't really matter."

"Like hell," she murmured. "It does matter, and somebody *does* know what you're up to."

"Bullshit." Again Flora laughed. "But obviously you'll try your best to make it seem like it."

The trouble was, if Eva jumped or fell, Flora getting away with this was all too possible. "I can't believe you think that you could get away with something like that."

"Why not?" She gave Eva a casual shrug. "Nobody gives a shit about you. I mean, you and your stupid childhood fantasies about that security man. He's way too much man for you." She sneered. "You couldn't even keep my nephew happy, and he's pretty damn easy." Flora shrugged. "You haven't learned feminine wiles at all. It's just pathetic."

Eva took a deep breath. "I'm still not jumping out the damn window."

"Actually you are," Flora stated, with a belligerent tone. "Otherwise I'll be going after your grandmother."

Eva hesitated, as she stared at Flora. "What do you mean?"

"Your grandmother is in her room," she noted. "And, if you think I won't go over there, shoot her, and be damned with the consequences, you're wrong. I'm sure I'll figure out a way to take her out without having to shoot her though," she said, with a smile. "It won't be hard to get some help if I need it. But then I'd have to share the money, and that won't happen at this stage. Not after everything I've done to get this far."

Eva studied the crazy woman, trying to figure out how in the hell Flora thought any money would be coming her way with the death of Eva and her grandmother.

"Although I could throw suspicion on them. Can you imagine who could it be? Maybe it's your former fiancé," she suggested, with a mocking laugh.

"No way. There always was something inherently decent about him. He might have had the poor luck of the draw in terms of his family, but he wasn't as badly poisoned as you were and Ron and Melody."

"You keep trying to believe that, Eva. You always were a fool."

"I don't understand the goal here for you. What good would my jumping do for you?" she asked.

"Just leave that to me. Now you better do it, or I'll go after your grandmother regardless."

Eva shook her head, frowning. "So you expect *me* to decide whether *you* keep Grandma alive or not? If I go out the window, you'll agree to not shoot her, and I'm supposed to believe that?" Eva said it with such horror and disbelief that Flora glared at her.

"You think you're so damn smart, don't you? What you don't know is, I'm not alone in the house."

And, at that, Eva's blood ran cold. Yet she had just said she didn't want to split the supposed money she was getting with anyone else. "I don't know who you've enlisted for help, but leave my grandmother out of this."

Even though it was daunting, there was at least a chance that her grandmother would survive if Aida went out her second-floor window, with no concrete below. Eva had no hope in hell that she would survive falling from her third-floor window though, whether the distance, the velocity, or her landing on a concrete walkway killing her.

Eva also knew that Carson should already be inside—or at least close to home, if that wasn't his headlights she'd seen earlier. He had promised to stop by and to see her, but he was probably debriefing Flynn first. That meant she had no idea when he would arrive. This was a problem with her extremely private studio. She locked herself up here all the time, and no one bothered her for hours.

Flora stared at her and smiled. "You're still looking for ways to get out of this. Haven't figured it out yet? There is no getting out of this."

"There is," Eva argued. "I know there is."

"No, you're just hoping," Flora snapped. "Now I can just shoot you or knock you out. By the time your body is found outside on the concrete, all smashed to bits, nobody'll know if there was a bullet in your skull or not." She laughed. "I haven't taken lots of shooting lessons for nothing," she added, with a sneer.

Eva considered this woman, whose level of betrayal defied logic. "All that hate," she murmured, "when you could have done something so much better."

"Yeah, like what?" she asked.

"You could have found a partner of your own. Somebody to love, somebody who would love you," she said gently. "Instead of always watching everybody around you having families, while you did without one yourself."

"I had a partner, but he was pretty damn useless. He took all my money and ran," she spat. "Believe me. I learned more from him than anyone else, and I also learned that I wouldn't become anybody's victim ever again. Now enough of this. Get over to that window."

"No. … If you're going to kill me, you'll have to do it, leaving a trail. Then at least I'll go to my death knowing you spent the rest of your life paying for your crimes."

"Nobody will know." Then she raised the gun. "Even if

they do, I don't give a shit," she muttered. "It'll be worth it to know that you're dead and gone and that Aida'll suffer the loss the rest of her life."

"How can you hate her so much?" Eva cried out.

"That woman … that absolutely useless woman took so much from me," she cried out.

"She took nothing from you," Eva countered, not understanding.

"No, but she sat there the whole time while her husband did."

"Were you hurt by one of Grandfather's business deals?" she asked warily.

She gave a brittle laugh. "I spent a lifetime telling my mother that it was okay, that we'd be fine. But you know what? The longer that sat inside my head, the more I realized that it wouldn't be okay. Now they're all gone except for me and my brother. And every time Ron hatched a method to recover some of the money, he blew it up. I'm still here, even after all these years, waiting and hoping, but I can see that my time is over. It's now or never, and, in this case, it's now. So enough of your bloody caterwauling. Get over to that damn window."

But Eva stood her ground. "No, I won't. I'm not responsible for anything my grandfather did, any more than my grandmother is," she stated. "I can see that the longer you live, the more it ate away at you, and I'm sorry that you lived like that, but I won't just sit back and let you kill me."

"That's the right answer," said a man from the door. And, sure enough, Flynn and Carson had arrived, guns out, facing Flora.

She stared at them and screamed, "No, no, no! You're not allowed to interfere." Stabbing a finger into the air, she continued yelling. "You're not allowed to interfere, do you hear me? You stay where you are! She'll go through that damn window, and that horrible woman downstairs will suffer like she's never suffered before."

"For what?" Carson asked. "Because you are greedy and selfish and want more money just given to you—or taken? Because you think that you are owed something more than you deserve? Even if her grandfather did cheat your family, that doesn't mean you were entitled to any of Aida's money," he stated. "Just like your brother, Ron, you're looking for an easy score, instead of being like the rest of the world and working for it."

"I worked for it." She stared at him in shock and anger, still holding onto her gun. "I worked my ass off."

"Then she helped herself to more," Eva shared quietly. "She made sure a little extra was in the household accounts for herself every damn week."

"Of course I did," Flora declared. "Why the hell wouldn't I? I barely made enough to live on as it was." Shaking her head, she raised the gun and, without any warning, fired at Eva.

Eva felt the bullet against her shoulder, as she tumbled to the ground, away from where the window was. But the gunfire after that stunned her. When she slowly raised her head, she saw Flynn at Flora's side, but Carson leaned over Eva, checking her wound.

"Don't move," he said. "Let me see how badly hurt you are."

"I'm fine." Eva reached up, wincing at her shoulder. "She just winged me."

"Good." He turned and stared at Flora. "Makes you wonder if it's worth having any money, doesn't it?"

"Yeah, is sure does," Eva admitted, using his hand to pull herself up to stand again. He opened his arms, and she threw herself in. "God. To hear her, … to hear her saying how bad we all supposedly are," she murmured. "It was terrifying. She's been behind it all. I was trying to figure out how many others were—" She stopped and frantically looked around, terrified. "Wait! You must go to Grandma," she cried out. "Flora talked about maybe getting help to kill Aida. I don't trust her. Someone else could be here now."

With that, Flynn took off.

Carson asked her, "If I leave you here, are you okay?"

"Yes, go to Grandma. Flora's not going anywhere."

"She's not dead," he noted.

"No? Well, maybe that's better," she murmured. "For Grandma, you know? She would prefer this mess not be a big public fiasco."

"Too late," he murmured, as he looked over at Flora.

Eva had to agree, as she sat down beside the injured woman, who started to moan in pain. Eva whispered to him, "Go save my grandmother."

And, with that, he was gone.

CARSON RACED THROUGH the hallways, catching up with Flynn just slightly ahead. "Do you know where Aida is?" Carson called out.

"She had gone to bed," Flynn replied. When the two of them burst into the master bedroom together, Aida was sitting up in the bed, looking at them in surprise.

"What's going on?" she asked.

They stopped and groaned. "Are you okay? Is anyone here besides you?"

"Nope, nobody here. Why?" She'd clamored out of bed, pulling on her robe.

"Because Flora just tried to kill Eva," Carson explained. "Flora was trying to make Eva jump out the window to her death."

She stared at him in shock. "Oh my God, are you serious? Eva!"

"She's fine," Carson murmured, "but obviously stressed, and she told me that it's possible Flora wasn't here alone."

"I'm going up there, and I'm going right now." Aida stepped into her slippers. The men waited as she made her way over to them and the door.

Flynn said, "I'll do a full search of the house. This place is a maze."

"Yeah, it's a hell of a house," Carson murmured. "I'll take Aida up to Eva." He quickly led Aida to Eva's studio. As Aida walked in, Eva quickly got up, and the two women hugged each other.

"Thank you," Eva whispered to Carson.

He nodded. "We didn't see anybody else yet, but Flynn is searching the rest of the house."

"There probably isn't anyone," Eva guessed. "It was probably just a threat to get me to jump." She looked down at Flora. "She's waking up."

Carson squatted beside the injured woman on the floor, now groaning in pain. At least she might answer a few questions. Carson needed answers now. "Is somebody else here?"

She shook her head. "No," she gasped, twisting in pain. "I was just trying to use that as leverage."

"We'll do a full search anyway," he stated, looking over at the two women. "Hopefully she's not lying this time."

"She has done nothing but play games, so we can't really trust anything she says," Eva stated.

"Go," Aida said to him. "We'll be fine here."

He looked at her doubtfully. "The cops are on the way," he told them, "and we'll hear them coming, but I want to make damn sure that nothing else is going on."

Eva called out, as he stepped out the door, "Wait." He turned and looked at her and she asked, "Could you check the attic first?"

He smiled, pulled down the stairs, and quickly searched the attic. By the time he came back down, he had a text from Flynn, saying everything was clear so far.

"I'm feeling better about this," he told them, "but let me go cross the *T*s and dot the *I*s with Flynn, just to make sure everything is secure." With that, he gave Eva a hard kiss on the cheek and left, leaving her staring behind him.

When he had realized what was going on upstairs with Eva and Flora, his heart had slammed against his chest. He had put Flora at the top of his suspect list right off the bat when he first arrived. Only because nobody else had the same access to the family and the house as she had. What he didn't know and hadn't been able to figure out until now was whether she was alone in all this or if she had others in on it.

He still didn't know the answers to that, but, now that the initial danger was over, he hoped he'd get the rest of the answers. Then they would finish setting up this place with an improved security system and get the access under control.

Together, Carson and Flynn searched the place from top to bottom, as Carson pointed out all the hidey-holes to Flynn. Finally satisfied that they were alone, the pair walked back to the front entryway just in time to let in the police and ambulance crew. Carson nodded at them. "The seriously injured person is upstairs on the third floor," he said, pointing out the elevator, so that they could get the gurney up there easier.

While Flynn filled in the police, one of them shook his head. "She actually tried to force somebody to go out a window at gunpoint?"

"Yes. I don't think she thought it through. She had hoped it would be easily accomplished but not so easy after all."

"No, probably not. Something must have triggered all this," the policeman noted.

"And I think I know what that was too," Carson suggested, stepping over to join them. "One day Aida and I were talking about getting Eva involved in the business side of things and easing the burden on Aida for the future. I'm sure now that Flora overheard that conversation and realized that her stealing from the household accounts would come to light. She had been skimping on the real expenses and skimming off the rest."

"*Great*," Flynn murmured. "Of all the reasons to try and kill somebody."

"There was more to it, I'm sure," Carson noted, "but we won't be sure of the details until we get a chance to interview Flora."

"Plus, we don't know what else she may have told Eva either," Flynn added.

"True. Let's head upstairs." Carson led the way, with the cops following, as they took the stairs to the third floor.

As it turned out, Flora had quite a lot to say, once she was fully conscious again. Even as she laid there injured, she spoke with Aida and Eva, while the cops listened in. Now that Flora was caught and too injured to escape, she seemed to be quite willing to talk. She was adamant about explaining to the women why she had done it. Pain was apparently a great motivator, as was getting caught and realizing that it was truly over.

Flynn looked at Carson and asked, "Will you stick around?"

"Yeah. We still need some answers. We'll also get the security system completely set up."

"When the cops are gone," Flynn noted, "I'll head home."

"You do that," he murmured. "I'll have a hell of a lot to bring Levi up to date on, but I want to make sure that Eva and Aida are okay first."

"You'll spend the night here though, right? They'll need to know that everything is fine."

"Yeah, I will. They're both a little shocked at this turn of events."

"With good reason," Flynn noted. "They've just been through a traumatic event. And it'll take them some time before they're ready to trust again."

"It's always that way, isn't it?" Carson said sadly.

"People like Flora always want what they want. They get jealous, thinking they should have the same as other people. It's the same old story about greed."

Carson nodded. "And laziness. Flora could have worked harder, smarter, and made more money, just like Eva and Aida did. Anyway, hopefully that'll be the end of the stalking and the threats for them. Once we get this security system set up, and they get familiar with it, they should be safe to be on their own again," he noted.

"Except for hiring honest staff."

"Well, staffing is always an issue."

"Apparently it's more than that," Flynn said, with a light laugh. "Apparently it's a killer."

Chapter 14

E VA STOOD AT the side of her studio door, watching all the chaos in front of her. Between the police and the paramedics, she was in the way but didn't want to get too far from her grandmother. Aida was sitting on Eva's bed, looking exhausted, but more from the shock and yet again another betrayal, this at a level no one would have anticipated.

Carson tugged Eva out of the way gently. "I'm sorry. You've just been threatened, and you found out something like this was going on right under your nose. It's just, well, ... it's really sad."

"Is it always about money?" she asked quietly.

"All too often, we find that it is," he murmured.

She looked at him and shook her head. "It's a sad world out there."

He pulled her into his arms and just held her close. "It is. I'm so sorry this happened to you and Aida." Dropping his chin to rest gently atop her head, she snuggled in close. "But still, that doesn't mean you should let it affect you."

She snorted. "How the hell do you not? I mean, it involved Ron, Melody, Flora, even my ex to a degree. This was just so much."

Carson nodded. "It would be nice if life wasn't such a bitch when it comes to this kind of stuff, but unfortunately there will always be those trying to take what you have from you."

She shook her head. "It's hard to imagine," she murmured. "I've really never had to deal with anything like this before."

"I think that's why your grandmother wanted to make sure you understood how the business is run."

"And I understand that so much more now unfortunately," she noted. "I really do know how badly I need to get a working knowledge about all this."

"Good," he said, "that's half the battle."

She smiled, then looked up at him. "What'll happen to Flora?"

"I don't know," he admitted quietly, "because this could go several ways now."

"Meaning?"

"Well, it's not just about the armed attack on you," he explained, "plus the cops are involved now."

She winced. "So we'll have to tell our personal stories to the police. I know that won't make my grandmother happy. Or me either."

"Of course not, but, at the same time, we also must make sure that none of this happens again. We don't want you to constantly deal with people like this."

"No." She groaned as she stared at the mess around her room. "This room feels very strange now."

"Of course it does. It was the scene of the crime and all. We'll also talk about those sketches." He stared at her.

Lifting her head back, Eva frowned at him, then looked around.

He watched as the color and the accompanying heat rolled up her face.

"Oh God, I was just looking at them when Flora barged in and pointed her gun at me."

"The artwork is interesting in itself," he noted, "because I had no idea you were drawing them."

"This will sound stupid, but I didn't really have the idea either, not until I'd started them and realized I couldn't *not* draw them," she explained. "For some reason, I seemed to capture your essence so very easily." She shook her head. "Then I couldn't stop. See? I don't draw faces. I've never been very good at it, but this was different. I'm sorry though. I should have asked you first—or at least told you."

He shook his head. "It's not even about that," he replied, as he studied the room, holding her firmly in his arms. "It was just a little unnerving to see so many of my own likenesses here."

She chuckled. "Any chance you'll get used to that?"

He looked at her in surprise. "Why?"

"Because, now that I've started, I think I'm addicted," she admitted. "You have a very compelling set of features."

"Oh no, I don't need to hear that," he groaned, yet gave her a teasing look.

"Too bad," she countered, with more spirit than she expected to feel. "But the artist in me is very interested in everything that your features have to offer."

"My features, huh?" Then he chuckled. "Can't say I ever expected somebody saying that to me."

She burst out laughing, and he hugged her closer. She loved that he tucked her in, making her feel safe and secure for the first time in a very long while. "I suppose you're leaving now," she murmured.

"Well, certainly not tonight," he said. "I want to make sure that you guys will actually get some rest after all this trauma. And we still have a full security system to set up and to get you trained on."

"Good. I can't say I'm looking forward to you leaving."

"And I get that," he stated. "You'll be nervous for a little while, but the fact that you know who was doing all this will end up behind bars will help."

"Maybe, but, in so many ways, it actually makes it worse because now we are aware that people do this crazy stuff, people we've known for years and years."

"Yeah, you're right, but you're a strong and very capable woman—as is Aida—and you'll both get through this."

"We will. I will," she stated, with a nod. "And you're right. We are strong and capable women. That doesn't mean that we don't necessarily want to have somebody at our side though."

He smiled, nodded. "Well, I can stay for a little bit longer but not much."

"Damn. Unless of course …" She looked up at him.

"What?" he asked, an eyebrow raised.

"Unless you want to spend some time with me," she suggested. "You know? Like personal time."

"Ah, and this from a woman who isn't ready to have a relationship?" he teased.

"*Well*, I might be persuaded to change my mind on that," she murmured.

"Might?" he asked, wriggling his eyebrows. "As much as I would like to have a real relationship with you and to get to know you a whole lot better," he murmured, "I need to know that you're committed, 100 percent."

"Unlike my last one, you mean?"

"Exactly." He smiled. "I know you're up for it. I just don't know if you're truly ready."

She nodded. "The only thing I can do is try to convince you that I am."

"I am totally open to being convinced," he murmured, tucking her up close. "Of course you're traumatized and under all kinds of stress right now," he noted, "so I wouldn't consider this the best timing."

She shook her head. "I've been thinking about this for a while, and a lot happened today. It's not as if this is a new thought for me."

"Are you sure though?" he asked.

"Absolutely."

"I mean, you won't fit me in the same space that you've got everybody else in your life, right?"

"No. God, no," she said. "You've actually already taken up more space than I've ever let anybody else have, just by being in my studio," she admitted, with a laugh. "But that doesn't mean that it's wrong, does it?" she asked.

"No," he replied cautiously, "not necessarily. It just feels strange to see myself all over your studio and in such interesting poses."

She laughed. "Is it the poses that bother you?"

"I'm not sure what it is. It's just mostly a shock to me—repeatedly."

She studied him. "I can see that. You'll get used to it soon enough." She smirked. He stared at her, as she shrugged. "Because really that's your only choice."

"What's my only choice?" he asked cautiously.

"I mean, if we're going out—dating or whatever you want to call it—obviously I'll want to have you as my model," she added.

"So, is it me you want, or am I just an object to fuel your artistic ambitions?" he asked in all seriousness. "I'm not just an image to draw, and that seems to be all you see me as right now. You know that, right?"

She burst out laughing. "You can be so serious. And I do want the whole relationship with you. However, since the only thing I have actually sketched so far is your face, and I don't know what surprises the rest of you may hold," she added, "I reserve the right to change my answer on that later."

Chuckling, he held her close.

"That's what was missing before," she murmured.

"What's that?"

"Laughter."

Still holding her as close as he could, he tilted his head back, so he could look at her. "That doesn't sound like much of a relationship then," he noted. "I think laughter and having fun together is really important."

"I do too, and now I see how much that was missing," she stated drily. "I guess sometimes you must figure these things out as you go."

"It's not always quite so easy to sort through some of this. So, if you need time, you just tell me, okay?"

"I don't need time," she stated. "I'm not as stupid as I may appear at times when it comes to people. But I feel like I've been waiting all this time for the right person, and that just didn't come about. It didn't happen, and I don't know if I just gave up or gave in. It's just … It didn't seem to matter anymore because I gave up hope for something better."

"Never give up hope," he murmured, as he pulled her right back to him and squeezed her tight. "That perfect person for you is always out there somewhere, but sometimes you must wait for that person to show up."

"Well, I was getting damn tired of waiting," she

snapped, rising on her toes and kissing him on the chin.

"You do realize we're having this conversation with a dozen people all around us, don't you?" he asked.

"So?" she said.

"And that the cops still need to talk to you."

She stared at him in horror and then sank against him. "God, I'm not looking forward to that."

"Maybe not," Carson agreed, "but you have to do it."

She groaned. "Will you stay with me?"

He nodded. "Of course."

"Good."

Just then a throat cleared behind her, and she turned slowly to see a cop standing there, holding a notepad. She groaned again. "Right. You have questions."

"I do," he noted. "We need to go over your statement."

She huffed out a breath. "Fine, but do you mind if we go downstairs to the dining room, so we can sit down and talk there?"

CARSON WAITED UNTIL all the cops were done and gone. Exhausted as Eva was, she was still up until everybody left, so she had time for just him.

As soon as the last one was out the door, she turned and looked at him. "Where's Grandma?"

"I sent her to bed a while ago," he murmured.

She nodded. "Thank you for that. It's probably the best place for her."

"She was looking pretty tired," he admitted.

"Of course she was. Hell, I'm tired too," she said, yawning.

"I'll bet. How's your shoulder feeling?"

"It seems kind of minor compared to all the drama, but it is definitely aching now," she admitted.

"Off to bed, you. Get some rest." He scooted her toward the stairs.

"Did you lock up?" she asked, as he followed her up to her floor.

"I did."

"And is the security system all set?"

"Yes, we've still got more upgrades to do. But, for now, you are safe with what we have installed so far."

"How long before I'll sleep without worrying about it?"

"Probably a long time," he admitted. "You've been through a lot and are dealing with several pretty significant betrayals."

"Yeah, I guess."

"Once we get the whole security system in, you'll see that it's not all that complicated. And it should give you some peace and a sense of privacy again."

"I'm not against that," she said, with a smile, stopping on the landing. "I guess security systems are big in your world, aren't they?"

"Yep. And, from now on, it'll be big in yours too." He wrapped an arm around her shoulders, nudging her upward.

She moaned. "I don't like the sound of that."

"Maybe not, but it's a necessary evil."

She nodded. "I get it. I don't like it, but I get it."

Back upstairs at her studio, he said, "Good night. Now lock yourself in, and I'll see you in the morning."

She looked at him. "Aren't you staying?"

"Yeah, I told you I was. I've got a few things to do, then I'll be in my room."

She shook her head, stepped closer, and wrapped her

arms around him. "I mean, aren't you staying with me tonight?"

"Oh. Well, that's a change in plans," he said, almost at a loss for words. But he already knew what to say. He wrapped her up and held her close. "I didn't want to intrude or to presume anything, especially considering how traumatizing this has been."

"No way," she argued. "All this really did was highlight certain things in my life that I need to change."

"Such as?"

"Such as, live a little more, stop obsessively planning and worrying about my career as an artist, step up and take some responsibility helping Grandma, and remembering to enjoy every day," she said instantly.

"Wow. You've really thought about this."

"Only a little bit," she teased. "As much as time would allow. I don't know what'll happen with all this latest fiasco," she murmured, "but I'm just happy to close the door on this mess, then turn a page or a corner, whatever you want to call it." She smiled. "I know that I can move on with my life, and I'm ready."

As she turned and looked at all the canvases in front of her, she added, "Apparently my soul already knew who I wanted to turn over that leaf with."

He chuckled. "Only if and when you're ready …"

She looked up at him, grabbed him by both ears, and tugged him toward her. "I'm ready now," she whispered. "There is absolutely nothing I want more than to spend the night with you … tonight." And she placed a finger against his lips. "Don't you dare question that."

He shook his head. "Hey, I'm no fool. I just wanted to be certain that you are sure."

She kissed him. "Come on. Take me to bed and help me forget."

"Now that I can do." He picked her up in his arms, making her shriek with laughter, then carried her to the bed and tossed her gently on the mattress. "Interesting bed."

"It's part of my childhood," she noted.

"That's all right by me. You'll leave it when you're ready."

"Or not," she teased, with a smile. "Maybe I'll never be ready."

"Or maybe you're ready now, and you just don't know it yet," he suggested.

She shrugged. "I don't know, but that's enough discussion for now," she said, as she hopped off the bed and stood in front of him. In a matter of seconds, she had stripped down, 100 percent nude.

His heart slammed against his chest, and his body responded instantly. His jeans were immediately way too tight. When he could speak, he muttered, "Jesus, give an old man a warning."

"Nope. Guys like you are always ready." She chuckled. Her hands went to his belt buckle, already finding the proof of her statement as she tried to strip down his jeans. He quickly brushed back her hands and said, "You're killing me."

"No, you're killing me."

Forcing her hands away again and struggling to undress as she kept trying to come back, he finally kicked off his boots and socks, then his jeans, and pulled his T-shirt up over his head.

"Now," she said, "that is much better."

He chuckled. "We don't have to rush it."

"Nope, we sure don't," she agreed. "And maybe next time we won't, but, this time, I'm not sure how much I'm ready to wait. It seems like I've waited a lifetime." She wrapped her arms around him and stepped up, pressing her hot skin against his, from thigh to chest.

He shuddered in place and noted she shivered as she whispered, "God, it feels so good ... just to be held."

"I hear you there," he whispered.

As he pulled back just slightly so he could nudge her toward the bed again, she stepped back. He looked over at her, then smiled. "We can at least take advantage of the bed."

She murmured something that he didn't understand and didn't bother to wait for an explanation, as he quickly picked her up and dropped her again on the bed. He immediately followed her fast enough that she couldn't pop up again. And there he stopped, feeling his heart swell as he held her close against him. "All I ever wanted," he murmured, "was to find somebody to love."

"And all I ever wanted," she replied, "was to find somebody who would love me."

"Well, in that case, it seems like we're both about to get what we wanted."

She nodded. "I didn't realize how much of what I wanted was directly affected by what I needed. And what I need is somebody like you."

"Somebody like me?"

"No." She frowned, shaking her head. "Scratch that. Not somebody *like* you. Just you. Only and exactly you." She wrapped her arms around his neck. "I realize we don't know each other very well yet, and we haven't been in this new relationship very long, but I am so looking forward to my future and finding out everything I can about you."

He smiled, then kissed her gently on the corner of her mouth, and whispered, "You and me both."

He lowered his head and kissed her with a passion that had been brewing ever since the first day he had met her. When he heard her gently crying beneath him, he lifted his head and whispered, "God, your shoulder. Did I hurt you?"

She shook her head. "No, never."

Her eyes were glazed with a heat that he hadn't seen before. "That was just me crying out in shock and surprise at my own need," she murmured, looping her arms around him. "Now, enough talking."

He burst out laughing, as he pulled her tighter against him and then proceeded to show her just what the future would bring them. By the time he had explored all of her with his tongue and his hands and his lips, she was trembling and crying out beneath him.

He slowly lowered his body until he possessed her completely. As she lay here, quivering in his arms, he whispered, "Are you okay?"

"Never better," she murmured. "But, if you don't start moving soon, you are so going to pay for teasing me."

He let out a shout of laughter and started to move, so deep and hard and all-encompassing and so damn perfect. By the time he felt her splintering beneath him, he was almost crying out in need himself. As soon as she came apart in his arms, he immediately followed her into nirvana.

When he collapsed beside her moments later, she whispered, "Dear God, … I didn't know it could be like that."

"It always should be like that," he stated, "at least when you find the right person."

"If I'd known that's what I was waiting for," she said, "I

wouldn't have wasted all week."

That struck him as funny, considering the week they'd had, and he couldn't stop laughing. Finally he got it under control. "Well, all those distractions aside, we don't have to keep wasting time now."

"No, but I just might need a tiny bit of rest first."

"You can have all the rest you need," he murmured gently. "What you really need is sleep."

She shook her head. "I don't think I need to sleep, and I definitely don't want to right now," she stated. "But there is something to be said for a restorative nap." And, with that, she closed her eyes and drifted off.

He held her close, then fell asleep himself. When he woke up later, he nudged her gently. "You still asleep?"

Her eyes opened, and she smiled up at him. "Well, I was. Unless you have something better you want to do."

He grinned. "I may have an idea."

She opened her arms in welcome, and he proceeded to show her all over again just how special she was.

Epilogue

LEVI SAT IN the kitchen of his compound with Alfred at his side, as they pondered work and life. "We're running at 100 percent," Levi noted. "Is that something we should be concerned about?"

"I have no idea." Alfred laughed. "But since everybody is happy and seems to have fulfilled some major dreams in their lives, I would say, no."

"Well, it's weird," Levi said. "We're still hiring men."

"But things are changing, families are happening, and guys want to stay home more," Alfred noted. "So that is to be expected."

"I get that," Levi agreed, "but it's also kind of weird because, once again, it's change."

"And you don't like change so much, do you?"

"Nope, I sure don't," he admitted, with a smile, "but obviously it'll happen sometimes."

"It sure does, and you're doing great adapting to it all." Alfred looked over at Levi and smiled. "Are you having any thoughts about retiring?"

"God no," Levi declared. "The more babies who come along, the more I'm in this for the long run."

"And that's a hell of a good thing, at least from my point of view," Alfred replied. As he looked at the stack of employment records in front of them, he asked, "So, Levi, who will you try next?"

"I hate to say it, but a part of me looks at this from the perspective of who'll keep my record going," he shared, with a laugh.

"I'm sure lots of guys are out there, searching for that right person to fill a hiring gap," Alfred stated, "but you can't be expected to find the right one out of the gate every time."

"No, I know that," Levi muttered sadly. "But when there's one who's single, my mind tends to go to—"

"What? You're thinking about—"

"Yep." Levi nodded. "I've known that man for a decade. He's been to hell and back, and maybe he needs a second chance."

"Everybody needs a second chance," Alfred agreed. "That doesn't mean he wants one though."

"Maybe not, but he can't sit there punishing himself forever."

"Are you sure?" he asked, with a knowing smile.

Levi nodded. "I'm pretty sure he would be the one who would say he should. However, just because his wife and child died while he was off in the military, that doesn't mean he's responsible for their deaths."

Alfred nodded. "I don't know that he has necessarily solved that one either. It's a cold case."

"It's also a cold case in his hometown."

"Which is?"

"Billings, Montana," he noted, with a tilt of his head.

"Interesting that it is in Billings, *huh?*"

"Yeah, just where our new case is too." Levi smiled broadly.

"Who are you sending with him?"

"I was thinking about one of the more experienced guys,

like maybe Tyson."

Alfred nodded. "You know what? That's not a bad idea, and he would at least understand the same level of grief."

"Yeah." Levi looked at his phone, picked it up, and called Dante. When an exasperated voice answered at the other end, Levi smiled. "Sorry, am I catching you at a bad time?"

"Hey, Levi. It's never a bad time for you," he said. "I'm just dealing with my nephew here. This kid is like a hacking king."

"Well, I don't want to pull you away from family time," Levi began, "but I was wondering if I could get you to do a job for us."

"*Huh*," he replied instantly. "Not sure I'm interested."

"I know. And it's not like you've asked for work either."

"Nope, and that's because I'm not certain I'm ready to go in that direction yet," he stated. "But, if you actually need my help, that's a whole different story."

Levi smiled. "That's kind of why I'm calling."

"Is it something that I'm even capable of doing?" Dante asked.

"Well, there's a reason why you're helping your nephew with computers."

"That's definitely my specialty," he admitted, "but you've got a lot of good people on staff."

"Yeah, but most of them have families or babies coming or something like that, and they don't necessarily want to travel so much anymore. So I've got to keep a larger pool to get the jobs done."

"Well, I don't have a problem helping you out, if it won't take too long."

"Most of these jobs don't tend to, but I can't be sure."

"So what's going on?" Dante asked.

"We've got a schoolteacher," Levi said.

"Oh, *great*, stick me with a prissy sixty-five-year-old, who'll tell me to mind my *P*s and *Q*s," Dante complained. "That sounds like a great combination."

"On the other hand," Levi countered, "it might take your mind off everything else going on in your world."

He snorted. "And of course you know about everything going on in my world."

"Hard not to in this field," he noted.

"Well, I walked out of the military because it was time," he snapped. "No other reason."

"And you'll stick to that, no matter what, right?" Levi laughed.

"Damn right," he said, a hint of laughter in his tone. "So what's this schoolmarm having trouble with?"

"She seems to think that somebody is hacking the student website," Levi explained.

"And that is of national security?" Dante asked. "What kind of jobs are you taking on these days?"

"She's a bit of a hacker herself," he added. "And she recognizes the signature but says it doesn't make any sense."

"And you know her how?"

"Let's just say that Mason's wife, Tesla, put us on this one."

"Oh, that's interesting. Is she one of Tesla's friends?" he asked, a spark of interest entering his voice.

"Ah, so that gives it more validity?"

"Well, Tesla is incredible at what she does, and God knows she's done plenty for us, so, if she's got a friend in need, I guess I'd sign up to help out," he decided. "But what the hell, Levi? You got me a schoolmarm?"

"I wouldn't worry about that so much. Times have been tough for her, and she's been trying to stay on the straight and narrow and to keep her head above water."

"If she's got serious hacking skills, what's she doing in front of a chalkboard?"

"I may just try to convince her to come work for me," Levi shared, "but first she wants to solve this mystery. I think it's been a pet peeve of hers for a while. I don't know how much you want to know about it beforehand, but there was that hacking incident some years back, and she got blamed for it. She wasn't charged, but it damaged her reputation, and she lost her job at the time."

"So ... she's always maintained her innocence but still had bills to pay, so she went to work at whatever she could get, I assume. She's probably been hot on that trail ever since too, so she can clear her name."

"Of course," Levi stated.

"So Tesla knows all about it?"

"Yeah, but Tesla is pregnant and can't really go to her friend's rescue right now."

"No, of course not," Dante agreed. "I can head out and lend a hand. So where am I going?"

"Billings," Levi replied innocently.

At that came a shocked silence through the phone. "Damn you, Levi," Dante murmured. "Billings fucking Montana? Are you kidding me?"

"Is that a problem?" he asked, trying to interject just the right amount of curiosity.

"No, *no problem*," he muttered, with a dark tone. "Just the way my luck runs."

"Well, if you can't do the job, it—"

"*I* can *do* the *job*," he gritted out in disgust. "Just seems like the universe thinks I've got a target on my back."

"Maybe it's a good time to get rid of that target," Levi suggested.

"Well, screw it," Dante said. "I'll do the job. When do I leave?"

"Yesterday."

This concludes Book 27 of Heroes for Hire:
Carson's Choice.

Read about Dante's Decision: Heroes for Hire, Book 28

Heroes for Hire: Dante's Decision (Book #28)

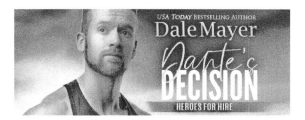

At Levi's request, Dante, with misgivings, returns to the one place he swore he never would come back to—Billings, Montana. The place where he lost his wife and daughter many years ago. If returning gives him a sense of peace or at least a way to reconcile what happened so he can move on, then fine. As it is, he finds more surprises in that department than he expected.

Laura needed a job. She had rent to pay and a teenager to feed. After being summarily ejected from her government-sensitive position, she was forced into teaching. But, when she sees something beyond odd in the high school website code, she knows someone has found her. Even worse, it's likely to be the same person who messed up her life the last time.

Maybe Dante can help her out, but it seems like he has bigger problems than she has, ... until her world flips completely out of control, and she needs him more than ever.

Find Book 28 here!

To find out more visit Dale Mayer's website.

https://geni.us/DMDanteUniversal

Other Military Series by Dale Mayer

SEALs of Honor

Heroes for Hire

SEALs of Steel

The K9 Files

The Mavericks

Bullards Battle

Hathaway House

Terkel's Team

Ryland's Reach: Bullard's Battle (Book #1)

Welcome to a new stand-alone but interconnected series from Dale Mayer. This is Bullard's story—and that of his team's. All raw, rough, incredibly capable men who have one goal: to find out who was behind the attack on their leader, before the attacker, or attackers, return to finish the job.

Stay tuned for more nonstop action as the men narrow down their suspects ... and find a way to let love back into their own empty lives.

His rescue from the ocean after a horrible plane explosion was his top priority, in any way, shape, or form. A small sailboat and a nurse to do the job was more than Ryland hoped for.

When Tabi somehow drags him and his buddy Garret onboard and surprisingly gets them to a naval ship close by, Ryland figures he'd used up all his luck and his friend's too. Sure enough, those who attacked the plane they were in weren't content to let him slowly die in the ocean. No. Surviving had made him a target all over again.

Tabi isn't expecting her sailing holiday to include the rescue of two badly injured men and then to end with the loss of her beloved sailboat. Her instincts save them, but now she finds it tough to let them go—even as more of Bullard's team members come to them—until it becomes apparent that not only are Bullard and his men still targets ... but she is too.

B ULLARD CHECKED THAT the helicopter was loaded with their bags and that his men were ready to leave.

He walked back one more time, his gaze on Ice. She'd never looked happier, never looked more perfect. His heart ached, but he knew she remained a caring friend and always would be. He opened his arms; she ran into them, and he held her close, whispering, "The offer still stands."

She leaned back and smiled up at him. "Maybe if and when Levi's been gone for a long enough time for me to forget," she said in all seriousness.

"That's not happening. You two, now three, will live long and happy lives together," he said, smiling down at the woman knew to be the most beautiful, inside and out. She would never be his, but he always kept a little corner of his heart open and available, in case she wanted to surprise him and to slide inside.

And then he realized she'd already been a part of his heart all this time. That was a good ten to fifteen years by now. But she kept herself in the friend category, and he understood because she and Levi, partners and now parents, were perfect together.

Bullard reached out and shook Levi's hand. "It was a hell of a blast," he said. "When you guys do a big splash, you really do a *big* splash."

Ice laughed. "A few days at home sounds perfect for me now."

"It looks great," he said, his hands on his hips as he surveyed the people in the massive pool surrounded by the palm trees, all designed and decked out by Ice. Right beside all the war machines that he heartily approved of. He grinned at her. "When are you coming over to visit?" His gaze went to Levi, raising his eyebrows back at her. "You guys should come over for a week or two or three."

"It's not a bad idea," Levi said. "We could use a long holiday, just not yet."

"That sounds familiar." Bullard grinned. "Anyway, I'm off. We'll hit the airport and then pick up the plane and head home." He added, "As always, call if you need me."

Everybody raised a hand as he returned to the helicopter and his buddy who was flying him to the airport. Ice had volunteered to shuttle him there, but he hadn't wanted to take her away from her family or to prolong the goodbye. He hopped inside, waving at everybody as the helicopter lifted. Two of his men, Ryland and Garret, were in the back seats. They always traveled with him.

Bullard would pick up the rest of his men in Australia. He stared down at the compound as he flew overhead. He preferred his compound at home, but damn they'd done a nice job here.

With everybody on the ground screaming goodbye, Bullard sailed over Houston, heading toward the airport. His two men never said a word. They all knew how he felt about Ice. But not one of them would cross that line and say anything. At least not if they expected to still have jobs.

It was one thing to fall in love with another man's woman, but another thing to fall in love with a woman who was so unique, so different, and so absolutely perfect that you knew, just knew, there was no hope of finding anybody else like her. But she and Levi had been together way before Bullard had ever met her, which made it that much more heartbreaking.

Still, he'd turned and looked forward. He had a full roster of jobs himself to focus on when he got home. Part of him was tired of the life; another part of him couldn't wait to head out on the next adventure. He managed to run everything from his command centers in one or two of his locations. He'd spent a lot of time and effort at the second one and kept a full team at both locations, yet preferred to spend most of his time at the old one. It felt more like home to him, and he'd like to be there now, but still had many more days before that could happen.

The helicopter lowered to the tarmac, he stepped out, said his goodbyes and walked across to where his private plane waited. It was one of the things that he loved, being a pilot of both helicopters and airplanes, and owning both birds himself.

That again was another way he and Ice were part of the same team, of the same mind-set. He'd been looking for another woman like Ice for himself, but no such luck. Sure, lots were around for short-term relationships, but most of them couldn't handle his lifestyle or the violence of the world that he lived in. He understood that.

The ones who did had a hard edge to them that he found difficult to live with. Bullard appreciated everybody's being alert and aware, but if there wasn't some softness in the women, they seemed to turn cold all the way through.

As he boarded his small plane, Ryland and Garret following behind, Bullard called out in his loud voice, "Let's go, slow pokes. We've got a long flight ahead of us."

The men grinned, confident Bullard was teasing, as was his usual routine during their off-hours.

"Well, we're ready, not sure about you though ..." Ryland said, smirking.

"We're waiting on you this time," Garret added with a chuckle. "Good thing you're the boss."

Bullard grinned at his two right-hand men. "Isn't that the truth?" He dropped his bags at one of the guys' feet and said, "Stow all this stuff, will you? I want to get our flight path cleared and get the hell out of here."

They'd all enjoyed the break. He tried to get over once a year to visit Ice and Levi and same in reverse. But it was time to get back to business. He started up the engines, got confirmation from the tower. They were heading to Australia for this next job. He really wanted to go straight back to Africa, but it would be a while yet. They'd refuel in Honolulu.

Ryland came in and sat down in the copilot's spot, buckled in, then asked, "You ready?"

Bullard laughed. "When have you ever known me *not* to be ready?" At that, he taxied down the runway. Before long he was up in the air, at cruising level, and heading to Hawaii. "Gotta love these views from up here," Bullard said. "This place is magical."

"It is once you get up above all the smog," he said. "Why Australia again?"

"Remember how we were supposed to check out that newest compound in Australia that I've had my eye on? Besides the alpha team is coming off that ugly job in Sydney. We'll give them a day or two of R&R then head home."

"Right. We could have some equally ugly payback on that job."

Bullard shrugged. "That goes for most of our jobs. It's the life."

"And don't you have enough compounds to look after?"

"Yes I do, but that kid in me still looks to take over the world. Just remember that."

"Better you go home to Africa and look after your first two compounds," Ryland said.

"Maybe," Bullard admitted. "But it seems hard to not continue expanding."

"You need a partner," Ryland said abruptly. "That might ease the savage beast inside. Keep you home more."

"Well, the only one I like," he said, "is married to my best friend."

"I'm sorry about that," Ryland said quietly. "What a shit deal."

"No," Bullard said. "I came on the scene last. They were always meant to be together. Especially now they are a family."

"If you say so," Ryland said.

Bullard nodded. "Damn right, I say so."

And that set the tone for the next many hours. They landed in Hawaii, and while they fueled up everybody got off to stretch their legs by walking around outside a bit as this was a small private airstrip, not exactly full of hangars and tourists. Then they hopped back on board again for takeoff.

"I can fly," Ryland offered as they took off.

"We'll switch in a bit," Bullard said. "Surprisingly, I'm doing okay yet, but I'll let you take her down."

"Yeah, it's still a long flight," Ryland said studying the islands below. It was a stunning view of the area.

"I love the islands here. Sometimes I just wonder about the benefit of, you know, crashing into the sea, coming up on a deserted island, and finding the simple life again," Bullard said with a laugh.

"I hear you," Ryland said. "Every once in a while, I wonder the same."

Several hours later Ryland looked up and said abruptly, "We've made good time considering we've already passed Fiji."

Bullard yawned.

"Let's switch."

Bullard smiled, nodded, and said, "Fine. I'll hand it over to you."

Just then a funny noise came from the engine on the right side.

They looked at each other, and Ryland said, "Uh-oh. That's not good news."

Boom!

And the plane exploded.

Find Bullard's Battle (Book #1) here!

To find out more visit Dale Mayer's website.

smarturl.it/DMSRyland

Damon's Deal: Terkel's Team (Book #1)

Welcome to a brand-new series from *USA Today* best-selling author Dale Mayer, where dark-ops SEALs have special senses and skills, needed to solve intrigue, betrayal, and ... murder. A series with all the elements you've come to love, plus so much more, ... including psychics!

ICE POURED HERSELF a coffee and sat down at the compound's massive dining room table with the others. When her phone rang, she smiled at the number displayed. "Hey, Terk. How're you doing?" She put the call on Speakerphone.

"I'm okay," Terkel said, his voice distracted and tight.

"Terk?" Merk called from across the table. He got up and walked closer and sat across from Levi. "You don't sound too good, brother. What's up?"

"I'm fine," Terk said. "Or I will be. Right now, things are blown to shit."

"As in literally?" Merk asked.

"The entire group," Terk said, "they're all gone. I had a solid team of eight, and they're all gone."

"Dead?"

Several others stood to join them, gathered around Ice's phone. Levi stepped forward, his hand on Ice's shoulder. "Terk? Are they all dead?"

"No." Terk took a deep breath. "I'm not making sense. I'm sorry."

"Take it easy," Ice said, her voice calm and reassuring. "What do you mean, *they're all gone?*"

"All their abilities are gone," he said. "Something's happened to them. Somebody has deliberately removed whatever super senses they could utilize—or what we have been utilizing for the last ten years for the government." His tone was bitter. "When the US gov recently closed us down, they promised that our black ops department would never rise again, but I didn't expect them to attack us personally."

"What are you talking about?" Merk said in alarm, standing up now to stare at Ice's phone. "Are you in danger?"

"Maybe? I don't know," Terk said. "I need to find out exactly what the hell's going on."

"What can we do to help?" Ice asked.

Terk gave a broken laugh. "That's not why I'm calling. Well, it is, but it isn't."

Ice looked at Merk, who frowned, as he shook his head. Ice knew he and the others had heard Terk's stressed out tone and the completely confusing bits and pieces coming from his mouth. Ice said, "Terk, you're not making sense again. Take a breath and explain. Please. You're scaring me."

Terk took a long slow deep breath. "Tell Stone to open the gate," he said. "She's out there."

"Who's out there?" Levi asked, hopped up, looked outside, and shrugged.

"She's coming up the road now. You have to let her in."

"Who? Why?"

"*Because*," he said, "she's also harnessed with C-4."

"Jesus," Levi said, bolting to display the camera feeds to the big screen in the room. "Is it live?"

"It is, and she's been sent to you."

"Well, that's an interesting move," Ice said, her voice sharp, activating her comm to connect to Stone in the control room. "Who's after us?"

"I think it's rebels within the Iranian government. But it could be our own government. I don't know anymore," Terk snapped. "I also don't know how they got her so close to you. Or how they pinned your connection to me," he said. "I've been very careful."

"We can look after ourselves," Ice said immediately. "But who is this woman to you?"

"She's pregnant," he said, "so that adds to the intensity here."

"Understood. So who is the father? Is he connected somehow?"

There was silence on the other end.

Merk said, "Terk, talk to us."

"She's carrying my baby," Terk replied, his voice heavy.

Merk, his expression grim, looked at Ice, her face mirroring his shock. He asked, "How do you know her, Terk?"

"Brother, you don't understand," Terk said. "I've never met this woman before in my life." And, with that, the phone went dead.

Find Terkel's Team (Book #1) here!

To find out more visit Dale Mayer's website.

smarturl.it/DMSTTDamon

Author's Note

Thank you for reading Carson's Choice: Heroes for Hire, Book 27! If you enjoyed the book, please take a moment and leave a short review.

Dear reader,

I love to hear from readers, and you can contact me at my website: www.dalemayer.com or at my Facebook author page. To be informed of new releases and special offers, sign up for my newsletter or follow me on BookBub. And if you are interested in joining Dale Mayer's Reader Group, here is the Facebook sign up page.
https://smarturl.it/DaleMayerFBGroup

Cheers,
Dale Mayer

Your THREE Free Books Are Waiting!

Grab your copy of SEALs of Honor Books 1 – 3 for free!

Meet Mason, Hawk and Dane. *Brave, badass warriors who serve their country with honor and love their women to the limits of life and death.*

DOWNLOAD your copy right now! Just tell me where to send it.

www.smarturl.it/DaleHonorFreeBundle

About the Author

Dale Mayer is a *USA Today* best-selling author, best known for her SEALs military romances, her Psychic Visions series, and her Lovely Lethal Garden cozy series. Her contemporary romances are raw and full of passion and emotion (Broken But … Mending, Hathaway House series). Her thrillers will keep you guessing (Kate Morgan, By Death series), and her romantic comedies will keep you giggling (*It's a Dog's Life*, a stand-alone novella; and the Broken Protocols series, starring Charming Marvin, the cat).

Dale honors the stories that come to her—and some of them are crazy, break all the rules and cross multiple genres!

To go with her fiction, she also writes nonfiction in many different fields, with books available on résumé writing, companion gardening, and the US mortgage system. All her books are available in print and ebook format.

Connect with Dale Mayer Online

Dale's Website – www.dalemayer.com
Twitter – @DaleMayer
Facebook Page – geni.us/DaleMayerFBFanPage
Facebook Group – geni.us/DaleMayerFBGroup
BookBub – geni.us/DaleMayerBookbub
Instagram – geni.us/DaleMayerInstagram
Goodreads – geni.us/DaleMayerGoodreads
Newsletter – geni.us/DaleNews

Also by Dale Mayer

Published Adult Books:

Shadow Recon
Magnus, Book 1

Bullard's Battle
Ryland's Reach, Book 1
Cain's Cross, Book 2
Eton's Escape, Book 3
Garret's Gambit, Book 4
Kano's Keep, Book 5
Fallon's Flaw, Book 6
Quinn's Quest, Book 7
Bullard's Beauty, Book 8
Bullard's Best, Book 9
Bullard's Battle, Books 1–2
Bullard's Battle, Books 3–4
Bullard's Battle, Books 5–6
Bullard's Battle, Books 7–8

Terkel's Team
Damon's Deal, Book 1
Wade's War, Book 2
Gage's Goal, Book 3

The K9 Files

Lovely Lethal Gardens

Arsenic in the Azaleas, Book 1

Bones in the Begonias, Book 2

Corpse in the Carnations, Book 3

Daggers in the Dahlias, Book 4

Evidence in the Echinacea, Book 5

Footprints in the Ferns, Book 6

Gun in the Gardenias, Book 7

Handcuffs in the Heather, Book 8

Ice Pick in the Ivy, Book 9

Jewels in the Juniper, Book 10

Killer in the Kiwis, Book 11

Lifeless in the Lilies, Book 12

Murder in the Marigolds, Book 13

Nabbed in the Nasturtiums, Book 14

Offed in the Orchids, Book 15

Poison in the Pansies, Book 16

Quarry in the Quince, Book 17

Revenge in the Roses, Book 18

Lovely Lethal Gardens, Books 1–2

Lovely Lethal Gardens, Books 3–4

Lovely Lethal Gardens, Books 5–6

Lovely Lethal Gardens, Books 7–8

Lovely Lethal Gardens, Books 9–10

Psychic Vision Series

Tuesday's Child

Hide 'n Go Seek

Maddy's Floor

Garden of Sorrow

Knock Knock…

Rare Find

Eyes to the Soul

Now You See Her

Shattered

Into the Abyss

Seeds of Malice

Eye of the Falcon

Itsy-Bitsy Spider

Unmasked

Deep Beneath

From the Ashes

Stroke of Death

Ice Maiden

Snap, Crackle…

What If…

Talking Bones

String of Tears

Psychic Visions Books 1–3

Psychic Visions Books 4–6

Psychic Visions Books 7–9

By Death Series

Touched by Death

Haunted by Death

Chilled by Death

By Death Books 1–3

Broken Protocols – Romantic Comedy Series

Cat's Meow

Cat's Pajamas

Cat's Cradle

Cat's Claus

Broken Protocols 1-4

Broken and... Mending

Skin

Scars

Scales (of Justice)

Broken but... Mending 1-3

Glory

Genesis

Tori

Celeste

Glory Trilogy

Biker Blues

Morgan: Biker Blues, Volume 1

Cash: Biker Blues, Volume 2

SEALs of Honor

Mason: SEALs of Honor, Book 1

Hawk: SEALs of Honor, Book 2

Dane: SEALs of Honor, Book 3

Swede: SEALs of Honor, Book 4

Shadow: SEALs of Honor, Book 5

Cooper: SEALs of Honor, Book 6

SEALs of Steel

The Mavericks